ELIZA MACE

ELIZA MACE

SARAH BURTON
JEM POSTER

DUCKWORTH

First published in the United Kingdom by Duckworth in 2024

Duckworth, an imprint of Duckworth Books Ltd
1 Golden Court, Richmond, TW9 1EU, United Kingdom
www.duckworthbooks.co.uk

For bulk and special sales please contact
info@duckworthbooks.com

A CIP catalogue record for this book is available from the British Library

Page design by Danny Lyle

Printed and bound in Great Britain by Clays Ltd Elcograf, Sp.A.

1 3 5 7 9 10 8 6 4 2

Hardback ISBN: 978-0-7156-5512-2

eISBN: 978-0-7156-5513-9

For Lyn, Sara, Zoe, Dave and Matthew

Although the hills
Are white with snow, although the evening sky
Gives warning of a deeper cold (the little
Crescent moon so sharp against the faint
And fading blue) she stands outside and stares
At the house she once called home, knowing there's nothing
To hold her there; knowing she may not leave.

(Laetitia Burrowes, 'Hearth and Home', 1867)

Tonight has been such a night as I have never known. There are
no words – or none that I can find – adequate to the terror of that
moment out there – the lantern splintered at my feet, the darkness
swelling around me, my body shrunk small as a hayseed – I am
trying to say how it felt – and the ground sliding away beneath
me. The wind – the wind sobbing and moaning in the branches
overhead, and me breaking away, pelting up the slope as if I
could outrun it, the terror, the thing I couldn't shake off because I
carried it with me in my mind's eye, as I carry it now, seared deep,
ineradicably mine. And these words are mine too, written not for
others but for myself alone – written in hope of getting a hold on
the thing, getting a hold on myself, so that when I sit at breakfast
or dinner, when I answer their questions or, as it may be, decline
to answer them, I shall not break down or fly in pieces, but stand
steady against it all, as though my life had not been plunged in
darkness, as though my world were still whole.

(From the notebook of Eliza Mace, entry dated 27 February, 1874)

One

It was happening again. Eliza burrowed deeper under the blankets, but the voices broke through – her father's, slow, emphatic, a little slurred, her mother's high and quavering.

'Why? Because I'm your wife, that's why.'

On the verge of tears, thought Eliza, wide awake now. She surfaced, listening. An indistinct murmur from her father, and then her mother again.

'Where's your sense of honour, Robert? You gave me your word. A solemn promise.'

'A promise you wrung from me. You make me say things I don't mean.'

'Don't mean, but should mean. I've a right to the promise.'

Moonlight falling on the sill and the washstand, an owl calling. Barely a glow from the embers in the grate: Eliza judged that she had been asleep for four or five hours.

She threw back the blankets, padded to the door and eased it open. The door of her father's room stood slightly ajar; a line of light lay at an angle across the corridor.

The sound of the wardrobe door being banged shut. A faint sob from her mother, and then a soft scuffling.

'For Christ's sake, woman. Get back to your room.'

'How long will you be away?'

'A few days. Maybe a week.'

'And you'll leave without a word to Elizabeth? What am I to tell her this time?'

Silence.

'Well? What shall I say?'

'Tell her the truth. Say I've had to leave on urgent business.'

'Business?' She had moved closer to the door and Eliza could hear the quick rasp of her breathing. 'What kind of business is it that always leaves you poorer than when you set out? What kind of business is it that you can't discuss with your wife? What kind of business is so urgent that you leave at dead of night without warning? Without a word to your daughter?'

'Let me pass, Hannah.'

'Not until you answer me.' Her voice was louder now, raw and edged with anger. 'I'm sick of your endless ducking and dodging.'

'I said let me pass.' There was a muffled thud and a sharp cry, and then the door slammed back on its hinges and her father, booted and in his travelling cloak, stumbled into the corridor, the bedroom lamp held high in his left hand.

Eliza made to slip back into her room, but he had already seen her. He lurched forward, and at the same moment her uncle emerged from his room at the far end of the corridor and began trotting towards them, faintly absurd in his long linen nightshirt, his bare soles slapping the floorboards. Her father swung round to face him.

'You stay out of this, James.'

Her uncle faltered, came to a stop. 'Someone called out,' he said. 'I thought—'

'I'm leaving for a while. On business. Hannah and I were discussing the matter. It doesn't concern you.'

Her mother closed the door on them. Eliza heard her weeping, quietly at first and then in long, shuddering gasps. James moved towards the door.

'You're overstepping the mark, James. You're a guest in this house.'

'Guest or not, I'm family. And Hannah—'

'Leave her to it.'

James hesitated. Robert stood half a head taller than his brother and was considerably more powerfully built, but that, Eliza knew, wasn't the point. There was something deeper at work. She had watched them together over the years, noticing the way James, so articulate in his conversations with her, stammered and mumbled like a nervous schoolboy when his brother addressed him, the way he seemed to shrivel under his gaze.

As now, taking a pace backward, his eyes downcast. Eliza moved in and gripped her father's sleeve.

'Wait until morning,' she said. 'Please.'

He peered blearily into her face as though trying to place her. His breath sour, a fine sheen of sweat on his forehead.

'I can't.'

'Surely a few hours wouldn't make any difference. If the business—'

'What the hell would you know about my business?' He tried to pull free of her but she held fast and, little by little, felt him slacken, felt the anger drain out of him. He leaned heavily against the wall and ran his hand across his face.

'I'm sorry,' he said. 'Eliza, I'm truly sorry.'

'Then you'll stay?'

He shook his head. 'My trunk's in the gig. Todd's waiting for me in the yard.' He broke away and moved unsteadily down the corridor towards the stairs, still clutching the lamp. Eliza stood for a moment in the deepening dark, listening to the thud of his boots on the treads, her mother's wild sobbing. James cleared his throat.

'Eliza—'

'Goodnight, Uncle James.' She slipped back into her room and went to the side window. Down below Todd sat slumped in the driving seat, his face a pale mask in the light of the gig-lamps, his breath rising on the frosty air. The door slammed and her father emerged from the porch, cramming his hat onto his head. He crossed the yard and clambered into the gig. Todd clicked his tongue and the horse started forward.

If her father had looked up he might have seen her there, her face so close to the pane that she felt the chill off it, but he seemed oblivious to her presence. She stepped over to the front window and stared after the gig until it swung out of the drive and its lights were lost to view.

* * *

It was dawn before she slept, and when she woke again Carys was in the room raking the ashes from the grate.

'I hope you don't mind, Miss. I didn't want to disturb you, only—'

'I know, Carys. There's no need to explain.'

The girl was run off her feet, piecing in her various duties wherever and whenever she could. Five years ago there had been three maidservants; now Carys was the only one. She was a wisp of a girl, but stronger than she looked; she went about her work as efficiently as circumstances allowed and, so far as Eliza knew, without complaint. When the second maidservant had been laid off, Mrs Pugh had threatened to leave, telling Eliza's mother in plain terms that a house the size of Edge Hall couldn't be run under the conditions she proposed. I'm a housekeeper, she had protested, not a miracle-worker; but she had been persuaded to stay, and the household had staggered on.

'Is my mother awake?'

'She's at breakfast with your uncle. If you'll pardon me saying so, Miss, she doesn't look well enough to be up and about – her face as white as the table linen and her eyes so red and swollen. And last night I heard her cry out, a terrible cry as if she was in pain. I hope—'

'Thank you, Carys. I imagine she would have sent for Dr Allen if it had been necessary.'

'And your father on his travels again.'

'You can leave that now. Please let my mother and uncle know that I'm dressing. I shall join them in five minutes.'

But ten minutes later she was still in bed, revisiting the events of the night, and by the time she entered the breakfast room Mrs Pugh was clearing the plates away.

'Is the tea still hot, Mrs Pugh?'

'I'll have cook make you a fresh pot. And an egg?'

Eliza shook her head. 'Just toast.'

Her mother sat hunched over her teacup, both elbows on the table. 'You're not eating enough,' she said as Mrs Pugh bustled away. 'There was a time, not so long ago, you'd eat as much as your father.'

And there was a time, thought Eliza, when her mother would have sat at table with her back stiff and straight as a ramrod, the cup's handle nipped elegantly between her forefinger and thumb. 'I'm not hungry,' she said.

'Even so,' said James, leaning back in his chair, 'the body needs proper sustenance. All the more so at times of rapid physical development. The bones are growing, the tissues changing, the system adapting to new biological needs.'

Her mother shot him a glance. 'I think,' she said, 'you might spare us the detail.' But the reproach seemed to Eliza to be at least half affectionate, and her uncle, acknowledging the intervention with a nod and a faint smile, gave no sign of discomfiture. This, she thought, scanning their faces, was the way it ought to be: a man and a woman at ease in one another's company, speaking out or keeping their counsel as they pleased. And it struck her suddenly that her mother might, in a different marriage, have been a very different woman, a woman at peace with herself and with the world around her.

By the time Mrs Pugh returned with the breakfast tray the post had arrived. She picked two letters from the tray and passed them across the table. 'Both for the master,' she said. 'And this one' – she placed a square cream envelope beside the teapot – 'is for Eliza.'

Eliza's mother drew herself up in her chair. 'Miss Elizabeth,' she said.

'I'm sorry, ma'am. I still can't get used to it. She'll always be Eliza to me.'

'You'll have to get used to it, Mrs Pugh. She's no longer a child.'

Mrs Pugh opened her mouth as if to speak and then clamped it shut. She set the butter dish beside Eliza's plate, touched her gently on the shoulder and withdrew.

'That wasn't kind,' said Eliza as the housekeeper's footsteps died away down the corridor, 'and I'm sure it wasn't necessary.'

'But it is necessary. If I've told her once, I've told her a dozen times. At sixteen a young lady should have left her childhood behind her, and a responsible servant should understand that.'

'It may be,' said James gently, 'that the transitional stage is difficult for both parties. For all parties, myself included.

I've been thinking about it a good deal recently. There will come a time, Eliza, sooner rather than later, when our excursions will seem inappropriate. I shall be desolate, but that doesn't mean I shall cling to the past. Change happens whether we like it or not, and if we don't adapt we lose our footing in the world.'

Eliza felt the tears prickling behind her eyelids. She lowered her head and busied herself with the butter knife, but her mother had evidently noticed nothing. 'Is that Charlotte's handwriting?' she asked.

Eliza made a show of examining the envelope. 'I believe it is,' she said.

'Aren't you going to open it?'

'I'll read it later.'

'I don't know why she doesn't address her letters to the whole family.'

Eliza said nothing. Her sister's marriage had been a gamble, a wild bid for freedom, and what she now had to say about it was not for her parents' eyes. *Out of the frying pan*, she had written on one occasion, *and into the doldrums*. Eliza invariably replied to her letters within a day or two of receipt, and then burned them.

She swallowed her toast, excused herself from the table and went straight down to the basement. Alice looked up from the pan she was stirring. 'She's in there,' she said, jerking her head towards the partition that separated Mrs Pugh's sleeping quarters from the rest of the room. 'Something's got her going.'

Eliza knocked gently on the panelling and Mrs Pugh emerged, dabbing at her eyes with a crumpled handkerchief.

'I'm sorry,' said Eliza. 'Mother didn't mean—'

'What isn't meant shouldn't be said. But the truth is, she's right. You're a lady now, and if I can't stop thinking of you as my little Eliza, the fault is mine.'

7

'I am Eliza. And we're as close as we ever were.'

Mrs Pugh shook her head. 'Maybe it's just that I don't want to see you grow up. You'll be married and gone from us before we know it.' The tears were flowing unchecked now. Eliza stepped forward and tried to take her in her arms, but she broke away. 'You won't want me blubbering all over you,' she said.

'There's nothing to cry over. It's all very simple. When it's just you and me, you call me Eliza. When my mother's there, you call me Miss Elizabeth. She's always called me Elizabeth, and I don't argue any more. I can't see that it makes any difference to who I am.'

'You think names don't matter? Let me tell you something. When I was first taken into service – and I was younger then than you are now – the lady of the house took me down to meet the staff. This is Ellen, she said. She'll be starting tomorrow. No, I said, thinking she'd made a mistake, and knowing no better. No, I'm Eluned. Not in this house you're not, said the lady, and she turned and walked out. I was never Eluned again, and when I think about it now, I see that I lost something of myself when I lost my name.'

She wiped her eyes and gave herself a little shake. 'This won't do,' she said. She turned to the cook. 'Is the stock ready, Alice?'

'Ten minutes,' said Alice.

Mrs Pugh gave a wan smile and tucked her handkerchief into her apron pocket. 'Thank you, Eliza,' she said.

* * *

Back in her room, Eliza settled herself at her dressing table and began to brush her hair. Darker and more unruly than ever, she thought, squinting into the mirror and lifting a hank of it to tease out the knots. Gypsy, the town boys had called after her when she walked down the high street as a child, and she had burned with a bewildering mixture of embarrassment and pride. She had once overheard her father comparing her with Charlotte: not as pretty, he had said, but more striking. At the time the remark had stung, but today, scanning her reflection as she brushed – the broad, smooth brow, the firm mouth and jawline, the eyes almost black but gleaming with an inward light – she found her father's judgement both apt and pleasing.

When she had finished she went to her desk, unlocked the drawer and took out a pen and the little leather-bound notebook her uncle had given her. Too lovely, she had thought, to be written in, but now she opened it up and dipped the pen. *Eliza Mace,* she wrote on the flyleaf, and then twice more, in a firmer hand: *Eliza Mace. Eliza Mace.* After a moment she closed the notebook, replaced it in the drawer and turned the key.

Two

Charlotte's letter was the usual mish-mash of gossip and grievance, largely unreflective and without any discernible sense of order or relevance. Bristol was busier and filthier than ever, Lettie had handed in her notice, the supposed joys of marriage were, for reasons too delicate to be discussed in a letter, still proving elusive, an evening at the theatre had been disappointing, Daniel had given her a puppy, Mr Proctor had brought round a packet of the most delectable Assam tea and the mice had been nesting in her sewing basket. *Just imagine me,* she wrote, *reaching for the pincushion and pulling out a little hairless creature no bigger than a grub. I screamed and Daniel came running from his study, puffing like a grampus – he has put on a good deal of weight since we were last at the Hall – and took me in his arms. I clung to him and sobbed like the heroine of a second-rate romance while he comforted me, kissing my face and neck and straining me to his breast. But then the questions, the discovery of the nest, the summoning of servants and, of course, the fizzling out of whatever momentary spark of passion had been struck in us. There are times, my dear Eliza, when I think longingly of early widowhood and a second marriage.*

A gentle tapping: her uncle's knock. She opened the door to find him standing against the opposite wall of the corridor, holding his hat and gloves awkwardly against his stomach.

'I wanted to apologise,' he said. 'For what I said at breakfast. I spoke thoughtlessly.'

'Did you mean it? That we won't be able to explore any more?'

'I said more than I intended, and I said it clumsily.'

'I couldn't believe it. Why does it have to change? You know what your company means to me. When you're not with me I still see the plants and the birds, but there's no-one to tell me about them. There's no-one to explain the tracks on the river bank. No-one to name the clouds or the constellations. Why shouldn't you go on teaching me for ever?'

'Nothing's for ever, Eliza. Even so...'

'Even so?'

'I was running ahead of events. It's one of my besetting sins – to dwell on anticipated sorrows when I should be relishing present pleasures. So I've come to ask whether you'd like...' He raised his hat to his head in quick, nervous dumb show and then lowered it again.

'A walk? You know I would.' The old excitement, mingled now with relief. 'I'll be down in five minutes.'

* * *

As they crossed the yard Brand came running from the barn to greet her. Eliza gathered her skirts and squatted on the cobbles, rubbing her knuckles against his blunt head while he circled her, purring and butting at her calves.

James looked on. 'You see,' he said. 'He's thriving out here. Cats are survivors.'

'Some are.' The rest of the litter had been drowned, in spite of her protests. Brand was alive only because of her intervention.

The name had been James's idea. A brand plucked from the burning, he had said, and though Eliza had objected that she had saved the kitten from water, not fire, the name had stuck. Eighteen months on, Brand was a swaggering hulk of a cat, a ferocious killer of rats and rabbits – not a house pet at all, she acknowledged now, though she had initially tried to persuade her parents otherwise.

Brand reared up on his hind legs and placed his forepaws against her skirts. 'Get down,' she said, buffeting him lightly away. 'That's enough.' She rose, brushing at the muddy pawprints with the back of her glove, and turned to her uncle. 'Let's go,' she said.

They struck diagonally across the parkland as usual, making for Top End Wood. It was a gentle rise, but the frosted grass was slippery underfoot and by the time they reached the edge of the wood they were both breathing heavily. Eliza leaned back on the gate and looked down to where Brand sat just outside the entrance to the yard, a black smudge against the orange brick of the wall.

The house could never have been described as grand but it was substantial, and until recently had been possessed of a certain understated elegance. Now, with the untended shrubbery pressing up against its windows and the ragged stalks of thistles standing stiffly upright in the lawns and borders that fronted it, the building seemed desolate. From where she stood, Eliza could see the damage inflicted on the roof by the previous winter's storms – the dislodged coping stone lying where it had fallen, the tiles around it cracked and slipping.

'It's horrible,' she said. 'Horrible to see the place so run down. Mother and Father don't seem to care what happens to it.'

'Oh, I think they care. Up to a point. But maintenance costs money.'

There was a long, uncomfortable silence. Below them, the curved line of the drive, with the parkland stretching out for almost a quarter of a mile beyond it and then, where the open prospect ended, the dark mass of Coptall Wood. 'All this land,' said Eliza at last. 'You'd think he might sell some of it if he needs the money to maintain the house.'

A commotion in the wood behind them: the agitated scolding notes of a blackbird above a hubbub of sharper bird calls, and then the harsh cry of a jay. 'They're mobbing an owl,' said James, turning to peer into the shadows. Eliza turned too, following his gaze, and at that moment the owl broke cover almost directly above their heads and skimmed along the woodland edge before dodging back among the trees thirty yards away.

Eliza loved her uncle's intimacy with the life of the woods and fields, his profound understanding of it. As a child she had looked upon it as a kind of magic – his sensitivity to the calls and rustlings in the trees and undergrowth, his ability to pick out half a dozen notes from a riot of birdsong and name the singer, his reading of the clues left in the soft ooze beside the river or along the woodland tracks. There's nothing mysterious about it, he had told her. It's simply a matter of observation. Keep your eyes and ears open, be receptive to the subtle vibrations in the world around you. And when you come across something you don't understand, keep worrying away at it until the understanding comes. Everything has an explanation, and it's a lazy mind that pretends otherwise. Science, he had insisted, not magic.

They kept to the high ground for another hundred yards and then followed the stream downhill, crossing the drive by the bridge and continuing towards the corner of Coptall Wood. Coptall had been the focus of her explorations since early childhood, and the centre of her imaginative world. Unlike Top End Wood – a narrow strip of ash and hazel, partially coppiced and amounting to little more than a windbreak – the lower woodland was unfathomable, dense, dark and almost pathless. Charlotte had always refused to accompany her into its depths, and as a child Eliza had grown used to exploring them alone until one summer day shortly before her ninth birthday, straying even further than usual, she had missed lunch and returned in the late afternoon to find her mother pacing the wood's edge, frantic with worry. Anything could have happened, Hannah had said. What could have happened? asked Eliza, genuinely perplexed. When you get lost you just keep walking until you come to the edge of the wood, and then you keep to the edge until you get back to the place you started from. And if you'd fallen, asked her mother, what then? What if you'd been trapped somewhere? I've had Todd out there searching the shaft in the ice house. What if you'd lost your footing there? From now on you stay out in the open, where we can find you.

For three months Eliza had roamed the parkland around the house like a lost spirit, sometimes skirting the forbidden wood, peering into its shadows, snuffing the mingled scents of growth and rot that breathed from it. And then, as if in answer to a prayer she had never quite managed to articulate, her uncle came to the Hall on the first of his extended visits and the matter was resolved. It wasn't simply that her mother was prepared to let her go into the woods in James's company, but that he was the perfect companion for her – thoughtful, knowledgeable and as willing to listen to her ideas as to share his own. She could see now that it was on those walks, not in her stilted exchanges with her governess, that her education had begun.

They ducked between the bars of the fence and entered the wood. She felt it at once, that subtle change in the air, the sense of a world at once more complex and more primitive than her own. Somewhere to her left a blackbird was turning over the dead leaves on the woodland floor, scratching and scuffling, the sound clear on the still air. Away to her right and at a greater distance, a shivering of the undergrowth and then the sharp crack of a breaking twig.

She gripped his sleeve. 'Deer?'

He shook his head. She craned forward, holding her breath. A figure detached itself from the shadows and came slowly towards them, eyes down, scanning the ground. The hunched shoulders and shambling gait were familiar.

'It's Fletcher,' she said.

The man started and straightened up. He hadn't seen them, she realised, watching the swaying movement of his head as he tried to pinpoint her voice. Then James stepped forward. 'Good morning, Fletcher.'

For a moment the man looked as if he were about to turn tail and run. 'Stay where you are,' said James, moving towards him. 'I know what you're up to.'

Fletcher flashed him an embarrassed grin and touched the brim of his hat with a grimy forefinger. 'Morning, Mr Mace,' he said. 'That's a relief. Just for a second I took you for your brother.'

'My brother and I think alike on the matter. Poaching's a crime.'

'You might think alike – difference is, the way you act.'

'Really? I could send for the constable this minute – in fact I've half a mind to do so.'

'Maybe, but that wouldn't be your brother's way, would it?'

'What do you mean by that?'

16

'You know what I mean. He'd have set about me by now. You see this?' He bent forward, pulling his shirt and coat back from his neck and ran his finger along his collarbone. 'See the dip there? Broken, and never mended right. That's what he did, the day he gave me notice.'

'I heard about it. But you attacked him.'

'Did he say that? Then he's a bloody liar.'

'Careful, Fletcher.'

'I'm telling you no more nor less than the truth. Listen. He walked up to me that morning – I was setting traps at the top end – and said the estate had no more use for a gamekeeper. My wife and I was to get out of the cottage by the end of the week. Just that, and then he made to walk away – no discussion, no apology. I grabbed him by the arm. I'm fifty-three years old, I said, and not as quick on my pins as I used to be – how am I going to find another job? Where am I to live? That's not my concern, he said. I tried to swing him round, tried to make him face me. Take your hands off me, he said, and brought his crop down on my arm. I slackened my hold but it made no difference – he was on me then, hacking at me like a madman until I fell, and kicking me where I lay. That's for your twenty years' miserable service, he said. For the vermin you're too lazy to kill, for the village rabble you turn a blind eye to, letting them take my rabbits and pheasants as they please.'

'You were never a good gamekeeper,' said James.

Fletcher shrugged. 'Maybe not. But I didn't deserve that kind of treatment. He beat me like a dog. I was ill for weeks after. Even now, I'm still not right.'

'But my brother had a point. Half the men of the village poached his woods with impunity.'

'I used to let a few get away with it. Folk have to eat.'

'Yes, but not at others' expense.'

'Isn't that what the rich do, Mr Mace? Eat at other people's expense? If the poor sometimes take a little for themselves—'

'That's dangerous talk, Fletcher. You can think what you like, but I'd advise you to keep your thoughts to yourself.'

Fletcher's face was flushed, his breathing heavy. It occurred to Eliza that he might have been drinking. 'I'll tell you something,' he said. 'This past year things have gone hard with me, but the folk I looked after when I had a job have helped me out now that I've none. God knows where I'd be without them. We don't have much, Mr Mace, but we stick together. Not like some I could name.'

James's face hardened. 'Empty your pockets,' he said.

Fletcher patted his side pockets. 'There's nothing in them.'

'I'm not stupid, Fletcher. Undo your coat.'

For a moment it looked as if he was going to refuse; then he slowly undid his buttons and held the coat wide. Two inner pockets, bulging visibly.

'Three rabbits,' he said. 'You'd never have missed them.'

'That's not the point. Hand them over.'

'No,' said Eliza. 'Let him keep them.' She felt the blood rising to her cheeks. James turned to look at her. 'Please,' she said.

A long silence before James turned back to Fletcher. 'Go on,' he said. 'Get out. I don't want to find you here again.'

Fletcher began to button his coat. 'Thank you, Miss Eliza,' he said. 'It's good to know there's some with a heart.' He turned and moved away.

'You hear what I say,' James shouted after him. 'You stay off the estate.'

There was no acknowledgement. Fletcher shambled back the way he had come and was quickly lost to sight among the trees.

'I'm sorry,' said Eliza. 'I couldn't bear to think of him going hungry.'

'Let's continue our walk as if nothing had happened to interrupt it.' James set off again, moving deeper into the wood. Eliza followed at his heels.

'But do you forgive me?' she asked. 'I know I spoke out of turn.'

James turned back to face her. 'There's nothing to forgive,' he said. 'Any true Christian would say you were in the right, and that I'm the one who behaved badly.'

'But I challenged you in Fletcher's presence. Father says—'

'I'm not your father, Eliza.' His expression softened; he reached out and placed his hand gently on her shoulder. 'Believe me, you did the right thing.'

It was trying to snow, a fine powder sifting through the bare branches. James turned up his collar. 'Come on,' he said, 'or we'll lose the best of the day.'

Three

They returned a little after midday to find Dr Allen's gig drawn up in front of the Hall. Eliza ran up the steps and burst into the hallway to find the doctor descending the stairs, his bag clutched awkwardly under his arm while he fumbled with the fastening of his cloak. He seemed barely to notice her.

'Mr Mace,' he said, moving briskly towards the door as her uncle entered. 'I understand that your brother is away on business. I wonder if I might have a word with you.'

'Yes. Is Hannah—?'

'It's nothing very serious. An attack of breathlessness – the result of a prolonged fit of coughing. You know, I presume, that there's an underlying problem – a congenital weakness of the lungs – but there's no indication that there have been any serious developments there. I'd like to ask you...' He broke off and glanced sideways at Eliza.

James reached out and drew her towards him so that she stood at his side. 'I think Eliza should be involved in any discussion of her mother's condition.'

'As you please. The fact is that your sister-in-law is in a state of considerable anxiety. I've probed the matter as far as is consistent with professional etiquette, but she's reluctant to discuss details. The sedative I've given her is a stopgap. What she really needs is a period of complete rest. I've advised her to keep to her room and leave the running of the estate and household to others. May I ask you to do what you can to ensure that she follows that advice?'

'Of course. I'll take charge of all essential matters until she's well again.'

'You're not expecting your brother to return in the near future?'

There was an awkward pause. 'It's a little uncertain,' said James. 'He'll be with us as soon as his business allows.'

'I'm sure everything will be in good hands meanwhile. And this little lady' – Dr Allen bobbed forward and pinched Eliza's cheek – 'will no doubt be able to contribute her penn'orth. If you have any concerns about Mrs Mace's condition, please send for me at once.' He gave James's hand a perfunctory squeeze and was gone, bustling out of the door and down the steps into the falling snow.

Eliza stared after him, rubbing her cheek. 'He's been doing that to me for as long as I can remember. It's time he stopped. Professional etiquette? He doesn't know the meaning of the phrase.'

James was smiling. 'Dr Allen isn't the most enlightened of men, but he means no harm.'

'He thinks I'm a child. Contribute my penn'orth? Does he think I've never had to run the household before? Mother's migraines, her monthlies – who does he imagine steps into the breach?'

'I don't suppose he imagined anything, Eliza. It simply wouldn't have occurred to him. Now I suggest you go up and see your mother. Assuming luncheon is on time, that gives you half an hour. We can talk further when you come down.'

* * *

Luncheon was not on time. They were already seated at the table when Mrs Pugh came in to let them know it would be delayed.

'By twenty minutes,' she said. 'Maybe a little more. What with attending to Mrs Mace and then the unpleasantness with the butcher's boy—'

'Unpleasantness?' James leaned forward. 'What kind of unpleasantness?'

'It's true there's money owing. But that's not the boy's business. And I believe your brother has come to an arrangement with the butcher.'

'No doubt,' said James drily. 'Thank you, Mrs Pugh.'

As the door clicked shut behind the housekeeper, James turned to Eliza. 'You can't be protected from all this,' he said. 'Whatever your mother thinks.'

'I'd have to be deaf and blind not to know that we're in trouble. And I don't need protection. I want a clearer sense of what's going on. You've always told me that ignorance is a curse.'

'And knowledge our salvation. Even so, it's natural for people to want to shield those they love from the harsher realities of life.'

'Why does father keep going away? When he says business, what sort of business does he mean?'

James sighed. 'I don't know, and neither does your mother. Your father has never been much inclined to take me into his confidence, and over the past few years he has grown increasingly secretive. When he goes away we don't even know where he is, let alone what he's doing there.'

'But we know he's in debt?'

'Well, the household owes money in town, of course – the butcher is only one of half a dozen tradesmen waiting to be paid. What's hidden from us is the extent of debts run up by your father in pursuit of his business affairs. It's your mother's fear that he may have suffered serious losses, and although I'm inclined to keep an open mind in the absence of evidence, I've become increasingly worried myself. And I know him of old. Money runs through his fingers like water – always has done. When I came back from India...'

He paused. Eliza heard the coals slip and settle in the grate.

'Go on.'

'I'm not sure I should tell you this. It's a story of bad behaviour on your father's part and perhaps a certain weakness on my own. Do you really want to hear it?'

'If it helps me to understand what's happening now, then yes, I do.'

'It's the answer I'd have expected from you, Eliza, and I applaud you for it. But I think of Pandora's box: once the words are out I shan't be able to call them back.'

'You've already opened the box, Uncle James. If you hadn't wanted to tell me the story you wouldn't have said anything at all.'

A tense silence, uncomfortably protracted; then James drew himself up in his chair.

'I imagine you know,' he said, 'that I inherited next to nothing when your grandfather died. What little remained of the estate went to your father, while I was left to fend for myself. India had never figured in my plans, such as they were, but an old schoolfriend who had gone out to manage a tea plantation wrote out of the blue to say that he had it in mind to appoint an assistant and wondered whether I might be interested in the post. I was there before the year was out.'

'I know you were in India, but you never talk about it. Why not? I've always thought you must have been terribly unhappy there.'

'On the contrary. I was happier there than I'd ever been before – or have been since. If I'm reticent about those times, it's perhaps because I want to keep the memories intact. Words take the bloom off such things. What I can say – what I want to tell you now – is that those two years transformed my view of the world and my place in it. From the moment I set foot in Bombay I experienced my surroundings with a new intensity. It was as if I'd been imprisoned in some dim cell, and now the door was thrown open. The streets and market places were a revelation. Everything pressing in on me – the jostle of bodies, the stench of rot and filth, the colour and fragrance of the spices heaped in bowls on the stalls, the incomprehensible cries and chatter. I remember noting in my journal that I was at last seeing the world in its true colours.'

'Wasn't it dangerous being out there alone? Weren't you afraid?'

'I remember fear, yes, but also a sense of exhilaration, stronger than fear – though that's not quite the right way to express it, because the fear was part of the excitement. It's difficult to explain. When I eventually arrived in Assam and was able to consider my experiences at greater leisure, I began to piece together a philosophy that might help me to understand what was happening to me, but the words I cobbled together in my notebook missed the essence of the vision, and I gave up.'

'At least you'd had the vision.'

'Yes, and I've never entirely lost it.'

'Yet you don't attend church with us.'

James frowned. 'What goes on in church here on a Sunday morning has no connection with my experiences in India. You'll learn more about life's mysteries in an hour's walk through the fields than from any sermon Mr Benson is likely to give. Nothing

I discovered in my travels seemed to me to reinforce the faith I'd been brought up in. On the contrary: out there in India I understood clearly for the first time that there's no heaven, and no need of it. The world is enough. The miracles lie all around us – in every twig, every feather, every blade of grass. The secret is to recognise them for what they are.'

Eliza unfolded her napkin and placed it on her lap. 'I'm hungry,' she said. 'You told me that my father—'

'I'm coming to that. Towards the end of my third year in Assam I fell ill. It seemed to be nothing serious at first, but after a month I was still feverish, and very weak – at times scarcely able to rise from my bed. When I first decided to return to England, it was in the hope of finding a specialist with the knowledge and skill to cure me, but by the time the ship docked in London it seemed more reasonable to assume that I was coming home to die. Your father…'

He fell silent, staring out of the window. He's regretting this, thought Eliza as the silence lengthened. 'I need to know,' she said.

'And I need to speak thoughtfully, without resentment. I don't say your father failed me. Not exactly. He found me lodgings in Hampstead and arranged for care and medical treatment. For well over a month he stayed nearby, visiting when his work permitted – some business he was conducting in the city – and in general keeping an eye on my progress. Rapid progress, as it turned out: by the time he left for home I was strong enough to take a regular morning constitutional on the heath and to resume control of my own affairs. That's when his misdemeanours came to light.'

'When you say misdemeanours—'

'Some would use a harsher term. A couple of days after my return your father asked me to sign a document giving him access to my savings. It hardly needs saying that I wasn't in full possession of my faculties at the time – as I recall, I was barely able to hold the pen – but the arrangement would have seemed, on the face of it, eminently sensible. He was to use the money to pay my bills until such time as I was competent to take matters back into my own hands. And if I died – well, we may have touched on the question once or twice during those first few days but I chose not to pursue it. Anyway the point is this: by the time I was well enough to handle my own finances again, there was nothing left to handle. The money was gone.'

'You're not saying he stole it from you?'

'He didn't think of it in those terms. When I confronted him – and you can be sure that I wouldn't have done so without detailed evidence – he told me he'd borrowed the money and would repay it in a few days. The days became weeks, the weeks months, and eventually he admitted that the money was lost – sunk in some failed scheme. It wasn't a fortune, but I'd done well in India and would have had enough to buy a house and a little land. All gone – the money, the dreams.'

'You didn't take him to court?'

'My own brother? I didn't even consider it. In any case I already suspected that his inheritance was gone, as indeed it was. He was in no position to return the money. I sometimes think, though, that I should have vented my anger, shown a bit more fight. As a grown man I behaved towards him in much the same way I'd behaved when we were young – pretending an insouciance I didn't feel – and I think that was harmful to both of us.'

'He should have paid you back later, when he had money again.'

'He never had money again. Don't you see, Eliza? When he married your mother he had nothing, and he has nothing now. Everything he has spent in the interim has been hers. He has run through the family funds, and would have run through a good deal more if he'd been able to get his hands on the estate. You have your grandfather to thank for putting that out of his reach.'

The door swung open and Mrs Pugh entered, with Carys at her heels bearing the Spode tureen. 'Stew,' she announced. 'Mutton stew.' She reached two plates from the sideboard and placed them on the table. 'Not as tender as it should be. It could have done with another half-hour, but I thought – stop dithering, girl, you'll have the whole lot on the floor. Set it down there.'

She removed the lid from the tureen and began to ladle stew onto the plates. 'Owen Meredith stopped by while you were out,' she said. 'He wanted to see the mistress but I told him she was indisposed and he'd have to speak to Eliza. Estate business, he said – prefers to speak with you. I hope you don't mind, sir, but I suggested you might be free to have a word with him this afternoon. If you'd rather not…'

'I'd be happy to oblige him. Thank you, Mrs Pugh.'

The servants were barely out of the door before Eliza let fly. 'He has no right,' she said. 'Does he think I'm incapable of discussing estate matters? Does he think I can't be trusted to take a message to my mother?'

James sighed. 'Patience, Eliza. You'll have responsibilities enough in due course – maybe enough to make you wish your childhood back. The fact is that Owen has asked, quite specifically, to speak with me. I've agreed. Let's leave it at that.' He picked up his knife and fork and began to saw at a wedge of meat.

Eliza watched him. 'Alice must have taken one of Todd's boots for a cut of mutton,' she said, and felt her anger lift like mist on a summer morning. That was the way of it when she was with her uncle: she could speak her mind freely and then move on. She smiled. 'You said something just now about my grandfather.'

'I was referring to the trust.'

'The trust?'

'You don't know what I'm talking about, do you? Something you said this morning made me wonder. It's simply this: your grandfather took legal steps in advance of your parents' marriage to ensure that your mother retained ownership of the estate. The Hall and its lands are hers alone, and will pass to you and Charlotte on her death. It was a prescient move – I think he had the measure of your father from the outset.'

'Why has Mother never told me about this?'

'Perhaps because whatever she said would have been likely to raise inconvenient questions. I imagine she was anxious to protect you and Charlotte from the knowledge that the marriage was flawed from the start.'

'She loved him, I'm sure of that. Maybe she still does. And I think he must once have loved her.'

James laid down his knife and fork. 'I can't eat this,' he said.

'I remember times when…'

What did she remember? Her father gazing across the room to where her mother sat sewing, his eyes following her small, quick movements with such rapt attentiveness that Eliza, watching from the window seat, felt her own heart quicken. An arm slipped round a waist, fingertips brushing a cheek, laughter from behind a closed door. Just a few odd fragments, it struck her now, precious by virtue of their rarity. 'But I suppose it was nothing,' she said. 'Nothing to speak of.'

A sharp rap at the side door, then voices drifting through the hallway. 'It's Owen,' said James. 'Would you excuse me, Eliza?' He folded his napkin and rose to his feet. 'We can continue the conversation later if you like.'

'Maybe. You've given me plenty to think about in the meantime.'

'Too much?'

She shook her head. 'Nothing I can't bear.'

Mrs Pugh put her head round the door. 'I know,' said James before she could speak. 'I'm coming.'

She heard her uncle greet the steward with breezy familiarity, heard the door slam shut. She was about to return to her meal when she became aware of voices beyond the window and looked up to see the two men striding out together across the lawn. As she watched she saw Owen throw back his head and laugh, at ease with her uncle as he never was with her father, and in that fleeting instant she caught herself wishing that her father would never return.

Four

E ven though Eliza banished the thought immediately, the remainder of the day was clouded by a superstitious anxiety. What if the wish, once formulated, proved irrevocable? What if it were granted? Sitting in her room as the late afternoon light faded from the sky she framed an appeal to a god whose existence she had recently begun to doubt. She hadn't meant it, she said; the thought had come unbidden and wasn't truly hers. Bring Father home, she pleaded, bring him safely home.

'Do you think,' she asked her mother that evening, 'that we can hurt people by thinking wrongly about them? By wishing for something that might harm them?'

Hannah eased herself back against the pillows. 'No,' she said. 'We think all kinds of unpleasantness, but it's only our actions that count. What did you have in mind?'

'Nothing. I was curious, that's all. Did you know that Owen was asking to speak with you earlier? I'd have found out what he wanted, only—'

'Your uncle is dealing with it. It's a complicated matter and there's no need for you to be involved. Your task is to keep the household running smoothly until I'm up and about again.'

'Are you feeling any better?'

Hannah sighed and pressed her hand to her chest. 'A little, maybe. Dr Allen tells me I need rest, but my mind's in turmoil. I slept this afternoon, but with such terrible dreams that I was glad to wake.'

'Is there anything I can do?'

'Nothing at all – the illness will no doubt run its course as usual.' She took her novel from the bedside table and opened it, forcing back the boards until the spine creaked. 'But if word comes from your father, let me know at once.'

'Of course.' Eliza bent over her mother and kissed her gently on the forehead. 'Sleep well.' She let herself quietly out and went downstairs.

She found her uncle in the drawing room, poring over an atlas. 'I've been wondering,' he said, looking up at her over his reading glasses, 'whether scientists might usefully devote more time to the study of the earth's oceans. When I think what life forms must be hidden there, far beyond land and at depths still unsounded, I feel a kind of giddiness – so much of our world still unknown to us, so much to discover.' He closed the atlas and motioned Eliza to sit beside him. 'Have you been with your mother?'

'Briefly. She didn't seem to want me to stay.'

'She's exhausted. It's hardly surprising. Your father's departure has naturally distressed her and as if that weren't enough, she has had to deal with an urgent matter of business.'

'The business you were discussing with Owen? Does that have to do with my father too?'

'It's understandable that you should want to know what's going on, Eliza. I sympathise, but your mother is anxious to protect you from what she refers to as the burden of knowledge. She hopes that whatever storms are raging now will have blown themselves out before explanations become necessary.'

'But you don't agree. I know you don't.'

The mantel clock ticked away the seconds. 'You're right,' said James at last, 'but I'm in a difficult position. You'll have to rein in your curiosity.'

'*Curiosity is a virtue, and don't let anyone try to persuade you otherwise.* That's what you told me.' She remembered the moment so clearly. They had been out at the far edge of the wood, looking across to the river and the hills beyond, and it had seemed to her then that there'd be no end to it – to the questioning, the exploring, the discoveries.

'Different circumstances, Eliza. We were speaking of the value of a scientific education, not about family matters.'

'But doesn't the principle hold good in all circumstances? How can anyone's interests be better served by ignorance than by knowledge?'

James smiled. 'It's the fate of teachers,' he said, 'to have their own lessons read back to them by their students. We see eye to eye on the matter, but your mother has other views and we have to respect them.'

'Even if they're wrong?'

'Even if they're different. She's an intelligent woman and I listen when she speaks.'

'And when I speak? I'm asking you to tell me—'

James rose suddenly to his feet – in anger, she thought at first, uneasily aware that she might have overstepped the mark; but catching his expression as he turned away, she realised that his agitation was something else entirely. He walked over to the fireplace and rested his forearm on the mantelpiece, staring into the flames. When he spoke again it was with an odd intensity; his hand, she noticed, was shaking.

'You must understand that I owe a debt of gratitude to your mother. An immense debt. If it hadn't been for her intervention at a crucial point in my life I dare say I'd be long dead. You may not realise it, but my initial visit to Edge Hall was at her invitation, not your father's.'

'I remember you arriving that first time. Young as I was, I knew something was seriously wrong with you. I was frightened by you, thinking you were dying.'

'I was ill, certainly – I thought at the time that I was suffering from a mild recurrence of the ailment that had brought me back from India – but that wasn't what troubled me. No, it was something else: some force or presence had lodged in my mind and I couldn't shake it loose. A shadow, that's how I thought of it – a formless shadow darkening everything I did and said, making me question the value of my life. Little by little I came to think that I was worse than irrelevant; I was an excrescence on the face of the earth, and the sooner I removed myself the better. The shadow told me in no uncertain terms that I must kill myself, and I was ready to comply. I went so far as to buy poison, and I believe I intended to use it.'

'But you didn't.'

'As you can see,' he said with a gesture – hands spread, a little bow in her direction – that might in other circumstances have suggested levity. 'But I came close. I can still see that small brown packet on my desk, and the glass of water standing beside it. If I tip the powder into the glass, I said to myself, I shall certainly swallow it. I sat staring at the packet from a little after midnight until the window lightened and the dawn chorus started up. Then I heard my landlady riddle the grate in the room below and something shifted in me so that I saw clearly how close I'd come to the edge of the chasm that separates the living from the dead, and I began to shake with terror. Even then, I didn't dispose of the packet. I slipped it into the desk drawer in case I should need it later. But I also picked up my pen and wrote to your father.'

34

'Did you tell him about the poison?'

'No. I said simply that I'd been suffering from a prolonged bout of neurasthenia and would value the opportunity to spend a little time with him. Perhaps I should have been more open. The letter he sent in reply was an invitation to stay here at the Hall for a week, but an invitation couched in terms so cold and grudging that I felt I'd be unable to accept it. And then, by the next post, I received a letter from your mother. You have to remember that at the time I barely knew her, yet she wrote with real warmth, and as though she had divined my predicament. You must come, she said. This time of darkness – it was as if she'd seen into my heart – will pass, but for the moment you need rest and company. The estate – a place conducive, as she put it, to the restoration of the soul – was mine to wander in as I pleased. I saw her then as a guardian angel, and her letter as my salvation.'

'Mother? A guardian angel?'

James's face creased into a smile. 'The phrase came to mind at the time. I don't believe in angels, but I do believe that human sympathy can help wrecked minds to heal. That letter changed my life. And I'm telling you this so that you'll understand the depth of my loyalty to your mother. Almost everything I value today – my place here, her friendship, the walks you and I take together – I owe to her.'

'So when she tells you I'm to be left in ignorance, you have to do as she says?'

'It's rather less straightforward than that. My loyalties in this case are divided. I know what your mother wants you to be told about the world you live in – frankly, not very much – and I know what you need to be told if you're to make sense of it. On the matter of the estate she was adamant: you're not to be involved in any discussion about it.'

'All I'm asking is that you tell me what Owen called to discuss this afternoon. It seems a small enough thing.'

'Seems, but isn't. Knowledge, of whatever kind, offers access to greater knowledge. You open a door and find yourself in a room. You look about you, map the room in your mind, and then you notice that there's another door in the far wall. Do you open it? Some would say no, others might weigh up the matter. But there are others again, and I suspect you'd be among them, whose curiosity would propel them straight through that second doorway. And so it goes on, doorway after doorway, room after room. Your mother would argue – I've heard her argue – that there's such a thing as too much knowledge, and even I recognise that knowledge may be a mixed blessing. Listen, Eliza: the simple answer to your question is that Owen called to discuss the felling of trees in the lower wood. Your father gave certain instructions before he left, and Owen rightly judged that he should speak with your mother before carrying them out.'

'Why would Father want the trees cut down?'

'Another question. Another door. You see what I mean, Eliza? Well, the simple answer is that he wants the money the timber will bring in.'

'But surely he can't—'

'Indeed he can't. Your mother has made that clear to him. When I brought Owen's message to her, she simply counter-manded the instruction. It's the thin end of the wedge, she said: the money would be useful, not least for repairs to the Hall, but the precedent would be disastrous. If, as she claims, the trees are part of the estate and therefore entirely under her control, that should be the end of the matter, but it doesn't take a fortune teller to foresee the trouble there'll be when your father returns.'

From the darkness beyond the window, the quavering hoot of an owl. James took up the poker and stirred the dying embers of the fire.

'I'm cold,' said Eliza. 'Cold and tired.' She rose to her feet.

'Just remember this, Eliza: you're bound to be affected by the discord in the household, but you're not responsible for it, and you shouldn't imagine that it's your task to set things right.'

'I don't. But I sometimes wish the pair of them would get together and set things right themselves. Don't they realise they're destroying each other?'

The tears came suddenly and without warning. James stepped forward as if to take her in his arms, but stopped short. 'It's nothing,' she said, turning away. 'Nothing a good night's sleep won't cure.'

'Of course. Goodnight, Eliza.'

'Goodnight, Uncle James.' She dabbed her eyes with the corner of her shawl and stepped out into the hallway.

Voices from the corridor: Carys and Alice. Incorrigible chatter-boxes, her mother had once called them to their faces, and it was true that they took every opportunity their duties allowed to huddle together in gossipy conversation. '...hardly waiting for the master to be out of the door,' Alice was saying. 'How long was he in there?'

'Five minutes. Maybe ten. As long as it took me to dust the banisters.'

'Five minutes is long enough for any man. More's the pity.'

Carys let out a little hiccupping giggle. 'You couldn't blame her,' she said. 'What she has to put up with from the master. But she wouldn't, I'm sure of it. She's not that kind.'

'Show me the kind who wouldn't, given half a chance. And when a gentleman has the freedom of a lady's bedroom, to come and go as he pleases, there's no saying what might happen.'

The girls were at the far end of the corridor, at the top of the kitchen steps, so deeply engrossed in their conversation that they didn't notice Eliza until she was almost upon them. They started guiltily and drew apart.

'We were just saying—'

'Thank you, Alice, I heard what you were saying.' Eliza felt the blood rising to her face. 'You were speaking about my uncle and my mother. Would you like me to tell them what I've just heard?'

Carys stepped forward and laid a hand on Eliza's sleeve. 'Please, Miss, please don't. What we said was said in jest. There was no harm meant.'

Eliza snatched her arm away. 'You should know better,' she said. 'Looking for scandal, scattering dirt. My mother has taken to her bed and my uncle was obliged to consult her on an urgent matter of business. That's all there is to it. Shame on the pair of you.' She turned on her heel and swept away with what she hoped was ladylike dignity, but as she reached the staircase she dropped all pretence and took the stairs at a run, stumbling over her skirts. She burst into her room, locked the door behind her and flung herself full length on the bed.

Five

The three of them were looking out from some high place, scanning the plain below. He'll come now, she thought, but her uncle placed a hand on her shoulder and turned to her mother. 'It's time to tell her', he said, and from some terrible resonance in the words she knew that her father was dead. She cried out and woke sweating among the tangled sheets.

Carys was laying the table in the dining room as Eliza entered. The girl was pale; her eyes were rimmed with red. She darted forward, mouth open, but Eliza cut in before she could speak.

'I want to hear nothing more about it, Carys, either from you or from Alice. We'll pretend it never happened.'

'Oh, thank you, Miss Eliza. I'm sure neither of us—'

'Nothing,' said Eliza sharply. 'Nothing at all. Carry on with your work. When my uncle comes down, tell him I've gone for a walk. I shall be back for breakfast.'

Out in the yard she stood and snuffed the air. The wind had veered round to the west, bringing a fine drizzle and that soft, deceptive fragrance that seems, in the depths of winter, to herald the arrival of spring. Todd was leaning in the doorway of the stable, as insubstantial as a shadow in the grey half-light. As she approached he took his pipe from his mouth and blew out a thin plume of smoke.

'You're up early, Miss Eliza.'

'I slept badly.'

'You'll be missing your father.'

A faint nickering from one of the stalls. 'Quiet, Tinder,' he said, half turning towards the darkness at his back. 'He wants his oats.'

'Of course. Don't keep him waiting on my account.'

'And Alice tells me the mistress has been taken poorly again. They say there's nothing goes right in a house that lacks a master.'

Eliza made to move on but the stableman seemed reluctant to let her go. 'Not that he's ever been master here,' he said.

'What do you mean by that?'

He shrugged. Something in the gesture – something close to insolence – unnerved her. 'A man like your father takes badly to the curb. Is it any wonder he spends so much time away from home?'

'Business,' she said. 'He travels on business.' She began to walk away.

'If he was truly the master – if he was allowed to be – his business would be here.'

He was watching her, she knew, waiting for her to turn back. She kept walking.

* * *

She was out for longer than she had intended and returned to find her uncle finishing his breakfast. 'I waited,' he said, smiling up at her, 'until hunger got the better of me. Have you been far?'

'Down to the woods. I had a restless night – worries, bad dreams. I wanted to clear my head.'

He rose and pulled out her chair for her. 'Have you told Carys you're back?'

'I'm not hungry.' She sat down, wanting to talk, not knowing how much to say.

'There's tea in the pot.'

She shook her head. 'I have a feeling...' she began. But it was something more than a feeling. She started again. 'Things are breaking down. The place is falling apart. I don't just mean the house – it wouldn't matter so much if that were all – but the whole household. I sense it in the way the servants behave towards us. It's as if they see it all – the bills piling up, the fields lying fallow, my parents' marriage crumbling – and feel they don't need to keep up appearances any more. When I went out this morning, Todd was loitering in the yard. Something in his manner, as well as what he said—'

'What did he say?'

'That Father wasn't the master here; that he chafes like a curbed horse. He didn't quite say that Mother was to blame, but his meaning was plain enough.'

'Todd's your father's man, Eliza – came with him and sticks by him. Owen and your mother have wanted rid of him for years, and though your father holds out for him I can't imagine Todd rests easy during his absences. He'll be relieved to see him back this evening.'

'Father's coming back?'

'Your mother received a telegram half an hour ago.'

She was crying again, quietly at first and then in long, shuddering sobs. If her uncle had asked she couldn't have told him exactly what her tears signified – relief, she might have said, but there was anger in her weeping too, and a suffocating grief. But he asked nothing; he simply took her hand and let her cry.

'I'm sorry,' she said at last. She pulled her hand free and fumbled for her handkerchief. 'I don't know what's the matter with me.'

There was a knock on the door and Carys entered. 'Shall you be wanting—?' She broke off, staring at Eliza, her mouth open. Eliza dabbed at her eyes and gave herself a little shake.

'Thank you, Carys, but I shan't be taking breakfast after all.'

She waited, listening as the girl's footsteps died away. 'I wonder,' she said, turning back to her uncle, 'whether Mother will be glad or sorry to see him back so soon.'

'And you? What do you feel?'

'I have letters to write,' she said, rising from the table.

* * *

Like a jack-in-the-box, thought Eliza, watching her mother bob up yet again from her seat by the fire and drag herself over to the window. James looked up.

'Sit down and rest,' he said. 'Please, Hannah.' He put down his newspaper and went over to where she stood staring out into the night.

'So late,' said Hannah. 'Todd left more than two hours ago.'

'The train may have been delayed. If so, Todd will have waited.' James took her gently by the elbow and guided her back to her seat. 'They won't be here any the sooner for your worrying.'

'Mid-afternoon, the telegram said.'

James straightened her shawl around her shoulders. 'He'll be home in time for dinner,' he said. 'I guarantee it.'

But by dinnertime there was still no sign of him and Hannah was trembling with anxiety. 'Suppose it's something more than a delay,' she said. 'Suppose there's been an accident.' Eliza saw it vividly in her mind's eye – the engine jumping the rails, the crumpling roll of the carriages down a brambled embankment, her father's body flung across the compartment in a rain of broken glass – but pushed the images aside. 'I think we should continue as normal,' she said. 'I'll ask Mrs Pugh to serve up.'

They were just finishing the soup when they heard the gig coming up the drive, and then the rattle of its wheels on the cobbles as it swung into the yard. Hannah started up and ran into the hall. Eliza made to follow her, but James caught her by the wrist.

'Give them a moment,' he said. Eliza heard the side door open, heard the click and scrape of her father's boots on the tiles. Something gruff, unintelligible, and then her mother's voice.

'What happened, Robert? Where have you been?'

'Dinner now, questions later.' He was moving along the corridor towards the dining room. 'Ham and pea soup, if I'm not mistaken.' He pushed open the door and stood leaning against the jamb. Eliza saw her mother dithering in the shadows behind him, her small hands fluttering.

'That's who I want to see.' Robert stepped unsteadily into the room and moved round the table, his hand trailing the chair-backs, until he stood over Eliza. 'How's my little girl?'

'I'm well, thank you, Father.' He bent to kiss the top of her head and she caught the fume of spirits on his breath. 'Was it a difficult journey?'

He seated himself beside her. 'Difficult enough. Cold and miserable. And I've had nothing to eat since yesterday. Hannah, would you mind?' He gestured towards the tureen on the sideboard.

Hannah stayed put. 'Mrs Pugh is about to bring in the roast,' she said. 'We've had our soup.'

'And now,' said Robert, 'you'll wait while I have mine.'

Hannah opened her mouth as if to speak and immediately closed it again. James rose, went over to the sideboard and began to ladle the soup into a bowl.

'I asked my wife to serve me.'

'Hannah has been unwell.' James brought the bowl to the table and set it in front of his brother. 'I'm happy to serve you.'

Eliza held her breath.

There might be a dozen such moments in any day spent in her father's company – moments of breathless stasis while everyone around him waited to see which way, as Mrs Pugh had once unguardedly expressed it, the cat was going to jump. So exhausting, thought Eliza, looking across at her mother's pale face; so unnecessary.

Five seconds, maybe a little more; and then her father took up his spoon and began to eat.

The mealtime passed uncomfortably in almost complete silence and as soon as she decently could Eliza excused herself and went up to her room. She had been in bed for some time, drifting uneasily between sleep and waking, when she became aware of her parents' voices, raised in argument. She padded over to the door and eased it open.

'...going cap in hand to them,' her father was saying, 'like some miserable beggar, while my wife sits easy on an inherited fortune.'

'There's no fortune. The money's gone.'

'The estate, Hannah. You know what I'm talking about.'

'No fortune nor, I can assure you, any ease. My task is to safeguard what we still have, and I'm worn out by the endless need for vigilance.'

'Worn out by your own stubbornness. Worn out from living hand to mouth when the sale of a dozen acres of grazing or a stand of timber would set everything straight. Don't you see, Hannah? We've hit a rough patch, but all we have to do is realise the value of a small proportion of the land and it'll be plain sailing again.'

'It was never plain sailing with you, and never will be. Your hopeless schemes, your cadging and wheedling, your lies and evasions – that's the man you are, Robert, and I'd be a fool to imagine you're ever going to change. You must pay your own debts. I'm selling nothing.'

A brief silence, and then her father again, weary and faintly tearful. 'I've tried, Hannah, but I've exhausted all possibilities. There's no-one willing to lend me anything – not even to stand surety for a loan.'

'And why do you think that is?' Another pause. 'Look at yourself, Robert. Go on, stand in front of that glass and take a good look.'

'Don't treat me like a child. You've no right.'

'No right? Until you learn to behave like a grown man, I've every right. No money you say, but you seem to have found enough to get drunk on.'

'I'm not drunk. Todd stood me a couple of brandies on the way home, that's all.'

'More than a couple, I'd say. And what sort of a master places himself in his servant's debt? You're sinking, Robert – sinking lower by the day.'

'Whose fault is that? I ask for help and you refuse it.'

'The fault's yours, and until you learn to take responsibility for your own actions there'll be no help from me nor, I imagine, from anyone else.'

There was a crash, as if some heavy object had fallen.

'Get out, Robert. Go and sleep it off.'

Eliza pushed the door shut. After a moment she heard the door of her mother's bedroom creak open, heard her father cross the corridor to his own room. From her mother's side, the sound of the lock clicking home.

No surrender, she murmured, seeing herself suddenly as a small child enveloped in light under the blue dome of the sky. It was a recurring image, a memory perfected over time but in essence true. Her eighth summer, and for a few weeks she had made it her custom each day to climb through the attic window on to the leaded roof of the bay. She would gaze out at the woods and meadows through a gap in the parapet or lie on her back staring up into the unstained blue as the sun beat down on her body and the heat rose from the leads. A month perhaps, certainly no more, before her mother, discovering her there one radiant afternoon, had ordered her back into the house and arranged for the window to be nailed shut. *No surrender* – the phrase, drawn perhaps from one of her father's books, had come to her as she sat in her room, listening to the hammer blows. *No surrender, no surrender*, as each nail was driven home.

She returned to her bed, drew up the bedclothes and lay staring into the dark, hearing the scuttering of mice behind the skirting, the quavering conversation of the owls. Midnight, one o'clock, two. When she heard the clock strike three she lit the lamp, went to her desk and took out her notebook.

I can do nothing to help them, she wrote. *I shall not let them drag me down. While I live here, it will be as far as possible on my own terms. When I leave, I shall not look back.*

Six

She had laid the box on the workbench and was picking through the jumbled tools. Brand was butting at her arm, trying to engage her attention.

'What would you want with that, Miss Eliza?'

She started, dropped the chisel she was holding. Brand leapt from the bench and made off towards the far end of the barn. Todd was standing in the doorway, one shoulder leaning against the frame.

'They're no good,' he said. 'Red with rust, the lot of them. Haven't been used since I don't know when.'

'This will do for my purposes.' She picked up the chisel and made to leave but Todd stood firm, blocking her way.

'And what are your purposes?'

'None of your business, Todd. Let me by.'

He stepped aside and she walked out into the light. 'I'm not a child,' she said, turning back to face him. 'Not any more. I'll not be questioned by servants.'

'You're your father's child, and I'm your father's servant. I've always kept an eye on you.'

'I know what kind of eye you keep on me these days, Todd. That particular duty – if it ever existed – ended with my childhood. Do you understand me?'

He lowered his gaze but said nothing.

'I mean what I say. You'd do well to heed me.' She marched into the house and slammed the door shut.

The flight of stairs leading from the landing to the attic was uncarpeted and she stepped carefully so as not to be heard. Ridiculous, she thought as she pushed open the door – acting as if she were still a seven-year-old, as if she might be bundled back down again, grabbing at the handrail, her feet drumming on the treads; but she entered with the same exaggerated care and closed the door softly behind her.

The window was smaller than she remembered. The job had been roughly done – a slender lath nailed into the recess behind the left-hand sashcord – and would be easy enough to undo. She slipped the edge of the chisel under the lath and levered it free.

The sash lifted easily, letting in a draught of fresh air. The chair she'd used all those years ago had been moved, but she wouldn't need it now, she thought, hitching up her skirts and raising her right leg to the level of the sill. But the folds of cloth hampered her, and after a few moments of positioning and repositioning she saw that she had already forfeited the supple ease of movement she had enjoyed as a child.

She was about to close the window when her father walked into view, sharply delineated against the trees of the lower woodland. At his heels trotted another figure, small and stocky, wearing a black hat and overcoat. His dress and demeanour made her think for a second or two that he might be a clergyman, but as he turned his head, looking back towards the house, she recognised him. She pulled down the sash and rushed downstairs, calling for her uncle.

James emerged from his room as she reached the landing.

'What is it, Eliza? What's the matter?'

'Mr Ellis,' she said. 'Mr Ellis is down there with Father. Down by the wood.'

'Mr Ellis?'

'The timber merchant. If Father is still planning to have the trees felled—'

'Your father's plans are irrelevant. Where's your mother?' James was already halfway down the stairs. 'Hannah!' he called. 'Hannah!'

Carys emerged from the drawing room with a feather duster in her hand. 'She went out,' she said. 'Not two minutes ago. Without her coat or bonnet.'

Eliza was first through the door but her uncle caught up with her as she ran through the yard gateway and out onto the drive. 'There,' he said, pointing down the long slope of the parkland. Hannah was picking her way cautiously over the tussocky ground, skirting the pockets of thawing snow. Robert had left his companion at the wood's edge and was moving up the slope towards her.

She was still some distance from him when she started shouting. What did he think he was up to, what was Ellis doing on her land, hadn't she made herself clear, wasn't she mistress of her own property? – her voice raw and shrill, the words delivered with vicious emphasis. Robert came to a stop in front of her, both hands raised in a placatory gesture.

'It's not the way it seems,' he said. 'Not exactly. Nothing has been agreed.'

'Of course it hasn't. You're in no position to agree anything.'

Robert looked up absently as Eliza and James approached but gave no sign of having noticed them. 'I'm exploring possibilities,' he said. 'That's all. What harm can there be in knowing the value of the timber?'

James hung back, but Eliza moved in to stand at her mother's side. Robert stared at her as though she were a stranger.

'What are you doing here?'

Eliza hesitated. Robert turned to his brother. 'Take Eliza back to the house,' he said. 'This isn't for her ears. And,' he added, glancing up the slope, 'you might tell Owen we shan't be wanting any interference from him.'

Eliza looked back. Owen was striding towards them, his coat unbuttoned and flapping about his legs. Her mother grabbed her by the elbow, held her close.

'I sent for Owen,' she said. 'And Elizabeth can stay. Let her see what I have to contend with.'

Down below, the timber merchant had evidently sized up the situation and was sloping off, keeping to the wood's edge. Owen came to a stop alongside James and stood stiffly attentive, as if awaiting instructions.

'There's no need for this,' said James. 'I suggest we all go indoors now, and talk about it later.'

Robert glared at him. 'Nobody asked you for your suggestions,' he said, 'and nobody wants them. The matter is between me and my wife. The rest of you can leave.'

'Owen's not leaving,' said Hannah. 'It's an estate matter. I want my steward here.'

Robert pulled a face. 'My steward,' he mimicked. 'Your toady. Your greasy lickspittle.'

James stepped forward. 'Come along, Hannah,' he said. 'Let's go in.' He laid his hand gently on her shoulder.

Eliza sensed it before it happened – everything slowing to a standstill as if the air had suddenly thickened around them. A breathless instant, the space, perhaps, between one heartbeat and the next, and then her father was upon her uncle, one hand gripping the lapel of his jacket, the other clenched, pummelling his face and chest. She cried out and moved uncertainly towards them, but Owen was there first, pushing between the two men, thrusting her father back and holding him at arm's length while her uncle scrambled clear.

'Get your filthy hands off me.' Robert brushed Owen's arm roughly aside, but Eliza saw at once that his rage was evaporating. He stood panting, rubbing his knuckles, his eyes downcast.

'I hope you're proud of yourself,' said Hannah. 'Acting like a bar room brawler.'

James stood with his head tilted, holding the back of his hand to his bloodied nose. Owen tugged a large linen handkerchief from his pocket and held it out to him. James took it without a word. As she watched him dabbing haphazardly at his face in a kind of daze it struck Eliza that it was up to her to restore some form of order. 'We're going in,' she said firmly. She took her uncle by the arm and began to walk him up the slope towards the house.

* * *

She entered her room late that afternoon to find Carys kneeling by the hearth, arranging the kindling in a neat pyramid at the centre of the grate.

'There.' Carys dusted her hands on her apron and rose to her feet. 'I won't light it yet. The coal's running out – just a few scuttle-fuls left. Your mother says we're to use wood now but the bedroom fireplaces won't hold more than a handful of sticks and I can't—'

'Thank you, Carys.' Eliza drew her shawl more closely around her shoulders. 'You may go now.'

She waited until she heard Carys's footsteps die away down the corridor; then she seated herself at her desk, dipped her pen and began to write.

My dear Charlotte,

You'll know from my recent letters that we're in a state of turmoil here – Mother and Father at loggerheads, Father absenting himself with increasing frequency, the few remaining servants struggling to keep the household running – but nothing I've written will have prepared you for what I have to tell you now. A fight – no, not a fight, an assault: Father attacking Uncle James, laying into him like a streetfighter, punching him so ferociously that I was afraid he might kill him. Imagine – his own brother, and completely without provocation. There's a sort of madness in him these days, a rage that seems to have infected Mother too. If you'd seen her standing out there in the cold, coatless and with her hair unpinned, screaming into the wind, you'd know what I mean. I'm not saying her anger is misplaced – Father's behaviour would try the patience of a saint – but there was something horribly frightening about its intensity at that moment, as if she had lost sight of who she was and who was around her.

Anyway, it turns out there's no great harm done. Uncle James cleaned himself up as soon as he came in and apart from a swollen lip and a bruised cheek seems little the worse for his beating. He was subdued at lunch – hardly spoke a word – but he ate well. Mother has taken to her bed again. Father stalked off immediately after the incident and hasn't reappeared.

I say there's no great harm done, but I'm still shaking at the thought of it all, still in the grip of the fear I felt out there this morning. I shall talk to Uncle James about it, but not yet. I wish I could see you now, Charlotte, I wish I could tell you what it's like here; I wish you could talk to me the way you did when I was small, when the night frightened me and I thought sleep would never come. I wish there were…

Eliza put down her pen and went to the window. Just childish whining, she thought – *I wish, I wish, I wish.* Asking someone else to make it better. Asking the impossible. A flock of sparrows rose suddenly from the cobbles of the yard in a blur of wings, and with the movement something shifted inside her, as though she were rising with them, lifted high above the outbuildings, above her own pettiness and the fret and fury of her parents' lives. She turned quickly and made for the door.

Lightly on the stair, lightly on the attic floorboards. This time she knew exactly what to do. She shed her clothes until she stood, barefoot and shivering, in her underwear; then she raised the sash, kicked herself clear of the floor and slithered head-first out onto the roof. She scrambled to her feet and stepped over to the parapet.

The air was damp and cold but even so, it seemed to hold a faint aftertaste of those distant summer days. She gripped the coping and looked out across the parkland. The sky was darkening and the jackdaws were swirling in for the night, crowding the trees, chattering madly as they settled. On the far side of the lane Morgan's boy was calling the dog to heel: *here, here, come here,* his voice clear and sweet on the wind. She leaned against the parapet, breathing deeply, taking it all in.

Five minutes and she was chilled to the bone. She clambered back through the window and dressed as quickly as she could, her fingers clumsy with the buttons. She was trembling, and not from cold alone. She felt again the pressure of her mother's hand on the nape of her neck and her own childish resistance – she had cried out, she remembered, in helpless fury, her feet slipping on the varnished wood of the staircase, her small hands grabbing at the rail – and at the same time she was filled with a wild excitement.

The world was wide and she would go where she wanted in it. No-one could stop her now.

Back in her room, she put a match to the kindling and stood a moment at the hearth, warming her hands. Then she took the letter from her desk and dropped it into the flames.

Seven

One more day of thaw, a slant rain melting the last of the snow; then the wind veered round to the east and the sky cleared. The cold bit deep and held, tightening its grip as the days passed. In the stillness small events loomed large – a fox running like a streak of flame across the parkland, a faint stirring of the sedges at the stream's edge, a flock of fieldfares dropping from the air to feed on the hedgerow berries. By day the sun shone brightly but without warmth; at night the frosted land gleamed pale as bone under the moon.

The cold invaded the house, stealing down the corridors, seeping under doors; the bedroom window panes were silvered with fronds and feathers of ice. Carys brought in box after box of wood to keep the drawing room fire blazing but Eliza, sitting reading with her feet on the fender and her cheeks glowing, could still feel the chill at her back.

The assault had deepened the gloom that hung about the household, but no-one seemed to want to discuss it. Her uncle and her mother kept largely to their rooms, coming down for meals and occasionally staying to warm themselves at the fire before retreating again. Her father slouched aimlessly around the house or took up a position a little to one side of the hearth, leaning on the corner of the mantelpiece. He would hover there without quite settling, staring into the flames or flipping back and forth through the pages of an illustrated magazine, a fidgety, disquieting presence at the margin of her vision. If she spoke to him he would answer, but he showed no sign of wanting to engage in conversation with her. One morning, coming down early to breakfast, she found him slumped at the dining table with his head in his hands. He didn't look up, but she knew he was crying. She stood for a moment in the doorway, then closed the door softly, went back upstairs and knocked at the door of her mother's room.

Hannah sat up as she entered. Her hair was dishevelled, her eyes wild. 'You startled me,' she said, putting her hand to her breast. 'I was dreaming – I don't know what, but the feeling... Has something happened?'

Eliza seated herself on the edge of the bed. 'Nothing to worry about,' she said. 'But Father seems unusually miserable.'

'Your father makes his own misery. There's nothing I can do about it.'

'I don't believe that.'

'Then believe this: there's nothing I wish to do about it.'

'He needs something to occupy him. Something to stop him moping about the house.'

'I'll tell you what's wrong with your father, Elizabeth. He's come to the end of the last of his absurd schemes. He has nothing left – no ideas, no funds, no credit – and he knows it. I warned him what would happen – spelt it out clearly enough and often enough – but he wouldn't have it. Well, perhaps he believes me now.'

She's pleased, thought Eliza, scanning her mother's face; she's relishing his suffering. 'Surely,' she said, 'you feel something for him? Some sympathy at least?'

Hannah sighed. 'Whatever I once felt,' she said, 'is gone. Long gone.' But her eyes filled with tears.

'Come down to breakfast now.' Eliza reached out and took her mother's hand. 'Please. Talk to him.'

* * *

'I was thinking,' said Hannah as Carys tidied away the breakfast plates, 'that we should have the ice house filled. The stream's been frozen hard for a week or more, and we don't know how long the frost will last. This time last year the job was already done.'

'This time last year,' said Robert, 'we had two labourers to call on. Who do you think is going to help Todd now?'

'Why don't the two of you spend the day on it? You could have the job done by nightfall.'

Robert set down his teacup with slow deliberation. 'Is that how it's to be? I'm your labourer now, is that it?' His hands, Eliza noticed, were shaking. Carys leaned over to take his plate, but he waved her away. 'Leave it,' he said. 'Come back later.'

'What Hannah meant,' said James when Carys had left the room, 'is that you can set Todd to work; you can supervise the operation. I'm sure there was no suggestion—'

'Since when have you been employed as my wife's interpreter? I know what she meant.'

Hannah glanced across the table at Eliza. You see how it is, her eyes said; you see what I have to deal with.

'In any case,' said Robert, 'it can't be done.'

'You mean you won't do it.'

'No, Hannah. I mean what I say. There's no way of transporting the ice.'

'The cart, Robert. We use the haycart.'

Robert shifted uneasily in his chair. 'The cart's gone,' he said.

57

'Gone? What do you mean?'

'Sold. I sold it six months ago.'

Hannah's face darkened. 'The cart wasn't yours to sell,' she said.

'We needed the money. We had no-one working the fields. In the circumstances I judged it best—'

'We needed the money, yes, but I saw none of it. And now we need the cart. What does your impeccable judgement suggest we should do about that?'

'The ice isn't important. If we had no ice house we'd get by without it, the way most people do.'

'We're not most people, Robert. And perhaps you'd like to go down to the kitchen now and let the servants know that we'll be without ice this coming summer? See whether Mrs Pugh thinks we can get by without it.'

James rose from the table, motioning Eliza to follow, but she ignored him. 'We can borrow Gwilym Morgan's cart,' she said. 'I'll go over and ask him now.'

Her father glared at her. 'You stay out of this,' he said.

'It's a reasonable suggestion,' said Hannah. 'Let her go.'

'Damned if I will,' he said, but Eliza was already on her feet and making for the door. He called out as she crossed the hall, but no-one followed her. She grabbed her coat and shawl from the stand and let herself out by the side door.

There was a time, she thought as she strode down the drive, when this would have been unthinkable – her defiance of her father's wishes, her father's inaction in the face of her disobedience. If things were changing – and she was certain they were – it was in part because of some change in herself, but she could see, too, that her father's grip on the world was slipping. It struck her suddenly that his attack on her uncle had been an act of desperation, an attempt to reassert his authority over a household in which he no longer had a place.

She crossed the lane and began to climb the track to the farm. It was familiar ground. For more than a year of her childhood she had made the journey two or three times a week, always with a sense of excitement or expectancy, her spirits rising as she climbed.

Rhiannon Morgan: eighteen months older than Eliza and, as Mrs Pugh once put it, too beautiful for her own good. Rhiannon's interest in her had seemed to Eliza, at the time, a fairytale aberration, as though a lady had stooped to befriend a dairymaid. It was only later that she came to see that her parents' barely disguised disapproval of the association might reflect an entirely different view of the matter. It's a tenancy, her mother had more than once observed in response to her casual references to the Morgans' land; they're not landowners.

What she found in the Morgans' household was a warmth lacking in her own. Rhiannon and her elder sister, Grace, conducted themselves with an ease unimaginable at Edge Hall, lively in their parents' company, speaking as and when they pleased. Eliza was at first shocked and then envious, hearing the two girls laughing and joking with their mother – Rebecca, so lovely, slight and carefree in those days that she seemed more like a third sister than a parent.

The change, when it came, was devastating. A difficult pregnancy undermined Rebecca's health and she withered like a nipped flower. The mood in the family darkened, the banter stopped. And the arrival of the baby seemed if anything to make matters worse: Rebecca kept to her bed for weeks after the birth, and both the farm and the house declined as Morgan struggled to cope. Grace was packed off to live with an aunt in Abergavenny while Rhiannon, preoccupied now with domestic duties and sometimes skipping school to attend to them, grew quiet and distant.

Young as she was, Eliza quickly understood that she couldn't expect the old connection to be restored, but it was some time before her visits stopped entirely. She was anxious to prove herself a true friend to the family in what she obscurely recognised as a time of need, and there was also the attraction of the new baby, a scrap of a thing with a round, pale face and a faintly disquieting gaze. While Rhiannon bustled around her she would sit in the rocking-chair, holding him as she'd been shown and talking to him in the sing-song voice he seemed to like: *Jevan, Jevan, little mite, tiny tiddler, fairy-child* – over and over, staring into his eyes, on the lookout for anything that might be construed as a response.

It was her father who had eventually brought the visits to an end. 'It would be best,' he said one morning as she pulled on her boots, 'if you stopped going to the Morgans' place. They've problems enough without having to look after you.'

'They don't look after me. I look after the baby so Rhiannon can get on with the housework. Mrs Morgan's too ill to—'

'You're not to go, do you hear me? I'll not have my daughter working as nursemaid to a farmer's wife.' And then, more gently: 'It's to your credit, Eliza, that you should want to help, but sometimes the kindest thing we can do for people is to stand back and give them the opportunity to address their own problems.'

She had wept, but her father was adamant. 'This is your family,' he said. 'This is your home. You've no call to be looking anywhere else.'

Mrs Pugh, finding her in tears in the yard some time later, had taken her down to the kitchen and given her biscuits and warm, sweet tea. 'You think your heart will break,' she'd said, 'but it doesn't. And six months on, you're a different person in a different world, and the hurt is gone.' At the time Eliza resisted the consolation, but as the weeks went by she came to see the wisdom of Mrs Pugh's words. Walking home from town one afternoon and seeing Rhiannon strolling up the lane ahead of her with Jevan on her hip, she had felt with sudden certainty that her own path would take her a long way from the Morgans' lives, and that she'd be a fool to wish it otherwise.

Now, as the farmhouse came into view at the top of the track, the dog began to bark, running back and forth along the house wall, its chain rattling as it ran. The door flew open and Morgan stepped out into the yard. 'That'll do,' he said, and the dog fell silent.

He stared at her for a moment, adjusting his spectacles on his broad nose, his eyes narrowed against the sunlight; then his face creased into a smile.

'Eliza! You've grown so fine I hardly recognised you. What brings you here?'

'I've come on an errand.' She fiddled with the fringe of her shawl, suddenly uncomfortable. 'To ask a favour.'

Jevan appeared in the doorway, a sturdy child now and tall for his eight years, sullen-eyed under a thatch of dark hair. 'Who's that?' he called.

'Eliza,' said Morgan. 'From the Hall. You remember Eliza?'

The boy shook his head. 'I used to visit the house when you were a baby,' said Eliza, 'but you wouldn't remember that. And I've met you in the lane a few times, walking with Rhiannon.'

Jevan stood staring for a moment, then ducked back inside the house. 'The lad's not much of a talker,' said Morgan. 'I suppose you know Rhiannon's married now?'

'My mother mentioned it.'

'A stonemason from Hereford way. A preening sort of fellow, not right for her. Just wait a while, I told her – there's better men will come along, but she was set on him. I gave my consent but I'd have been hard put to it to give my blessing.'

'Is she well?'

Morgan shrugged. 'She writes now and again, but tells us next to nothing. Will you come in?'

'Thank you, but they'll be expecting me back.'

'A favour, you said. Did your father send you?'

'Not exactly, no. But he needs the loan of a cart, and I thought—'

'Tell him I'll come down to discuss it later.' His expression had hardened. 'And to discuss the outstanding business. Tell him that.'

'The outstanding business?'

'He'll know what's meant.' There was a long silence and Eliza, feeling that the conversation was at an end, turned to go. But Morgan reached out and gently touched her sleeve. 'I'm in the wrong,' he said. 'Your father's debts and dealings aren't your concern, and I shouldn't have made you party to them. Just tell him I'll be down shortly.'

She nodded. She could feel him watching her as she walked away, and it wasn't until she was halfway down the track that she heard the door slam shut.

* * *

The knock startled her, a quick rat-a-tat at the side door. She put down her book and rose from her chair but her father, who must have been lurking in the hallway, was already on his way down the corridor. She heard his boots rapping on the floor tiles, heard the door swing open.

A muttered greeting from her father, and then Morgan's voice, as firm and forthright as if he were speaking to a member of his own family.

'Eliza tells me you've a favour to ask of me. The loan of a cart, she says. I'm not ruling it out, but you should know that any loan in present circumstances would be subject to conditions.'

In the long pause that followed she could hear Todd whistling tunelessly in the yard. 'I wonder,' her father said at last, 'whether we might discuss the matter outside.' She heard the door click shut and then, glancing out of the window, saw the two men rounding the corner of the house and moving out into the parkland. 'The fact is,' she heard her father say, 'that Eliza's visit to you...' – but he was striding on and his words were lost.

Eliza rushed upstairs, burst into the attic and eased open the window. Morgan's voice rose clear on the still air. 'No doubt,' he was saying, 'but if you need the ice, you need the cart.'

'Need it? It depends what you mean. We don't need the ice, whatever my wife says, but she'll make my life a misery if we don't get it. You know how it is with women.' He let out a sharp bark of laughter, but there was no answering laugh from Morgan.

Eliza leaned out as far as she could, straining upward. She was unable to see them, but sensed that they had stopped at a little distance from the house.

'I said there'd be conditions,' said Morgan, 'and you know well enough what they are. I want nothing for the loan of the cart – I'd do as much for any neighbour – but the money you owe me is to be paid in full without further delay. It's as simple as that.'

'Not as simple as you might think. But I'll do what I can.'

'You'll do what you must. The money's mine by right, and if you don't come up with it, I'll go to law to get it.'

'That won't be necessary. I've told you I'll pay.'

'You've told me, right enough. More times than I can count. But I don't want your promises any more, Mr Mace, I want cash. You know how it's been with us the past few years – doctor's bills for Rebecca, the boy always hungry, the farm hardly paying though I'm labouring dawn to dusk. I know what's due to me, and the law will back me up. Whether you borrow the cart or not, I'll have my money.'

'Give me a month.'

'I'll give you a fortnight. As for the cart, you can have it until Tuesday evening. I can't say fairer than that.'

It seemed that the discussion was at an end. Morgan's burly figure came suddenly into view, walking briskly away towards the gateway. Eliza ducked inside and quietly lowered the sash.

She hurried downstairs and settled back in her chair by the fire. She was about to return to her reading when her father pushed open the door and peered in.

'I'm going out,' he said. 'If your mother asks where I am, tell her I've gone with Todd to bring down Morgan's cart. Tell her she'll have her ice. And in future...'

'In future?'

'Don't take your mother's side against me, Eliza. I made it abundantly clear that I didn't want you asking favours of Morgan and you chose to ignore me.'

'I wasn't taking sides, I was taking action. You and Mother block each other at every turn and the result is that nothing gets done. I decided to do something, that's all.'

'And you think you've addressed the problem? I know you want to help, Eliza, but you don't understand the ins and outs of it all. How can you? The fact is, I struggle to understand it myself – the mess we've made of things, your mother and I.' His voice was softer now, and his perplexity so obviously genuine that for a moment she wanted to take him in her arms the way a mother takes a hurt child, to make everything well again. Tenderness and shame – shame at her impatience, the disobedience, the eavesdropping – and then the moment was gone. Her father withdrew, closing the door behind him.

Eight

As a child she had loved to watch the ice splintering as the men drove at it with their picks, to hear the creaking and cracking as they levered it up, the cold clatter as they heaved the shards into the cart. And then she'd follow them down to the ice house to see them fill the shaft. Twenty feet deep, Todd had once told her, holding her by the waist as she leaned over, and the thought of that long drop into the dark had filled her with an excitement almost as strong as her fear.

Now, she thought, stumbling over the frozen tussocks in the late afternoon sunlight, it was all changed. The labourers had moved on and Todd, stooping there in the bed of the stream, swinging the pick wildly, alternately coughing and cursing, seemed to bear no relation to the lithe figure she remembered from her childhood, striding out at the head of the two great carthorses as he led them down the long slope to the wood.

'Mother asked me to bring you some tea.' She had been clasping the little earthenware flask to her breast for warmth but something in Todd's gaze made her uneasy and she stepped quickly forward and set it down on the bank.

He grabbed it and straightened up. 'Made by your own fair hand, I hope.'

'The tea? Mrs Pugh made it.'

'Well, that'll have to do.' He pulled out the cork and took a swig. 'Not a bad brew. No more than I deserve, mind. Three days heaving and carting and not a soul to help me out apart from Cally – and he's not the horse he used to be, poor old boy. It's not just the hard work – it's the lack of company. Time was, remember, there'd be five of us on the job – two down here, two shovelling on the bank, and me with the cart. We'd be done in a few hours. And the two down on the ice trying to keep their footing, and us up top laughing and poking fun, so the time seemed to fly by. Well, it's no joke now. Look at this.'

He pulled up the leg of his breeches to reveal a mess of blood and bruising on his right shin. 'I swung wide and went over.' He jabbed with his boot at the head of the pickaxe. 'Came down hard on the point.'

'The wound needs cleaning. When you go up, ask Mrs Pugh to boil a pan of water for you. Tell her you need the iodine bottle and a clean cloth. Have you much more to do?'

'If this isn't the last load, the next will be. The shaft's full, near enough.' He clambered up the bank and moved towards her. 'Come with me,' he said. 'I'll take you down and show you.'

'I'm afraid I don't have time, Todd. Bring the flask when you come up.' She turned to leave but he reached out and caught at her arm.

'You liked me once,' he said. 'You had time then.'

She shook herself free. 'What do you mean by that?'

'Five years ago. Six. You were always hanging around me.'

'I liked watching you work. What of it?'

'Watching, yes. And talking, nineteen to the dozen. You weren't afraid of me then.'

'I'm not afraid of you now.'

'But you won't stop and talk. Hardly give me the time of day.'

'I'm as civil as I need to be. But I'm not a child any more. I don't loiter around watching grown-ups going about their business. I have business of my own.'

He was eyeing her closely. 'No,' he said, 'not a child. I've seen the change in you these past few months. I'd say now there's not a lovelier woman for twenty miles around.'

'That's enough, Todd.' She took a step back, but he reached out and gripped her wrist. 'Let go,' she said. 'Let go now or I'll tell my father.'

'Your father owes me money.'

'It seems my father owes everyone money. That doesn't give anybody the right to lay hands on me.'

'Around seven shillings by my reckoning. But I'd let it all go by for one kiss from your pretty mouth. What do you say?'

'What do I say? I say you must be a scoundrel to suggest such a thing and a fool to think you'll get away with it.' She tried to twist free but he held on and drew her close.

'Where's the harm? One kiss, that's all.' Still holding her by the wrist, he brought his other hand up behind her, fumbling at the back of her head.

She struck at his face with her free hand and kicked out at his injured leg. He stumbled back with a cry, and as she turned to run she saw him slithering down the bank, grabbing for a handhold on the brittle sedge.

She hoisted her skirts and raced towards the house, stopping only when she reached the gateway to the yard. Glancing back, she saw Todd watching her, one hand shading his eyes, but as she looked he turned away and bent to his work as if nothing had happened.

She had hoped to get up to her room unnoticed, but as she crossed the yard the side door flew open and her father rushed out to meet her.

'Eliza! What the devil's the matter?'

She bent forward, trying to catch her breath.

'You came pelting up the drive like a hunted hare. What is it?'

'Nothing.'

'What do you mean, nothing?'

She straightened up. Her mother had come to the door and stood on the threshold staring at her.

'I mean I don't want to talk about it.'

'I'm sorry, Eliza, but I insist that you do. Something's amiss and I want to know what it is.'

'Let the girl come in, Robert. She's shaking like a leaf.' Hannah held back the door to let her through and followed her into the hallway. 'Your dress,' she said. 'What happened?'

Eliza looked down. A ragged tear in the fabric a little below knee level, the hem hanging askew.

'I don't want to talk about it now,' she said. She turned and began to climb the stairs. 'Would you ask Carys to bring a jug of hot water to my room?'

* * *

When she had washed and changed, Eliza sat on the edge of her bed in the fading light, trying to calm herself. After a while she heard the sound of Cally's hooves on the cobbles outside and went to the window. Todd was leading the carthorse into the stable, speaking to him with such gentleness that she could almost believe that the incident at the streamside had been a dream; then, as though sensing her gaze, he glanced up, and as his eyes met hers she felt the panic return, flaring in her like wildfire, taking hold. She ducked away from the window and slumped back onto the bed.

A knock at the door and her mother entered. She crossed over to the window and looked down into the yard; then she lit the lamp and drew the curtains.

'You'd better tell me,' she said. 'What's been going on?'

'Todd tried to kiss me.'

'I'm afraid that doesn't surprise me. Unsuccessfully, I hope.'

'Of course.'

'There's no of course about it, Elizabeth. A man like that is apt to take what he wants, and you can be sure he wants more than a kiss. Did he touch you? Did he put his hands on your body?'

It came to her again – Todd drawing her close, the pressure of his fingers around her wrist, the stink of tobacco on his breath, the horrible proximity of his flushed face. 'Nothing happened,' she said. 'Nothing I couldn't deal with.'

'You're still shaking.' Hannah sat down beside her and draped an arm around her shoulders. 'Poor dear. But I've warned your father. Time and again I've said it – the man's a ruffian, I'd tell him, and one day you'll be sorry you defended him against me, sorry you kept him on. Well, Elizabeth, that day has arrived. Perhaps he'll listen now. Come down with me to the drawing room. I want you to tell him what you've just told me.'

'I'd rather not speak to Father about it.'

Her mother tightened her hold. 'He needs to know. He needs to hear the truth, and it's important that he hears it from you.' She rose to her feet, drawing Eliza with her, and walked her towards the door.

Her father was at the drawing room window, staring out into the dusk. He turned as Eliza was ushered in.

'It's Todd,' her mother said without preamble. 'Todd, trying to get his filthy hands on her.'

'Is that true, Eliza?'

'He wanted to kiss me.'

'And you refused? Well, of course you did. So no great harm done, but Todd must be made to understand clearly that behaviour of that kind is completely unacceptable. I'll have a word with him tomorrow.'

'Have a word with him?' Hannah stepped forward, interposing herself between Eliza and her father. 'For God's sake, Robert. We're talking about your daughter. We're talking about a man who has just made an attempt on her virtue. Have a word with him? You'll get rid of him, that's what you'll do. You'll go out there at once and give him his marching orders.'

Robert flushed. 'Todd is my servant,' he said, 'not yours. We can discuss the matter later.'

'No discussion. I want him off my property and out of our lives.'

'You're making too much of this, Hannah. A man chances his luck, asks a girl for a kiss. These things happen to pretty girls, and Eliza is growing to be a very pretty girl indeed; but she's also a sensible girl, and can be trusted not to have her head turned.'

Hannah drew herself up, her fists clenched as though she were about to strike him. 'You're a fool,' she said. 'You saw the state of her when she came in. We're not discussing a conversation that took place between Elizabeth and a young gentleman after a society dinner. Our daughter has been put upon by a servant, a man more than twice her age and known – by the rest of the world if not by you – for a rogue. What are you going to do about it? There are fathers in this town who'd take a horsewhip to the man, yet you can't even bring yourself to let him go.'

Robert glanced at Eliza. 'I wonder whether it might be better—'

'Elizabeth stays. You might be interested to hear what she thinks about the matter. Tell him, Elizabeth.' Hannah reached for Eliza's arm and dragged her forward.

Eliza stood silent for a moment, considering. I'm being used, she thought, used in the service of an argument I want no part in. Hannah gave her arm a little shake. 'Go on,' she said.

'There's not much more to be said. I was frightened. I thought I knew him, and now I realise I don't.'

'You're still frightened. I can feel you trembling. You'll be frightened for as long as he's around, and with good reason.'

'Maybe so.'

'Do you hear that, Robert? Are you prepared to let your daughter walk in fear for the remainder of her time in the family home? What kind of father would countenance such a prospect? Go out now and tell Todd to pack his bags.'

Robert cleared his throat. 'The fact is,' he said, 'that if we send Todd away he'll find it difficult to get by. He has no money to speak of – certainly not enough for more than a couple of days' food and lodging.'

'That's not our concern.'

'I'm afraid it is. The problem is that I'm in debt to him. I'm in arrears with his wages, and then there are the sums I've borrowed from him at various times over the past few months. I don't think he'll go quietly if I don't repay him, and I simply don't have the means to do so.'

'How much do you owe him?'

A second's pause. 'Fifteen shillings, near enough.' A faint flickering of the eyelids, a downward glance; nothing Eliza would have noticed if she hadn't recognised the lie.

'A small price to have him gone. I'll go into town for the money first thing tomorrow. You'll pay him off and have him out of the cottage by noon at the latest. Is that understood?'

Robert sighed. 'You drive a hard bargain,' he said.

'It's not a bargain, Robert. It's an ultimatum.' Hannah gave him a vicious stare; then she turned and marched out of the room, with Eliza in tow.

* * *

Sleepless in her bed, watching the moon's slow progress across the sky, Eliza told herself that the matter of the money was unimportant. If the discrepancy between Todd's calculation and her father's claim had been much greater she might have felt obliged to confide in her mother. But her mother had been pleased to pay the sum and her father appeared to have agreed to her conditions. Why intervene? Tomorrow Todd would be gone and she'd be able to go about her business with a quieter mind. There was nothing to be gained by complicating matters.

Clear enough, but her thoughts continued to circle and snag. Tainted, she thought suddenly, and saw, as if it were a physical fact, her father's dishonesty seeping into her, spreading like a bloodstain. She lay staring at the window until the stars faded and the farmyard cocks began to crow.

Nine

T he eggs were fresh enough, but something about the smell of them turned her stomach. She pushed her plate away. James leaned over and placed his hand gently on hers.

'You're not ill, are you, Eliza?'

She shook her head. 'I'm tired,' she said. 'I had a restless night.'

'Even so, you need to eat.'

Hannah shot him a warning glance. 'You may not be the best judge of Elizabeth's needs,' she said. 'A woman's body is more finely balanced than men seem to realise.'

'Of course.' James withdrew his hand and returned to his breakfast.

'I have business in town,' said Hannah. 'Elizabeth may wish to accompany me. No doubt a dose of fresh air will do her a great deal more good than a plateful of bacon and eggs. What do you think, Elizabeth?'

Eliza felt a wave of fatigue wash over her. 'I think a walk would be helpful,' she said diplomatically, 'but for the moment I'd rather rest. I may go out later.'

'As you please.' Hannah rose from the table. 'If your father comes down before I return, tell him I've gone for the money.'

When she had left the room James turned to Eliza. 'Your mother tells me Todd has been making a nuisance of himself,' he said. 'She says your father has agreed to dismiss him.'

Making a nuisance of himself: delicately phrased, she thought, wondering whether the delicacy was her mother's or her uncle's. Did he know what had happened, or would she be obliged to explain?

'There's no need to talk about it,' he continued, as if overhearing her thoughts, 'but if you should ever want to, you'll find me ready to listen.'

'Thank you, Uncle James. Someday, perhaps.' She folded her napkin. There seemed so little to tell, yet as she rose to her feet she realised that she was shaking again, and by the time she reached her room she was on the verge of tears. She threw herself on to the bed, buried her face in the pillow and gave herself up to a fit of weeping.

She had calmed down and was dozing lightly when her mother returned. She heard her footfall on the stairs and then the rustle of her skirts as she passed along the corridor.

'Robert! Are you awake? It's ten o'clock.'

A muffled response from her father's room, and then the sound of the door being opened. 'Here's the money,' said Hannah. 'That concludes my part of the bargain. Now I want you to attend to yours.'

'What you want, Hannah, is to crush me under your thumb like an insect. Most wives see it as their bounden duty to offer support when their menfolk fall on hard times. Not you. The further I sink, the more heavily you bear down on me.'

'By noon, Robert. He's to be out of the cottage by noon. That's the agreement, and your grievances have no bearing on the matter – none at all.'

The door slammed shut.

On with the day. Eliza stepped over to the washstand and splashed her face with a handful of icy water from the jug. She examined herself for a moment in the mirror, pinned her hair up in a makeshift coil and went downstairs.

Her mother was pacing to and fro in the hallway. 'If he refuses to go through with it,' she said, 'I shall never speak to him again.'

Like children, thought Eliza – two vengeful children so completely caught up in their own squabbling that as far as they were concerned the rest of the world could go hang. 'Has he taken the money?' she asked.

'With unseemly haste. He all but tore the purse out of my hand.'

'Then he'll no doubt honour the agreement.'

'You've no idea, Elizabeth. Your father's life is a patchwork of broken promises.' But as she spoke Robert appeared at the top of the stairs. He came hurrying down, snatched his cloak from the stand and, without a word to either of them, strode out of the house.

'You see?' said Eliza. 'He may not want to, but he'll do it.'

'Maybe. I'll believe it when I see Todd walk down the drive with his belongings in tow. Where your father's concerned I've learned to wait until my chickens are fully fledged before I start counting them. He has let me down time and time again – I could give you a hundred instances.'

'I think,' said Eliza, crossing quickly to the hallstand, 'I might take that walk now.'

'Very sensible. Hand me my coat.'

'I'd like to walk alone.'

'No. Absolutely not. Not until Todd's off the premises.'

'I'm not worried about Todd. Not now. And I need time to myself.'

Hannah sighed. 'You don't listen to me any more, Elizabeth. You were always headstrong but now there's no gainsaying you.'

Eliza was already buttoning her coat. 'I'll be back within the hour,' she said.

* * *

The temperature must have dropped further overnight; it seemed to Eliza that she had never known cold so intense. There was scarcely a breath of wind but the air on her cheeks and forehead was like a blade of ice, and by the time she reached the lower wood she was shivering uncontrollably. If her longing for solitude had been less acute she would have turned at the wood's edge and made her way back to the house, but she pressed on, picking her way along the familiar pathways between the trees until she stood looking out at the frosted meadows and the long curve of the river beyond.

This was what she needed, she thought, feeling her mind settle, watching her breath rise on the quiet air – to be alone in a world uncontaminated by the presence of fretful humankind. But even as she framed the thought she became aware that she might not, in fact, be alone. Nothing she could put her finger on at first – just a vague sense of a watcher at her back; then a soft rustling, the snap of a breaking twig.

She turned in time to catch a movement in the shadows. 'Who's there?' she called.

A tense silence and then, as she craned forward, Fletcher slouched out from behind a hollybush. He shambled over and came to a stop directly in front of her, his teeth bared in a sly grin. He patted the pockets of his coat. 'Empty,' he said. 'I swear it.'

'If you've caught nothing,' she said, struggling to suppress the tremor in her voice, 'it won't be for want of trying.'

'I can see I've frightened you, Miss Eliza, and I'm sorry for that. You were good to me when we last met, and I don't forget it.'

'I felt sorry for you. I wasn't giving you licence to roam the estate as you please. My uncle warned you off, and you'd do well to heed the warning. Next time it may be my father who catches you here, and you know how he deals with these matters.'

Fletcher put his hand to his collarbone. 'I know well enough,' he said, 'and it's worse than you might think. I'll tell you something he's never likely to tell you. A few years back he got it into his head that we should bring the old mantraps down from the hayloft, oil them up and set them here in the woods. You can't do that, I told him, it's against the law. So is poaching, he said. I suppose you know, I said, that the jaws will smash a man's leg so it looks like something you'd find on a butcher's slab. That's the idea, he said.'

'He couldn't have meant it seriously.'

'He was serious, right enough, but I stopped him in his tracks. What about Miss Eliza? I said. Suppose it's her leg gets smashed in the trap. Suppose it's your own child who never walks straight again. He just gave me a hard look, but I could tell he'd never so much as thought about it. Anyway, the whole business was dropped, and it was as well for him that it was. When word of what he'd been planning got about – and I couldn't help talking about it – there were those in town who wanted to come up and teach him a lesson he wouldn't forget. Leave it, I said, there's no need. I brought them round in the end, and no doubt I did right, but there's been times I've wished I'd let them go ahead, let them break his legs as they wanted to. You'll blame me for thinking that, Miss Eliza, but you can't understand how it feels – knowing my life's as good as over, knowing he's the reason.'

Eliza opened her mouth to speak and immediately closed it again. Fletcher was undoubtedly a rogue and might well be a liar, but his stories about her father had the ring of truth. What defence could she offer?

'Whatever goes unpunished in this world,' said Fletcher, 'will be dealt with in the next. That's my consolation.'

'What consoles you, Mr Fletcher, would trouble me deeply if I had any belief at all in the afterlife. Would you excuse me? My mother is expecting me back at the house.'

He stood aside to let her pass. 'You be careful,' he said. 'Careful you don't end up following in your father's godless footsteps.'

'I'm on my own path,' said Eliza. 'I stopped trailing after my parents long ago.'

* * *

She was through the wood and climbing the slope towards the house when she saw Todd emerge from the yard and set off along the drive. He was limping noticeably and his back was bent under the weight of a bulging sack he carried over his shoulder. She adjusted her course to take account of his, but he set down his burden and stood waiting, too close to the house for her to be able to avoid him.

'You'd be better off sitting by the fire,' he said as she approached. 'It's no weather for walking.'

It irritated her that he should try to engage her in casual conversation, as if the events of the previous day had never taken place. 'I don't mind the cold,' she said, 'just as long as I can walk in safety.'

'You're talking about yesterday? You were in no danger.'

'I expect that's what you've told my father. And I expect he believes you.'

'He can't find it in his heart to blame me. That's what he says, and I take him at his word. He says it's on account of your mother that I have to go.'

'And what about me? What about my feelings?'

'Your feelings, Miss Eliza? He didn't mention those.'

The rage that flared up in her at that moment was extraordinary. She wanted to slap, to punch, to cudgel – to lay into Todd, yes, but it was her father's face she saw in her mind's eye, raw and disfigured under the punishing blows. She felt the blood hammering in her chest and throat. And then, as suddenly as it had arisen, the fit passed and she was her public self again, the daughter of the house seeing off a troublesome servant.

'Where will you go?' she asked.

'I've a mate in town will probably put me up for a day or two. After that, I shall walk the roads until I find work. There'll be nothing for me in these parts, things being as they are.'

'But you have resources, haven't you?'

'Resources?'

'Funds. Belongings.'

Todd let out a bark of mirthless laughter. 'Bless you, Miss Eliza, you've no idea, have you? I've nothing but this' – he indicated the sack at his feet – 'and the clothes I stand up in.'

'As well as the money my father has returned to you. That should tide you over.'

'How far do you think three shillings is going to take me? I'll be through it in a week, and then what?'

'Three shillings? But I thought you said—'

'Oh yes, he owes me more – as much again, and then some. He'll send it on, he says, but he won't tell me when, and there's no knowing where I'll be by the time he gets around to it.'

It crossed her mind that she might confront her father on Todd's behalf, but she dismissed the thought. The debt wasn't hers, she told herself, and Todd had forfeited his right to any assistance she might have given.

'Well, Todd,' she said, 'I hope you find work before too long. I'm not sorry you're going but I wish you well.'

Todd shouldered his sack again, touched his hat brim and moved away. Watching his halting progress down the drive, she felt the stirrings of something like pity, but she hardened her heart and walked briskly into the house.

Ten

It might drive the sanest mind to distraction, thought Eliza, listening over luncheon to the dull clink of cutlery on china, feeling her parents' wordless anger darkening the air like a stormcloud. She tried to engage her uncle in conversation but he seemed unable or unwilling to respond, and she was relieved when her father pushed back his chair and rose from the table.

Hannah looked up sharply. 'Some of us are still eating,' she said.

'I'm glad you have the leisure to dawdle over your food, Hannah, but someone has to feed and water the horses. Who did you imagine would do that once Todd was gone?' He flung down his napkin and stalked out of the room. They heard the side door slam and then the stable door grating on the cobbles.

'Todd should have fixed that hinge,' said Hannah. 'I must have told him a dozen times.'

James laid down his knife and fork. 'I'm loth to enter the fray,' he said, 'but it's obvious that someone will have to carry out Todd's duties. It's equally obvious that Robert can't be expected to take on work of that kind for any length of time.'

'As author of the family's misfortunes he might reasonably be expected to make a few sacrifices. Everyone else in the household has been obliged to do so.'

'He's not a stable lad, Hannah, and there'd be a certain danger in treating him as if he were. If you harbour any hopes of reconciliation in the future, I'd advise you not to add to his catalogue of grievances.'

There was a long, uncomfortable silence. Eliza rose and went over to the window.

'The cart's still out there,' she said. 'Down by the stream. Who's going to deal with that?'

Hannah gave a dismissive wave of her hand. 'All in good time, Elizabeth. The cart isn't one of our more pressing concerns.'

'It should be. Father has agreed to return it by this evening.'

'If Morgan needs it urgently, he'll doubtless come for it.'

'Oh yes, doubtless. But he has done us a kindness, and I can't imagine a shabbier way to repay him.'

'I don't like your tone, Elizabeth. In any case, it's not your concern.'

'It doesn't appear to be anyone else's. And look – the cart's still piled high with ice. Who's going to unload it? Do you want to add insult to injury by asking Mr Morgan to finish Todd's work for him?'

'The best plan,' said James, 'might be for someone to go and see Morgan – to explain the situation, to ask for a day's grace while we sort matters out. I'm sure he'll understand.'

'Very well. Robert can go when he's finished attending to the horses. Would you mention it to him, Elizabeth?'

'I think,' said Eliza, 'that it might be better if I were to go and speak to Mr Morgan myself.'

Her mother stared angrily at her for a moment, then spread her hands in a gesture of resignation. 'As you please,' she said.

* * *

Her father was saddling up in the yard when she went out, his head down and his cheek pressed hard against Tinder's ribs as he fumbled for the free end of the girth. The horse was restive, uncooperative. Robert was cursing under his breath, but he stopped and looked up as Eliza approached.

'Your mother can say what she likes about Todd,' he said, 'but you'd look a long time before you found a better stableman. He had a way with the horses, no doubt of it – very easy with them but wouldn't take any nonsense. You see that?' Tinder was pulling away from him, hooves slipping on the icy cobbles. 'Now if it were Todd saddling him the brute would be standing stock-still, steady as a rock.'

'Nobody doubted Todd's skills as a stableman, Father. You know why he had to go.'

'The trouble with your mother,' he said, drawing the horse back towards him, 'is that she doesn't think anything through. We've lost a good man, and I'm the one paying the price. I could be sitting snug indoors now if I didn't have to exercise this miserable animal.'

James had hit the mark, thought Eliza: her father had a new grievance and would resist any attempt to divert him from it. 'I'm going over to see Mr Morgan,' she said. 'I shall ask him to let us keep the cart until tomorrow. He'll be expecting it back.'

'True enough. By this evening, in fact. It had slipped my mind.' He had hold of the girth now and was pulling it tight. 'Well, I imagine tomorrow will do. Thank you for seeing to it, Eliza.'

She was about to go when he straightened up and stepped over to her. 'One day,' he said, 'I'll make it all up to you.' It might have been the biting cold, but his eyes were filmed with tears. He gripped her by the shoulders and bent to kiss her brow. 'I'll make amends for all this mess. I swear it, Eliza.'

'There's nothing I need from you,' she said, turning away in sudden agitation, embarrassed by his intensity. She tugged her shawl tight about her shoulders and set off down the drive.

In the days to come she would return obsessively to that moment, hearing again the pain in her father's voice, fretting over the inadequacy of her response, wondering whether she might, in some obscure way, have contributed to the events that followed. But now she lifted her head and marched through the parkland, breathing the chill air deep into her lungs, feeling her spirits rise with every step.

The dog started barking before she was halfway up the track to the farm, and by the time she reached the yard Morgan was already at the door. He beckoned her in.

She hesitated. 'Come on,' he said. 'Rebecca's down and sitting by the fire. She was sorry to miss you last time.'

Eliza stepped inside. Woodsmoke and, beneath it, a sour smell like the inside of an unwashed churn. Rebecca was hunched on a chair with a blanket over her knees. Her face was hollow and worn, but her eyes lit up as Eliza approached, and she held out her hands. Eliza took them in her own, shocked to find them as frail and bony as an old woman's. 'We've missed you,' said Rebecca. 'And because I don't go out any more...' She sighed and trailed off as though the effort of speaking had already tired her.

'You were good to me. I felt at home here.'

'We were glad to have you,' said Morgan. 'And when he was a baby' – he jerked his head towards the table, where Jevan sat reading – 'you were no end of a help to Rhiannon. I remember you holding him in your lap, singing to him, keeping him happy.'

Jevan looked up briefly from under his tangled mat of hair and then returned to his reading. 'He's a regular bookworm these days,' said Morgan. 'And doing well at school.'

Rebecca gave a weak smile. 'Yes,' she said. 'He took to book learning right away. He's quiet, but he's clever.'

'You'll be here for a reason,' said Morgan. 'I'd guess that I'm not going to get my cart back today. Am I right?'

Eliza felt a rush of shame, as though the fault were her own. 'I'm sorry,' she said, 'truly sorry. My father had Todd shifting the ice, but Todd's gone – dismissed – and the cart's still loaded up, and I know Father won't have it emptied by this evening. Maybe tomorrow, but—'

'Steady now, Eliza – it's no disaster. But who's going to unload the cart tomorrow?'

'That's the problem. Owen, perhaps. I don't know. There have been difficulties.' She lowered her eyes, unable to meet his gaze.

'How far did Todd get with the job?'

'He told me it was all but done.'

'Then I'll tell you what I'll do, Eliza – and I'm doing it for you, mind, not for your father. I'll come over with Bess, deliver the load to the ice house and have the cart back here by nightfall. That way you can go home now and forget all about it. I'll not have you troubled by business your father should be attending to himself.'

'It's very kind of you, Mr Morgan. I know Father will be grateful.'

'I doubt it, but that's no matter. Tell him it's in hand.'

A soft moaning sound. Rebecca was leaning forward in her chair with one hand pressed to her waist. 'She's up and down,' said Morgan, 'but never what you'd call right.' He squatted beside her chair. 'Do you want your medicine, Becky?'

'I must go,' said Eliza.

Rebecca straightened up. 'I'm glad you came,' she said. For a fleeting instant her face was lit with the old sweetness, and then her gaze faltered and her body folded again. Eliza stooped and lightly touched her shoulder, finding nothing to say.

* * *

She returned to find her mother still sitting in the dining room, staring moodily out of the window. 'Your father has gone out,' she said. 'Rode off without a word.'

'He's exercising Tinder.'

'Did he tell you that? Exercising his drinking arm, if I know anything about him. As far as I could see, he was making for town. If he finds anyone there fool enough to stand him a few drinks—'

'Please, Mother – you'll wear yourself out fretting about him. Come into the drawing room. We'll set up the card table in front of the fire, the way we used to, and play a few rounds of cribbage.'

'Don't treat me like a child, Elizabeth. If the need arises I can find my own distractions.'

'Please. It can't do any harm to put your worries aside for half an hour.'

In the event they played for far longer. Dusk was falling when Hannah totted up her imaginary winnings and rose from the table. 'You see,' said Eliza. 'You've enjoyed yourself.'

'I wouldn't call it enjoyment. A couple of hours' forgetfulness, that's all. And now it's almost dark and your father's still out.'

'He may be back by now. I'll go and see.'

Eliza threw a shawl over her shoulders and went out to the stable. Cally nickered softly in the darkness as she entered, but there was no sound from Tinder's stall, and she knew at once that it was empty.

That was neither surprising nor, in itself, alarming; but as she turned to leave, the darkness seemed to deepen and envelop her, isolating her from her surroundings and filling her with a dread so intense that she had to bite her underlip to keep herself from crying out. She leaned against the wall and gulped deep breaths of stale air, pressing the flat of her hand to the stonework. There's no reason for this, she kept telling herself, no reason at all, and after a while the trembling in her limbs diminished and she was able to make her way back to the house.

Mrs Pugh came bustling down the passageway with a tray of cutlery as Eliza closed the side door behind her. 'Gracious, child,' she said, peering into her face, 'whatever's the matter? You're as white as a bedsheet.'

'It's nothing. I frightened myself out there in the stable, that's all – let my imagination get the better of me.'

'Wandering about in the cold and dark – it's no wonder. Go and sit by the fire. I'll bring you a hot posset in a moment.'

'Thank you, Mrs Pugh, but there's no need. I'm feeling better already.' The housekeeper's solicitude, the smell of roast meat rising from the kitchen, the spill of yellow lamplight from the hall – all worked together on her, filling her with a gratitude as profound, in its way, as her recent terror. 'Really,' she said. 'It was nothing.'

But dinner, served late in her father's continuing absence, was a sombre affair. Hannah picked at the food on her plate but ate next to nothing; her anxiety seemed to grow by the minute, settling on the room like a blight.

'Anything could have happened to him,' she said.

'Yes,' said James, 'but the likelihood is that he's sitting comfortably in the Bull, too far gone to make the journey home. You know his ways.'

'Indeed. I know he drinks himself stupid from time to time. I also know that they won't put him up at the Bull overnight until he's paid off his debts there, and because he has no money he may end up sleeping under a hedge. He's done it before, but if he tries it tonight he'll be dead of cold by morning.'

'The fact is,' said Eliza, and faltered, aware that the circumstances justified disclosure but uncertain how best to begin.

'What is it?' asked James.

Eliza took a deep breath. 'He does have money. He asked Mother for more than he needed and paid Todd less than he owed.' She glanced at her mother, but Hannah sat rigid, with her lips pursed, and said nothing.

James dabbed at his mouth with his napkin and stood up. 'I shall walk into town,' he said, 'and search him out. I should be back within the hour, and we'll all sleep sounder for knowing where he is.'

Eliza pushed back her chair. 'I'll come with you,' she said.

James shook his head. 'It's not a suitable errand for a young lady.'

'He's bound to be the worse for drink. Suppose he takes it into his head to attack you again?'

'All the more reason for you not to be there, Eliza.'

'I could talk to him. He listens to me.'

Hannah brought her hand down hard on the tabletop. 'You're not going, Elizabeth, and there's an end of it.'

James was already making for the door. 'I'll take Owen with me,' he said.

* * *

It was well past midnight by the time James returned. Hearing voices in the yard, Eliza ran to the door, but it was Owen, not her father, who stood there with her uncle by the stable wall. She knew, from the silence that fell between them as she approached, that they had no good news to give her, and for a moment she imagined the worst.

'I'm afraid,' said James, 'that we haven't managed to track him down.'

Hannah leaned out from the doorway. 'Come on in,' she said. 'You too, Owen.' She led them through to the hall and turned up the lamp at the foot of the stairs. 'Have you no information at all? Someone must have seen him.'

'He's been seen,' said James, 'but we've found no-one who saw him after he rode away from the Bull at about four o'clock. That's not necessarily bad news, but the circumstances of his leaving give some cause for concern.'

Hannah clutched at the newel post and then lowered herself gently to sit on the bottom step of the stairs. 'Tell me,' she said.

'What's certain is that he spent the afternoon drinking in the Bull. He had money – you were right about that, Eliza – and plenty of it. He sat in the corner by the fire and ordered drink after drink, paying on the nail each time. If you're so flush, Dan Davies told him, you can pay me what you owe for the drinks you've had on tick – all this we heard from Davies himself – and Robert put his hand in his pocket and threw down two florins. Take what you think's yours, he said, and bring me another brandy. At that – and everyone we spoke to bore witness to this – there was a kind of commotion. Todd came forward from the far end of the bar – it seems he'd been there for an hour or so, also spending freely and somewhat the worse for drink himself – and stood in front of Robert. Since you're paying out, he said, what about seeing me right? And that gave rise to an argument that ended with Robert storming out. I'll not drink in the same bar as a liar, he said – I paid you off fair and square.'

'But that's not true,' said Eliza. 'Not unless Todd lied to me.'

'Forgive me, Eliza, but everything we heard suggested that by the time the conversation took place your father was in no state to differentiate between truth and falsehood.'

'So we know nothing of what happened after he left the Bull?'

'Very little. One of the tinkers, Donnelly, went out after him – says he tried to persuade him to stay until the drink wore off a bit. Apparently Robert wouldn't listen. In the end Donnelly helped him into the saddle and then went back into the bar.'

'So Donnelly was the last to see him?' Hannah rose to her feet, visibly agitated. 'Supposing he harmed Robert? Supposing—'

'No,' said James. 'Davies was watching through the window. He saw nothing untoward, and Donnelly was back inside within minutes. It's Todd I'm worried about. After Robert had left, Todd finished his drink, and then wandered around the bar telling anyone who'd listen how he'd been turned out of his job with no notice and an empty promise in lieu of back pay. It appears that he became increasingly intemperate, and a couple of the fellows heard him say – what exactly was it, Owen?'

'If the fellows remembered right – and they were agreed on the matter – Todd swore that his master – begging your pardons – was the greatest cheat and swindler he'd had the misfortune to come across in all his days on God's earth. Then he said – and they told me these were his exact words – *I have that in my fist as will make him pay his dues.* An empty threat, I said, knowing Todd for the coward he is, but they went on to tell me—'

'It appears,' James cut in, 'that Todd had no sooner uttered the threat than he grabbed his overcoat and ran out. Whether or not he followed Robert nobody knew, but it seems probable that he did. And if he came upon him in the state he was in – well, it doesn't take much in the way of courage to rob a helpless drunk.'

'Robbery is one thing,' said Hannah, 'but the point is that Robert has gone missing. We should be out there looking for him.'

'Between us, Owen and I have searched every road out of town. There's no sign of Robert, nor of his horse.'

'Then,' said Hannah, 'you should be searching the fields and woods around.'

'We've discussed that, but thought it best to wait for daylight.'

'And suppose he's lying out there, freezing to death? Every minute matters. If you won't go, I will.' Hannah stepped over to the hallstand and made to reach down her coat, but James prevented her.

'We'll go,' he said. 'You should try to get some sleep. You too, Eliza. I'll wake you if there's any news.'

'Thank you, James. Thank you, Owen.' Hannah tried to smile, but her face creased suddenly, and tears ran down her cheeks. James hovered awkwardly at her side but she waved him away. 'I shall be all right,' she said. She turned and made her way slowly up the stairs.

Eliza went through to the dining room and stood by the window, watching as the men's lanterns bobbed down the drive and then out across the parkland. Even when the lights had vanished she went on staring into the darkness, as though the intensity of her concentration might bring her father home.

Eleven

She had anticipated a wakeful night, but had barely settled her head on the pillow when she fell into a deep sleep. She was woken at first light by her mother's voice, shrill and angry, echoing up from the hallway.

'Wait? Wait for what? We should notify them immediately.'

A murmured response from her uncle, and then Hannah again: 'Owen, would you attend to it?'

Eliza dressed quickly and hurried downstairs. Her mother and uncle had moved into the dining room. Hannah was leaning forward over the table, talking in low, urgent tones but looked up and fell silent as Eliza pushed the door wide.

The sight of her mother's grey, strained face frightened her. 'What is it?' she asked. 'What's happened?'

'Nothing,' said James. 'I mean, we've found no sign of him. Whether that's good news or bad depends on your point of view. I'm worried, certainly, but in the absence of any definite information I'm inclined to hope for the best.'

'Your uncle takes a more optimistic view than I do. For as long as your father's missing, I feel we have to assume the worst. I've sent Owen into town to inform the constabulary, and – what are you doing out there, girl? What do you want?'

Carys was hovering just outside the doorway. 'Please ma'am, I don't want to interrupt, but Mrs Pugh was wondering about breakfast. She says everything will be at sixes and sevens and she's not sure—'

'What does Mrs Pugh know about the matter?'

'Only that the master's missing and the police sent for.'

'Then she knows more than I've thought fit to tell her. Please inform her that we'll have breakfast served as usual.'

Carys gave a little dip of her head and scurried away down the corridor. 'Eavesdropping and tittle-tattle,' said Hannah. 'They'll all be at it.'

Eliza seated herself at the table. 'You could hardly have expected,' she said, 'to keep this a secret from the servants. Any minute we'll have the constable at the door – how could you stop them seeing that something's wrong? And it's better that they know the truth than that they start inventing their own stories.'

'Eliza's right,' said James. 'The servants are bound to be involved. They may have seen or heard things we've missed, and if the constable knows his job he'll want to speak to them.'

Hannah sighed but said nothing. She sat in silence through breakfast, leaving her food untouched, staring out of the window as she sipped her tea.

Carys was clearing away the plates when Owen returned. He let himself in and entered the dining room without knocking. Hannah turned in her seat. 'Where's the constable?' she asked.

'He'll be with us shortly, Mrs Mace. It's the new man.'

'The new man?'

'Constable Pritchard. Up from Cardiff, I believe – arrived a month ago.'

'Then I wouldn't have thought he's quite the man for the job. Someone with local knowledge would be better. Where's Sergeant Williams?'

'Busy, apparently, with another case. But I imagine he'll intervene if Pritchard proves inadequate in any way.'

But nothing about Constable Pritchard suggested inadequacy. Watching from the window as he approached the house, Eliza was struck by the vigour of his stride, the confident tilt of his head and his open gaze. His uniform was crisp and neat. He didn't hesitate for an instant as he marched up the front steps.

'Who does the man think he is?' demanded Hannah. 'James, send him round to the side door.'

'I'll go,' said Eliza quickly, and was out of the room before her mother could stop her. She ran to the front door and threw it open.

The constable removed his helmet and looked her up and down. 'Would you tell your mistress—'

'I'm Eliza Mace. It's my mother who sent for you.' She led him though the hall and ushered him into the dining room.

Her mother shot her an angry glance, but the constable was already introducing himself.

'Pritchard,' he said, with a stiff gesture somewhere between a nod and a bow. 'Dafydd Pritchard. I understand that your husband is missing.' He took a notebook and a well-sharpened pencil from the pocket of his tunic. 'I'm sorry, Mrs Mace, but you'll need to give me a few details. Do you mind if I sit down?'

James rose and pulled out a chair for him. 'I'm James Mace,' he said. 'Mrs Mace's brother-in-law. I should say at once that our anxiety isn't without foundation.'

'I'm sure it isn't. A man goes missing—'

'On the one hand, my brother's behaviour has sometimes been erratic, and occasionally rather secretive. On the other, he has never left home without informing his wife of his departure. And there's one particular circumstance you should be aware of. It seems there was an altercation between him and a former servant – a man he had recently dismissed – in the Bull yesterday afternoon. The landlord can give you a fuller account than I can, but the nub of it is that my brother left the inn in a state of inebriation at about four o'clock, and the servant – Jacob Todd – a short time afterwards. I understand that in the moments between my brother's departure and his own, Todd threatened violence.'

'In what terms?'

James glanced across the table at Owen. 'As I heard it from others,' said Owen, 'he said he had that in his fist as would make the master pay his dues.'

'Pay his dues?'

'My husband owes money,' said Hannah. 'We don't know the full extent of his debts, but when a man borrows from his servant you can be sure he has exhausted his credit everywhere else.'

Pritchard was writing quickly, in a small, neat hand. Eliza stepped over to the table and was about to sit down when her mother reached out to block her. 'I think,' she said, 'it might be better if you occupied yourself with domestic matters. Go and have a word with Mrs Pugh about the arrangements for luncheon.'

Eliza stared down at her. 'Mrs Pugh knows how to prepare luncheon,' she said. 'I need to be here.'

She saw the blood rise to her mother's face, but as Hannah opened her mouth to speak, Pritchard cut in. 'I shall want to speak to your daughter later. I can see that there are delicate matters to be discussed, and it's important that everyone should feel able to speak freely.' He raised his eyes to meet Eliza's. 'Eliza, would you mind?'

There was, of course, the authority conferred on him by his uniform, but that, she reflected later, wasn't the only reason for her acquiescence. Something in his gaze warned her that he was a man unlikely to brook opposition. She left without another word, closing the door quietly behind her. 'When you describe your brother as erratic,' she heard Pritchard say, but she was already making for the stairs, and heard nothing more.

Back in her room, she seated herself at her desk and took up her pen. *My dear Charlotte*, she wrote,

I've no wish to alarm you, and there may indeed be no cause for alarm, but I feel I should let you know that Father has gone away, leaving us with no idea of his whereabouts. Nothing new about that, I hear you say, but the circumstances on this occasion have given rise to anxiety, particularly on Mother's part, and the police have been called in. The constable is downstairs as I write – a new man, quite young and not entirely likeable, but with an air of efficiency that makes me hopeful that Father will be found before this letter reaches you. I might have spared you the worry but I know in my heart that you'd wish to be informed.

Please, dear Charlotte, do nothing at the moment – nothing at all. There's no need for you to make the journey to Edge Hall: all that can be done is being done, and I shall write again as soon as there is anything further to report. I expect we shall have

She heard the door of the dining room open. Her uncle's voice, barely audible, and then the constable's, rising firm and clear above it: 'You might usefully search the grounds again – you may find in daylight what you missed in the dark.' Eliza laid down her pen and ran to the head of the stairs.

Pritchard looked up. 'I'm going now, Eliza. There's work to be done. If our search is unsuccessful I shall want to speak to you this afternoon. I naturally hope that won't be necessary.' He gave her a perfunctory nod, turned on his heel and allowed James to shepherd him down the passageway to the side door.

* * *

The light was already fading from the sky by the time Pritchard returned. Eliza was at the dining room window, staring anxiously out across the parkland, when she saw him turn in at the gate. His step was as brisk as before, but something in his demeanour told her that he wasn't bringing good news. James must have been watching from another room: he was out of the door and waiting on the drive by the time the constable reached the house.

'Nothing to speak of,' she heard Pritchard say as he came into the hallway. 'We've found no-one who saw him after he left the Bull, so unless Todd—'

'Yes, what did Todd have to say for himself?'

'We haven't found Todd either, though I'm certain we'll be able to track him down. We know he spent last night at Clem Weston's cottage, but according to Weston he wasn't able to sleep – talked half the night, then packed his bags and left. He was out of the house well before dawn.'

'A guilty conscience?'

'Not necessarily. He's desperate to find work, Weston tells me, and doesn't believe he has any prospect of employment here, or for twenty miles around. That's enough in itself to rob a man of his sleep and send him out on the road before anyone else is stirring. Even so, I feel he's likely to hold the key to your brother's disappearance. I wonder whether I might ask Mrs Mace a few questions about him?'

'She's in bed, trying to rest. It might be better not to disturb her.'

'You'll remember that when I asked her about the circumstances of Todd's dismissal this morning she brushed the question aside – an irrelevance, she said. Forgive me for broaching the subject again, Mr Mace, but in a case of this kind anything may prove relevant. Could you tell me what you know about the matter?'

'I think,' said James, 'we should continue this discussion in a more private place.' A pause, and then the sitting room door creaked open, clicked shut. Eliza heard the key turn in the lock.

She stood watching the sky darken, listening to the cries of the jackdaws as they flocked in to roost for the night. She was lost out there, caught up in all that wheeling hubbub, when her uncle called her name from the hallway. She started like a wild animal.

'I'm coming.' She stepped, blinking, into the light of the hall.

'I'm sorry, Eliza. Were you asleep?'

She shook her head. 'Just thinking,' she said.

'About your father?'

'In a way, yes. It's strange – when he's here I often feel it would be better for everyone if he weren't. Now, I'd give anything to see him walk through the door.'

'There's nothing strange about it, Eliza. We all want to know he's safe. We're not dealing simply with his absence from the house, but with the possibility that he has been prevented from returning to it. Constable Pritchard is taking his disappearance very seriously indeed. He says he'd like to ask you a few questions.' James led the way to the sitting room and pushed back the door, standing aside to let her pass. 'I'll leave you to talk,' he said.

'Aren't you coming in with me?'

Pritchard rose from his seat by the fire. 'I prefer,' he said, 'to speak privately to each witness. In cases of this kind everyone has his own particular story to tell, and I've found that witnesses speak most directly, and most helpfully, when they're not distracted by other people's stories.'

She heard the door close behind her and felt a flutter of panic. 'Witness?' she said. 'Is that what I am?'

'Everyone in this house is a witness, Eliza. You've all seen things, you've all heard things. It's my job to listen to your stories, to examine them, to compare them. I'm looking for fragments that might fall into place alongside others to give me a clearer idea of what has happened to your father. Please sit down.'

'So you do think something has happened to him?'

'What I've heard about your father's past behaviour leaves room for hope. It's possible that he has simply gone away on one of his business excursions, and my mind remains open to that explanation. But I have to say that the information I've gathered so far inclines me towards a more worrying possibility.'

Eliza found that she was shaking uncontrollably. She sat down in the chair opposite him and began to cry.

'I'm sorry to have upset you,' he said. He dipped into the pocket of his tunic, pulled out a neatly folded handkerchief and handed it to her. 'I thought it best to be honest with you.'

'Yes, I want that. And what you say doesn't surprise me – I've been thinking all day that something must be badly wrong. It's just that hearing it from you makes it seem more real.' She wiped her eyes and drew herself up in her chair. 'I'll answer your questions now.'

'Thank you, Eliza. I need to touch on a rather difficult matter. Your uncle tells me that Todd' – he hesitated, cleared his throat – 'that Todd behaved improperly towards you. I understand that you weren't seriously harmed, but the question I'm asking myself is whether serious harm was intended. Did you feel at the time that Todd posed a danger to you?'

'He tried to kiss me. I made it clear that I didn't want to be kissed. It was all over in seconds.'

'That doesn't quite answer my question. Did he desist when you asked him to?'

'I didn't ask him, I told him. When he persisted I kicked out at him and ran.'

'That suggests to me that the danger was real, and that you knew it. Were there other incidents of that kind? Or anything else in his behaviour that made you fearful for your safety?'

'He'd never laid hands on me before.'

'Did he ever give you cause to think that he might?'

She considered the question. 'No,' she said at last, 'but lately I'd been feeling uneasy about him. It's hard to say what it was, but something was different in his dealings with me.'

Pritchard was writing, his head bowed over his notebook. His features, thought Eliza, matched his speech: strong and definite, with a touch of refinement that marked him out from most of the local men. She grew absorbed in her contemplation of him, and when he set aside his notebook and looked up, meeting her gaze, she started as if she'd been guilty of some misdemeanour.

'Thank you, Eliza. You'll understand why I needed to discuss the matter with you.'

'Of course. You believe that Todd is responsible for my father's disappearance.'

'I wouldn't put it quite so strongly, but I regard him as – at the very least – a crucial witness. And I have to say that the information you've given me this evening strengthens my view that he may turn out to be something more than that. Would you say you know him well?'

'Not exactly, but I've known him all my life. He was attentive to me when I was a child – talked to me, let me watch him work. I liked him then.'

'And now? Do you still like him?'

She stared at him. 'How can you ask that?'

'My questions may sometimes seem foolish or clumsy, but they serve a purpose. You would tell me, wouldn't you, if you knew of his whereabouts?'

'Of course I would. I don't understand why you're asking.'

'You've been a great help, Eliza. I may want to speak to you again tomorrow, but that will do for now. Would you mind asking your uncle to give me a few more moments of his time?'

James was sitting on the bottom step of the stairs. He's been waiting, she thought, waiting, like a naughty child, to be summoned back into the room. 'He wants to speak with you again,' she said, making as if to return to the dining room; but when James had closed the door behind him she doubled back to the sitting room and stood outside, listening.

'Yes,' Pritchard was saying, 'very useful. In particular, I think I can now rule out the possibility that she's in any way entangled with Todd.'

'I don't know how you could ever have imagined—'

'I have to imagine every possibility, Mr Mace. I have to ask awkward questions. A girl of her age can be very impressionable – and vulnerable if she falls under the influence of an unscrupulous man. I needed to satisfy myself on that score.'

Eliza's face burned with rage and shame. She flung Pritchard's handkerchief down on the hallstand beside his helmet and stormed up the stairs to her room.

Twelve

Had she returned to her letter that evening she might have been tempted to pour everything out to Charlotte – her view of the constable's contemptible suspicions and general presumptuousness, her distress at the thought of her father somewhere beyond reach under the cold stars – but she judged it wise to wait until the following morning. She rose at first light, put on warm clothes and went straight to her desk.

I expect we shall have... What had she meant to say? She knew she had planned to end the letter on a vaguely reassuring note, but now the phrase seemed lame and unconvincing, and she had no idea how she might plausibly follow on. She struck it out and began a new paragraph.

Another day, and no news of Father. I should, in honesty, tell you that the constable is treating his disappearance with a seriousness that seems, when I reflect on it, more worrying than reassuring. You know I have no aptitude for prayer, but I think perhaps you still have the necessary faith. If so, you might pray for him.

Your loving sister,
Eliza

She slipped the letter into the pocket of her coat and was out of the house before the others were down. The sun was rising above the hills, bathing the valley in an orange glow that made her think of firelight, though the air cut like a knife blade. A profound stillness lay over the land, disturbed only by the swish of her skirts and the brisk tap of her boots on the drive's frosted surface.

Halfway down the hill, where the curve of the lane brought the town into view, she saw Pritchard striding towards her. He raised his hand in a salutation jaunty enough to make her think, for a fleeting instant, that he was bringing good news.

'Nothing to report,' he said as he drew close. 'We'll continue the search today. The weather's against us, I'm afraid. In normal conditions we'd expect to pick up a trail – footprints, hoofprints – but the ground's as hard as stone. I'm not surprised we've drawn a blank there, but there seem to have been no sightings, either of Todd or your father, after they left the Bull, and that does surprise me a little. We've combed the town for witnesses. There's plenty of information about the argument in the bar but precious little beyond that.'

'Have you spoken with Gwilym Morgan? He farms the land across the lane from us. He'd lent us a cart and was due to collect it on Tuesday. I don't know what time he came over, but the cart was gone by yesterday morning. He might have seen something.'

'Might have done, but didn't. I called on him yesterday evening, at your uncle's suggestion. Morgan told me he'd gone for the cart just before dusk on Tuesday, so – if we assume your father set off for home on leaving the Bull – the timing would have been about right. But Morgan says he neither saw nor heard anything out of the ordinary. That doesn't help us very much, but it may suggest that your father didn't, in fact, set off for home or, if he did, that his journey was interrupted before he reached his destination.'

She was silent, imagining the interruption – her father dragged from his horse and bundled to the side of the road, blows aimed at his fuddled head, his hopeless resistance, his terror and bewilderment, his cries fading into silence in the darkness. Pritchard must have read something of her distress in her face: he softened his tone.

'Forgive me,' he said. 'I should have spoken more thoughtfully.'

'No – I want to know. I want to know what you know. You mustn't keep anything from me.'

He looked hard at her. 'You're very young, Eliza, and you've no idea what you're asking. A girl of your age—'

'I'm not a girl, Mr Pritchard, though you treat me as if I were. You call me Eliza, yet you scarcely know me. That's the freedom of an adult addressing a child, not the familiarity that friendship allows.'

He smiled. 'And how old are you, Miss Mace?'

'I shall be seventeen this coming summer.'

'And I shall be twenty-six. You'll at least admit that I'm likely to know a little more of the world than you do.'

'No doubt, but that wasn't the point I was making.'

'I'm guilty of a breach of etiquette – was that the point?'

'Not exactly. It's that I want to understand the world – the good and the bad of it – and I can't do so while I'm kept in the dark by people who imagine I'm a child in need of protection. Or by those who think they can probe my character on the sly.'

'What do you mean by that?' But he knew exactly what she meant, she was sure of it: his eyes flickered sideways and his neck reddened above the collar of his tunic.

'You told my uncle you thought I might be entangled – isn't that the word you used? – entangled with Todd. No-one who knows me could imagine such a thing, and no gentleman would enquire into it.'

'I've lived here for barely a month, Miss Mace – how should I know you if not by asking questions? And I'm not a gentleman, of course – I'm a police constable, doing my job to the best of my ability, mapping the ground as thoroughly as possible, blind alleys and all. I'm not sure why your uncle saw fit to discuss the matter with you.'

'He didn't discuss it. I overheard your conversation.'

'You did? And how close to the door was your ear when you overheard it?'

'I had a right to know what you were saying about me – what you were thinking. You weren't honest when you spoke with me. You asked questions that seemed direct, but weren't. Something was being kept from me. You scuttled around behind my back when you might have looked me in the eye.'

'You think I was being devious; I thought I was being tactful.' He had recovered his composure and was preparing to move on. 'You know, Miss Mace, none of this is going to help us to find your father. If I've offended you, I apologise, but now I have work to do at the Hall. More questions, I'm afraid.'

'Will you have questions for me?'

'Possibly, though it's your mother I particularly want to speak with. When will you be home?'

'Very soon. I have to post a letter, that's all. Please understand that I want to help you to find my father – of course I do – but I had to speak my mind.'

'A sharper mind than I'd given you credit for.' He was scrutinising her with an intensity that made her uncomfortable. She pulled up the collar of her coat and made to move away.

'Just one more thing, Miss Mace. I'm wondering whether you might have picked up any information about your father's business affairs? Your mother seems reluctant to discuss them, but they may be important.'

'I'd say it's not reluctance, or not only that. My parents' marriage...' She trailed off, staring out across the town to the hills beyond.

'You've asked me to tell you what I know, Miss Mace, so it seems fair to turn the tables. Tell me what you were about to say.'

Eliza took a deep breath. 'Only that my parents never seem to confide in one another. I'm fairly certain that my mother knows nothing, or next to nothing, about my father's business interests. I also think...'

'Go on.'

'I've a feeling that my father's recent excursions have been nothing more than hopeless attempts to fend off his creditors – not business in the usual sense at all.'

'I don't suppose you've ever heard him mention any names – people he visited during his absences from home?'

She shook her head. 'We didn't even know where he'd gone. Todd might have known that much – he drives him to and from the station – but I doubt whether he'd have known more. It's hard to explain how it is with my father – the secrecy, the unpredictability. It's so much a part of him that I've come to accept it, though I know that there's something wrong with him, something wrong with our family.' She had begun to shiver. 'Do you mind if I go now? We can talk later, can't we? I mean, if you think I can help.'

'I do think so,' he said. 'In fact, I'm sure of it.'

*　*　*

Pritchard's voice reached her from the sitting room as she entered the hallway on her return. '…and it's only a matter of time,' he was saying, 'before we turn over the right stone.' And then Hannah's voice, faint and a little weary: 'Maybe, but meanwhile we've nothing to cling to, nothing at all. And while you're here questioning us, they're a man short out there.'

'Believe me, Mrs Mace, my questions are an essential part of the search for your husband. Sergeant Williams has taken charge of the wider search.'

'I'd like to speak to Sergeant Williams. Could you ask him to call in?'

'What reason should I give?'

'I think you'll find, Constable Pritchard, that my request will be reason enough for Sergeant Williams.'

'Of course. I'll ask him to come as soon as he can, though he may not be back before nightfall.'

Eliza tapped on the door and pushed it open. Her mother had clearly been crying; her uncle was staring gloomily into the fireplace with his chin propped on his hand. Both looked up as she entered, but neither spoke.

'Please come and join us, Miss Mace.' Pritchard was writing busily in his notebook. 'We've been discussing Isaac Fletcher, and a possible connection with your father's disappearance. Is there anything you've witnessed or overheard that might be relevant?'

'I raised the matter,' said James, 'of our meeting with Fletcher in the woods the other day. His diatribe against your father didn't seem particularly significant at the time, but in the light of subsequent events we need to take it seriously.'

She turned to Pritchard. 'But I thought you were looking for Todd,' she said.

'We are. At this stage we're looking for anyone who might know where your father is. We're also looking for the person or persons who may be responsible for his disappearance. On both counts I shall certainly want to question Fletcher, but that doesn't mean that I'm any less interested in tracking down Todd.'

'But Fletcher isn't likely to have harmed Father. He said that while he was employed here he'd once prevented others from attacking him.'

James frowned. 'I don't recall him saying that,' he said.

'You weren't with me on that occasion. He told me about the time Father wanted him to set mantraps in the woods – he was gamekeeper at the time. Fletcher dissuaded him, but word got round, and a band of men – he didn't say who, or how many – wanted to come over and teach Father a lesson. A lesson he wouldn't forget. They wanted to break his legs' – she saw her mother flinch – 'but Fletcher wouldn't let them.'

James glanced across at Pritchard. 'I'd be inclined to believe Fletcher's story,' he said. 'My brother has a hatred of poachers quite disproportionate to the harm they do. I doubt whether I'm the only one who has heard him say that the world took a turn for the worse when the mantrap was outlawed. It seems quite possible that a group of ruffians wanted to attack him, and equally possible that Fletcher dissuaded them. But times and circumstances change. While Fletcher was employed here it was clearly in his interest to protect his employer, but he might well have seen the matter differently once he was out of the job – all the more so because of the manner of his dismissal. He has at least as much reason as Todd to hate my brother, and he undoubtedly keeps more dangerous company.'

Something stirred at the back of Eliza's mind: Fletcher telling her there were times he wished he'd let his cronies go ahead, wished he'd let them do as they wanted with her father. She opened her mouth to speak, but decided against it.

Pritchard snapped his notebook shut and stood up. 'I'll know more when I've spoken with him. I shall go back into town now and search him out. Would you see me to the door, Miss Mace?'

Eliza ushered him into the hall. 'I wonder,' he said quietly, 'whether you'd do me the favour of accompanying me to the end of the drive.'

They were well clear of the house before he spoke again. 'I hope you don't mind,' he said, 'but I'd like your opinion on a matter that puzzles me. Tell me a little about your uncle's place in the household.'

'It might be better to speak to him about that.'

'I have spoken to him about it – to your mother too. But every observer sees things from a different angle, notices details that others have missed. Tell me how you see it.'

'I expect you know that he's here at my mother's invitation rather than my father's. I think my mother finds life a little easier when he's around.'

'But your father doesn't.'

'Father and Uncle James are very different from each other.'

'Would you say they actively dislike one another?'

She hesitated. No well-bred family, her mother was apt to say, washes its dirty linen in public.

'I suppose I've already heard enough,' said Pritchard, 'to be able to answer that question for myself. But what I can't quite fathom is why the arrangement has continued for so many years.'

'My father has no choice in the matter. The house belongs to my mother.'

'Even so, I'd have thought he'd be able to exercise sufficient leverage to have his brother ejected.'

'There are complications. My uncle lost a good deal of money when he returned from India. I believe he may find it difficult to provide for himself.'

'But that's not a problem your parents are obliged to address. Your uncle is responsible for his own losses.'

'That's not true. My father is directly responsible for my uncle's losses.'

Pritchard's expression barely changed, but he stopped suddenly in his tracks and turned to face her. 'I've heard nothing about this,' he said. 'Tell me more.'

Eliza looked back towards the house. 'If my uncle hasn't seen fit to tell you about it,' she said, 'it's hardly my place to do so.'

'I'd put it differently. If your uncle hasn't told me, it may be your duty to do so.'

'But these are family confidences.'

'The withholding of information can seriously affect the outcome of an enquiry of this kind – it can even mean the difference between life and death. Do you want us to find your father, Miss Mace?'

'Of course I do. How can you ask? But I'm sure that what my uncle told me wasn't intended for anyone else's ears.'

'No doubt you're right, and in normal circumstances I'd applaud your discretion. But these are not normal circumstances, and I now have two alternatives. Either I go back to your uncle and ask him, more or less directly, to tell me in what way his brother is responsible for the present state of his finances, or I get the necessary information from you. Which would you prefer?'

A wild crying overhead – a skein of geese, sharply delineated against the luminous blue of the sky. She watched their progress until they were lost to view behind the wood.

'If I tell you,' she said, 'you're never to let anyone else know that I've done so.'

'I can promise that anything you say will remain confidential unless circumstances dictate otherwise.'

'Unless circumstances dictate otherwise? That's hardly a promise at all.'

Pritchard sighed. 'I have great respect for you, Miss Mace, and I very much regret having to put you in this position. But the more I can discover about your father and his connections, the sooner we'll find him. And the sooner we find him, the greater the chance of finding him alive.' He fumbled in his pocket and fished out his notebook and pencil. 'Please tell me what you know.'

She was aware in the telling that the story wasn't quite as her uncle had told it – her version was scrappier and more abstract – but she felt that she was conveying its essence. Pritchard didn't interrupt but listened carefully, occasionally jotting down brief notes.

'It sounds,' he said, when she had finished, 'as though your father is paying for his sins. Forced to live alongside the brother he has wronged, reminded daily by his presence of events he might prefer to forget, and – forgive me, Miss Mace, but am I right in inferring that your mother prefers your uncle's company to your father's?'

'She has always been more at ease with my uncle.'

'And if that was apparent to you, it must also have been apparent to your father. It seems to me that he must have been living in torment. Tell me,' – he was moving on now, drawing her with him – 'did he ever give you the impression that he'd had enough, that he wanted to be out of it all?'

'You think he might have killed himself?'

'I didn't say that. Not exactly. But people who are tired of living may seek out the means to bring their lives to an end. They don't always know that they're doing it, but they take chances, even going out of their way to place themselves in danger. It's a matter I know something about.'

'I've come to see how far my father's grip on the world has been loosened over the past year or two. If you're asking whether he has been suffering, then yes, I'm sure of it. But we've all been suffering.'

They had reached the gate. He turned to look at her and she saw his features soften. 'I realise that,' he said, 'and I'm very grateful for your help. I shall be back shortly, and I hope to see you then.'

'What do you mean when you say you know something about people putting themselves in danger?'

'That's a conversation we may have time for in the future. Goodbye, Miss Mace.' His tone was businesslike, but the smile he gave her was so warm, so unguarded, that she seemed to feel the glow of it on her skin.

'Do you know,' she said, 'I preferred it when you called me Eliza. I'm afraid I behaved rather badly when we spoke earlier.'

'My own behaviour wasn't irreproachable. You were right to point out that I hadn't treated you with the respect you deserve. I shall do better in future.'

'Thank you, Mr Pritchard.'

He was already through the gate, but he turned to face her again. 'Dafydd,' he said. 'Call me Dafydd.'

Thirteen

They were sitting late over breakfast next morning when Carys knocked on the dining room door. 'Sergeant Williams is here,' she said. 'Shall I show him into the sitting room?'

'This won't take a moment,' said Hannah. 'I'll see him here.'

Carys pushed the door wide and the sergeant entered, hulking and awkward, his helmet clutched to the bulge of his belly. He cleared his throat noisily before speaking.

'I'm sorry to hear about your husband, ma'am. A worry for you, I don't doubt – for all of you. But I can assure you that we'll find him, and I have high hopes he'll be alive and well when we do.'

He's been practising that little speech on the way up, thought Eliza, catching the faint hint of artifice in the sergeant's delivery. James drew out a chair and motioned him to sit down. 'I'm grateful to you for your reassurance,' he said, 'but I have to say that our own hopes are beginning to fade.'

'Men go missing from their homes now and then, Mr Mace, and they're as likely as not to return to them in due course. You don't want to jump to conclusions, nor to frighten yourselves without need.'

'And yet,' said Eliza, 'Constable Pritchard seems to be preparing us for the possibility – the probability, I've come to think – of bad news.'

Hannah shot her an unmotherly glance. 'The reason I've asked to see you,' she said, turning back to Williams, 'is that I'm not entirely happy with the way Constable Pritchard is handling the matter. He seems to feel a constant need to interrogate us, often about private matters, when he might be far better employed in searching the lanes and villages round about or questioning staff at the local railway stations.'

'That's all in other hands, ma'am, and what Constable Pritchard does, he does with my blessing. He comes to us with something of a reputation.'

'What kind of reputation?'

'He's razor-sharp, they say – misses nothing. Keeps at it – searching, questioning – when others have given up. They say—'

'I don't know who "they" are, Sergeant Williams, but it sounds to me as though the constable hasn't yet proved himself here.'

'He's had very little opportunity, ma'am, but everything I've seen so far suggests that his reputation is well deserved. And he's an educated man, as these things go – has a way with words – so I thought he'd be likely to hit it off with you.'

'I should prefer a local man. In fact, I should like you to take charge.'

The sergeant stiffened. 'I am in charge, ma'am, and I use my men as seems best to me. Constable Pritchard will continue with his enquiries, reporting back to me in the usual way.' He rose to his feet. 'Was there anything else?'

Hannah was staring fixedly ahead of her, her mouth a hard line. James leaned forward in his chair. 'No, nothing else. You'll understand my sister-in-law's concern to move matters forward as quickly as possible, but we naturally trust your judgement. Thank you for calling in to see us. Eliza will show you out.'

'My mother isn't entirely herself,' said Eliza as she stepped out into the yard with the sergeant. She closed the door softly behind her. 'In my opinion it would be a great pity if Mr Pritchard were to be taken off the case. Whatever my mother says, it's obvious that he's doing what's necessary to – why are you smiling?'

'I was wondering whether you'd be speaking up for the constable that way if he didn't cut such a fine figure. He turns heads, no doubt of it. There's quite a few women in town—'

'The world is full of foolish women, Sergeant Williams. I'm not one of them.'

'Forgive me, Miss Mace, I meant no harm. And of course you're right – we've very little to guide us at the moment, and the constable's questions are our best way forward. I hope we'll have news of your father very soon.'

'Thank you, Sergeant.' Eliza turned on her heel and went back into the house. Despite the cold, her face was burning.

* * *

She was in her bedroom that afternoon, keeping out of her mother's way, when she heard the sound of hooves on the cobbles below. She rushed to the window and looked down.

The light was already failing, but she recognised Tinder at once. *Father*, she breathed, but the word was still on her lips when she realised her error. The man in the saddle was Pritchard. She watched in a state of almost unendurable turmoil as he dismounted, hitched the reins to the hook in the stable wall and crossed the yard to the door.

It was Carys who let him in. Eliza heard her voice rising indistinctly from the hallway and then Pritchard's voice cutting through: '…better that I speak directly to Mrs Mace, but yes, I do have news.'

Eliza reached the stairhead just in time to see him being shown into the sitting room. She raced down the stairs and was at the door before Carys had closed it. She barged in and stood, breathless, in the doorway.

Pritchard half-turned, but her mother and uncle seemed hardly to notice her presence. 'Tell me,' said Hannah. Her face was white and her hands moved restlessly in her lap, alternately crumpling and smoothing the fabric of her dress. 'Tell me, is it bad news?'

'That's not yet clear, but it certainly looks as though we're a step closer to finding your husband. We've found a horse answering the description you gave us. Bought on Wednesday, by a dealer in Ludlow, from a man who rode in from this direction. First of all, I need confirmation that we have the right horse, and I wonder whether you'd mind stepping outside to—'

'That's Tinder,' said Eliza. 'Father's horse. I saw him from my window when you rode into the yard.'

'You're sure?'

'Absolutely.'

'Then we're definitely on the right track. On the strength of the dealer's account we've already made an arrest. We now know we have the right horse; assuming we also have the right man, we should be able to move forward.'

James looked up. 'And are you going to let us know the fellow's name?'

'Not until I've spoken further with him – clarified a few important details. The dealer has given us a description of the man who sold him the horse, and we've arrested someone who fits that description but denies all knowledge of the matter. That's as much as I feel able to say at present.'

Hannah pulled a handkerchief from her sleeve and dabbed at her eyes. 'It's a dreadful thing,' she said, 'not knowing what's happened to Robert. I think I'd rather know he was dead than go on living with this uncertainty.'

'That's understandable.' Pritchard's voice was softer now. 'I hope things will be a little clearer tomorrow, Mrs Mace. I shall come by as soon as I have any definite news.'

He turned to leave, and Eliza stepped back to let him pass. 'I'll come out with you,' she said. 'I must see to Tinder.'

The stars were beginning to appear, pale pinpricks in the fading blue of the sky. Tinder whickered softly and strained towards her as she approached.

'I heard what you said in there, Dafydd, but I have to ask. The man who sold Tinder – it's not Todd, is it?'

'The person we're questioning isn't Todd.'

'Is it Fletcher, then?'

A pause, just long enough to suggest that she had hit the mark. 'Until I know more,' he said, 'I don't want to speak about it. You'll have to be patient. And now I suggest we get the horse stabled before we lose the last of the light.' He stepped forward and began to unbuckle the girth.

'I've no need of help. You can go – get back to your duties.'

'You're angry with me, Eliza, but you've no call to be.'

'I'm not angry – just upset. When I looked down from my room and saw Tinder, I thought Father was back. If you ask me what I really believe, it's that he's gone for ever, but just at that moment it seemed that the impossible had happened, and that everything would come right again – though goodness knows nothing's been right for years. And then, seeing it wasn't him at all, the confusion I felt – the finding and the losing all packed into an instant, joy and sadness jammed together so tightly that they seemed to be one thing. And all the more confusing because my father wasn't a good man – he wasn't trustworthy, he wasn't careful of others' feelings, he didn't provide for us as he should have done – yet I can think of many times in my childhood when I was certain of his love for me, and certain that I loved him in return. It's hard to explain to anyone who doesn't know.'

Dafydd lifted the saddle and placed it on the ground. In the quiet before he spoke Eliza could hear the rats scuttling across the boards of the hayloft.

'I wasn't much above your age when I lost my own father. He was a miner, and still young when the black lung got him. He was a hard man, not inclined to spare the rod, and there were times I hated him with a passion, but as the sickness sapped his strength a kind of tenderness enveloped us both, and I came to understand him more deeply. I'd always known that he wanted me to better myself – to get the education he'd had no chance of – but I hadn't properly understood his reasons. Another way of controlling me, I'd thought – and perhaps that wasn't entirely untrue, but there was more to it. He wanted to save me from having to follow him into the pit, and the childhood beatings were as much part of his plan as the sacrifices he made later, trying to keep me in school. Sitting by his bedside in those last weeks I came to see that the force that had driven it all was love. These things are never simple, Eliza, and it's small wonder we're confused by them.'

In the gathering dusk she could barely make out his features, but she imagined them gentler than usual and more contemplative. She moved to pick up the saddle, but he was there before her, hoisting it onto his shoulder. 'I'll put this away,' he said. He was settling it on the rack when the side door opened and her uncle stepped out into the yard.

'Your mother asked me to see if you needed help.'

'Thank you, Uncle James, but Dafydd is helping me. Tell her we'll be finished in five minutes.'

'Not even that,' said Dafydd, emerging from the stable. 'We're almost done.'

James craned forward. 'Constable Pritchard? I thought you had work to do.'

'Indeed I have.' Dafydd unhitched the reins and led the horse in.

James moved forward to stand at Eliza's side. 'Your mother's real concern,' he said quietly, 'wasn't that you needed assistance, but that you might be receiving it from an inappropriate quarter. Finding that she was correct in her assumption makes me just a little uneasy. You will be careful, won't you?'

'There's nothing to worry about. You know me well enough to know that.'

'Where such matters are concerned, Eliza, we're lucky if we even know ourselves.'

'You surely don't imagine—' She could hear Dafydd stumbling through the stable towards the door. 'Tell Mother I'll be in as soon as I've seen to Tinder.'

'I've no idea when the horse last ate,' said Dafydd as he stepped out into the yard, 'but he could certainly do with a good feed now.'

'We'll see to it,' said James. 'Goodnight, Constable.'

'Thank you, Dafydd,' said Eliza. 'Thank you for all your help.'

'Glad to have been of service,' said Dafydd with a decorous bow in her direction. 'Goodnight, Eliza. Goodnight, Mr Mace.'

Eliza went into the stable, lit the lantern and filled a nosebag with oats. 'Tinder,' she murmured, slipping the strap over the horse's ears. She set her cheek against his neck and listened to the deep, slow sounds of his body, trying to steady her own unquiet heart.

Fourteen

She had run down the drive to meet the postman and was stuffing Charlotte's letter into her coat pocket when Pritchard turned in at the gate. She stood waiting as he approached.

'Good morning, Eliza.'

'Is there any news? The man you were questioning—'

'All in good time. Is your mother about?'

'Tell me now. I need to know.'

'I should say at once that I've no news of your father. What I can tell you is that, as you guessed, the man we've arrested is Isaac Fletcher. When I came over last night he was still holding out on us, but once you'd identified your father's horse we were able to push him towards a confession.'

'He's confessed?'

'To the theft of the horse, yes. I was hoping to be able to bring you information about your father by now, but Fletcher's adamant that he knows nothing of his whereabouts.'

'But if Fletcher sold Tinder he must know what has happened to Father.'

'Not necessarily. He says he found the horse. At first he told us that he came across it wandering riderless in the lane – had no idea who it belonged to and decided that he had as much right to it as the next man. As we continued to press him, the story changed. He said he'd found the horse tethered to a tree down there' – Pritchard nodded in the direction of the lower woodland – 'and he admitted that he knew perfectly well who it belonged to. In this version he'd taken the animal as compensation for the injuries inflicted by your father at the time of his dismissal. Your uncle had already told me about the beating, but since his information came from Fletcher himself, that can't be seen as corroboration.'

'We've no reason to disbelieve Fletcher's account of the incident, have we?'

'Fletcher's a habitual criminal and, like most of his kind, he lies when it suits him to do so. We have to treat everything he says with caution. Still, let's assume that he did, in fact, suffer a beating at your father's hands. He presents the incident as justification for the theft of the horse, but anyone with any intelligence will recognise the connection between the desire for compensation and the longing for revenge. If it turns out that your father has come to any harm, Fletcher's defence – such as it is – could rebound on him.'

Eliza felt suddenly cold; she drew her muffler more closely around her throat. 'Listen,' she said, 'there's something I should have mentioned earlier. You remember I told you about the mantraps and how Fletcher said he'd stopped a gang of men from coming up to attack Father? Well, he actually said a little more than that. He told me it had sometimes crossed his mind that he should have let the attack go ahead – should have let the men do what they wanted. I suppose that's important, isn't it?'

'It's one of a number of matters that might be considered relevant if he were ever brought to trial for anything worse than horse stealing. But I have to say – forgive me – that a fair few of the men I've spoken to in the course of my enquiries seemed to think that whatever mischance might have befallen your father would be no more than he deserved. One of the things that makes this case so difficult is the number of people who have it in for him, and don't mind saying so. Fletcher's view is by no means unique.'

'But Fletcher's the one who took Tinder.'

'Indeed. Which is why he's the one we're questioning. And now I need to speak to your mother. Are you coming in?'

'Is there more to say? More than you've just told me?'

He smiled. 'You don't want to miss anything, do you? No, there's nothing more.'

'Then I won't join you. I want to walk a little.' She turned away and struck off across the parkland towards the wood.

* * *

Always that sense of stillness at the wood's heart, a dark, inhuman calm. She sat on a fallen ash trunk, breathing deeply. Odour of rotting wood, damp leaf-mould; and then, faint but unmistakable, the delicate sweetness that presages thaw. The scent brought with it a memory of childhood – her father entering the hall after some long journey and gathering her roughly into his arms. She felt, as vividly as if she were back in the moment, the scratching of his cheek against hers and the fragrant air blowing into her face through the open doorway.

She imagined for a moment that it was part of the memory – an insistent pressure at her elbow – but it was Brand, there on the trunk beside her, rubbing his muzzle against her sleeve. She hauled him onto her lap and sat for a long time fondling his neck, finding comfort in his warmth and solidity.

A scuffling deep in the undergrowth and the cat was off again, moving stealthily towards the sound. Eliza watched until he was lost to sight in the shadows; then she rose to her feet, dusted down her coat and walked back towards the light.

Dafydd was squatting beside the fence at the wood's edge. His head was down and he appeared to be oblivious of her approach, but as she emerged from the wood he looked up and called her over.

'There are signs of disturbance here,' he said. 'You see – the grass has been heavily trampled. Perhaps this is where an attack took place.'

'This is the access to the ice house. Look.' She slid one of the moveable rails sideways in its slot. 'We have to be able to cart the ice through. Since that's what Todd was doing the day before Father went missing, the trampling tells us nothing. I'm not saying an attack couldn't have taken place here, but we know for certain that the carthorse drew the cart through at exactly this point, maybe half a dozen times each way, and that alone could account for the state of the ground.'

'Of course.' Dafydd's embarrassment was palpable. 'I should have been looking more closely and thinking more clearly.'

'It's just that I know these things. I can help you.'

'I don't doubt it. Are you going back to the house?'

'Luncheon will be ready soon. But I wanted to ask you something. When you spoke the other day about unhappy people taking chances with their lives, you said it was a matter you knew something about. You didn't mean that you'd taken chances with your own life, did you?'

'There are always dangers in my line of work, Eliza – we take that for granted. But there was a time when I was half crazy, running risks I shouldn't have run, seeking out trouble for trouble's sake. That's why I'm here in this godforsaken spot, squelching through muddy lanes when I might be walking the pavements of Cardiff.'

'You don't like it here?'

'At first I hated it. Now I'm beginning to see the place in a different light, though for an ambitious man it doesn't offer much. But I had to get out of the city, and I see now that I could have done worse than to fetch up here.'

'When you say you had to get out—'

'I'd probably be dead by now if I'd stayed. It's as simple as that.'

'It can't be as simple as that. There's something you're not telling me.'

'It's not a story I'm particularly proud of but I don't mind telling it. When my father grew too ill to work, his plans for me went to pieces. There had been an idea that I might read for the law – my teachers had always said I was clever, and with time I had become a diligent pupil – but the funds he'd put aside were needed for food and medicine and we had to drop the notion. I joined the police for the pay, and with the vague idea of working my way up and out. I was good at my job, no doubt of it, but I wasn't particularly well-liked, and my hopes of promotion faded as time went by. What I most enjoyed was working alone on a case, piecing together clues the way a detective does, sharing nothing with my colleagues until I'd got to the bottom of things. The one-man force, they called me, and it wasn't meant entirely as a compliment, though no-one could deny that I got things done.'

'Perhaps they were jealous of you.'

'A little, maybe. But they saw me as self-serving and stand-offish – the station sergeant told me as much quite early on – and I think that's what really rankled with them. Anyway, about a year ago there was a spate of warehouse thefts down on the docks. Not petty pilfering – that goes on all the time – but theft on a grand scale. Whole crates were going missing, and the thieves seemed to have a nose for the most valuable items. We had a fair idea who was involved, but they were clever: we must have made a dozen or so raids on various houses without finding anything incriminating. It seemed obvious that we needed to catch the culprits in the act, and that became a kind of obsession for me. I took to walking the dockside when I went off duty, on the lookout for any suspicious activity – on the lookout for danger, I see now, and desperate to find it. Night after night in all weathers, back and forth until my feet were chafed to ribbons – a kind of madness, though at the time it all made sense to me. The longer the crimes went unsolved the more I came to feel that I was the only one capable of bringing the gang to justice. I imagined myself a lone hero – the kind you read about in the penny magazines – and I had some hazy idea of finally getting the promotion I'd been denied. But it didn't work out that way.'

'You didn't catch the thieves?'

'Oh, I did, and more besides. One night, about an hour after I'd come off duty, I was walking down one of the streets that run behind the warehouses. There was a full moon, I remember, rising clear above the dockyard cranes. The air was cold and still – not a breath of wind – and I could hear raised voices from one of the side-alleys further on. I crept to the corner and peered down. Two men arguing, apparently about money. Five, said one of them, it's always five, and the minute I heard the voice it struck me that I knew it, though I couldn't have said then whose it was. Four, said the other, take it or leave it. They went on, back and forth, until the first man gave way. Four tonight, he said, but I won't do it again for that, and you can tell them so.

'They didn't see me until I was almost upon them. The first man was pocketing something, head down, but as I came up to him he raised his eyes. I knew him then, right enough – a colleague from the station – and he knew me. He was in uniform but bareheaded, his helmet dangling from his hand. Edwards, I said, and at that moment the other man broke away and sprinted towards the quay. Edwards was blocking the alley but I barged him aside and gave chase.

'I caught up soon enough – heard the man's breath wheezing in his chest where he was crouched in the shadow of one of the gantries. I hauled him out, wishing I had the handcuffs with me. He was a small man but lithe, like a weasel, and he kicked, punched and bit as I dragged him across the cobbles. Police, I said. I'm taking you to the station. That made him struggle the more, and I hit him then – hit him hard in the face to quell him. Three or four times, which to be honest was more than was needed, but I was raging, not quite in control of myself. In any case, it worked. I got a firm grip on his collar and marched him forward at arm's length.

'As I passed the end of the alley Edwards came out of the shadows and fell into step beside me. Whatever you thought you saw there, he said, I'd be grateful if you'd not mention it back at the station. I know what I saw, I said. Maybe so, he said, but you might forget it. He reached into his pocket and drew out two sovereigns. Two-way split, he said. Two for me, two for you. Put the money away, I said. You'll need it when they kick you out of the force.'

'And did they?' asked Eliza. 'Did he lose his job?'

'Of course. When I reported what I'd seen they had to investigate. Edwards went to prison, convicted on my testimony. And after they'd questioned the man I'd brought in, there were other convictions – five members of the gang. So you might think I'd have been the hero of the hour, but it wasn't like that. Edwards was popular with his colleagues, and there were those whose sense of comradeship ran a good deal deeper than their sense of public duty. One evening I was standing by my locker when one of his mates came up close behind me. Did you know, he said, that Edwards has three children? No, I said, I didn't know. Three hungry children, he said. I said nothing to that, thinking it over, wondering how best to answer him. Well, Pritchard, he said at last, I hope you have eyes in the back of your head or you'll never see the blow that fells you.'

Eliza leaned back against the fence in a state of strange excitement. What would it be like, she wondered, to live in the shadow of that threat, to walk the city streets knowing that each step might be your last?

'You're shivering, Eliza. I'll walk you back to the house.'

She shook her head. 'Not yet. Didn't you tell anyone you'd been threatened?'

'I reported the incident to the sergeant, who was so obviously unwilling to take action against the man that there seemed little point in pursuing the matter. I thought it would all blow over, but I was wrong. One night I was on duty in Butetown when I sensed that I was being watched or followed – nothing I could pin down, and the street was deserted except for three dockers larking about outside the public house, but the feeling was too strong to ignore. And because I've learned to trust such feelings I was already on my guard when I saw him.'

'Saw who?'

'My attacker. He stepped out of a sidestreet and came straight for me, not seeming in any hurry but bearing down on me with an air of purpose. It was as though he were striding over to greet me, but even in the miserable light from the streetlamp I could see that he was nobody I knew – a tall man, powerfully built and with a huge head that seemed to twist a little to one side. As he came close I saw the gleam of something half-hidden in his sleeve, and I just had time to pull my truncheon from my pocket before he drew out the knife and lunged at me.

'I sidestepped and the blade went by me but he was quick to get his balance and he grabbed me by the arm, wrenching it upward so that the truncheon dropped from my grip. He lunged again with the knife and I made to catch him by the wrist but missed and caught the blade instead. I can feel it now – the edge slicing deep into my palm as he tugged it from my grasp and the horrible certainty, as I stumbled and fell, that the next thrust would be the end of me. I rolled sideways and tried to scramble to my feet, but more from some vague notion of facing death head-on than with any hope of escape.

'What happened then was confused, but I heard the sound of raised voices, boots pounding the cobbles; a heavy blow, a flurry of curses, and then my assailant turned and ran, with the dockers at his heels. Just three young rowdies seeing the chance of a fight, I imagine – certainly none of them paid any attention to me, down there on my knees with blood pouring from my hand – but if it hadn't been for them I doubt whether I'd be here today.

'They gave me a fortnight's leave for the injury to heal, but I couldn't rest. I got it into my head that Edwards' cronies would see to it that my attacker wasn't brought to book, and after a few days I was back on the streets, not officially but on my own account, trying to track him down. I wasn't entirely lucid, but I can recall the feeling of those days and nights – walking my own private beat in a frenzy of rage and terror, hoping I'd stumble across the fellow, hoping I wouldn't. And an aching and throbbing from my fingertips to my shoulder, so that I wondered at times if I was going to lose the arm.'

'Did you find him?'

'I didn't, and by the time I returned to work I was in a worse state than when I'd gone on leave. I tried to settle back into the job, but everyone could see I wasn't right. One morning the sergeant called me over to his desk. You can't go on like this, he said. You're sick. I know it, I said, but I need to work. What about working somewhere quieter? he said – I can help you find another post and I can give you a testimonial second to none. He wanted rid of me, I could see, and it seemed I had no alternative. That evening he wrote a letter to an old friend – Sergeant Williams – and here I am, reasonably sound and a good deal safer than I'd be in Cardiff.'

'Would you really still be in danger if you'd stayed?'

'I'm certain of it. In time I came to think that I might have overestimated the influence of Edwards' cronies, but I've never doubted that I was the intended target of the attack. A constable in any large city is exposed to violence often enough – when he's breaking up fights, when he's making arrests – but this was different. The man was after me, no question about it. Somebody wanted me dead. Gang members, crooked policemen, an unholy alliance of the two – I've learned to stop wondering who or why. And if they wanted me dead then, there's a good chance that they still do.'

'So you'll stay here?'

'For the time being, at least. I feel the place is healing me.'

'Your hand – is it still—'

'No, that has healed, as far as it's ever going to.' He held his right hand towards her, palm upward, and she saw the puckered scar running diagonally across it. 'What I meant was that my mind has steadied. There were times back there that I thought I should go mad with it all – the fear and the anger, the imaginings, the nightmares. I felt I'd be blown apart if I couldn't let it out, but it seemed impossible to speak of it. I didn't trust my colleagues and I knew better than to burden my wife with such things.'

A slight dimming of the world around her, as though a rag of cloud had passed across the sun. 'So why,' she asked, 'are you telling me?'

'Maybe because you listen. Because I think you really want to know.' His hand was still extended towards her, but now he dropped it to his side. 'I'm keeping you from your meal,' he said. 'You'd better go.'

Fifteen

She was hanging up her coat when the dining room door opened and her mother bustled out into the hall.

'Luncheon has been ready this past half-hour,' she said. 'We've been waiting for you.'

'I was walking.'

'That's not all you've been doing. I've been watching from the window. You're spending too much of your time with Constable Pritchard.'

'We were talking.'

'What would the pair of you have found to talk about that's so important it keeps him from his duties? The man's supposed to be searching for your father, not exercising his charms on gullible young ladies.'

Eliza felt the blood rush to her cheeks. 'I was helping him,' she said. 'There was something he didn't understand and I was able to give him the information he needed.'

'Information? Information it took twenty minutes to convey to him? I'm sorry, Elizabeth, but I simply don't believe it.'

'We spoke of other things too.'

'What kind of things?'

'Things that had happened to him before he arrived here. We had a conversation. I don't see what's wrong with that.'

'That's exactly my concern, Elizabeth – that you don't see at all what any sensible person would see at once. Let me enlighten you. A young man – handsome, plausible – finds that his duties bring him into contact with a young lady of considerably higher birth than his own. She's impressed by him, flattered by his attentions, perhaps believes herself a little in love with him. He'll take advantage of the situation, mark my words. Do I need to speak more plainly?'

'You're speaking quite plainly enough, thank you. I'm sorry you've delayed luncheon on my account – let's not delay it any further.' Eliza pushed open the dining room door and held it back for her mother. 'I suppose you know,' she said as Hannah brushed past, 'that Constable Pritchard is married?'

James looked up as they entered. 'Even so,' he said, 'you should be more thoughtful. Your mother has worries enough without you adding to them.' He dipped his soup spoon and raised it to his lips. 'Stone cold,' he said, 'but no matter.'

They'd been talking about her, she knew – knew it from something still hanging in the air as they ate. And when, at the end of the meal, her mother excused herself from the table and left her alone with her uncle, she felt certain that the manoeuvre had been planned.

She sat back in her chair. 'Mother wants you to give me a talking-to, doesn't she?'

James smiled. 'She thinks you're getting out of hand – her words, not mine. She wants me to ask you to consider your behaviour, and to think how it affects others.'

'I know what she wants, but I'm not a child any more and she can't bring me to heel the way she used to. And I won't be spied on either – watched from windows as though I might be about some mischief or other. What does she imagine I'm up to?'

'Her worries are those any mother might have about her growing daughter, though perhaps in heightened form. If your father had been a more attentive parent she might be a less anxious one.'

'But you must see that I have to live my own life, not the one she wants me to live.'

'I do see it, Eliza, believe me. But listen: I have to leave for a while, and I'm asking you to give your mother the support she needs while I'm away. That's not too much to ask, is it?'

'Where are you going?'

'London. Your mother believes your father may have gone to beg money from one or other of our relatives there. It's the slenderest of possibilities – I can't think of a single family member who'd be willing to see him, let alone help him – but it may be worth following up. At the very least, it gives me something to do. We can talk further when I return, but I need to pack now.'

'You're leaving today?'

'Owen will drive me to the station in about half an hour. I want to get to London tonight. Will you bear in mind what I've said?'

'How long will you be gone?'

'A few days at most, I should imagine.' He was already on his feet and making for the door, but as he passed he rested his hand momentarily on her shoulder. 'Listen to your heart,' he said, 'but not to your heart alone.' She wanted to speak – to acknowledge the gesture – but missed the moment.

* * *

She watched him go, gazing from the window as the gig drew away down the drive, and only then did she remember Charlotte's letter. She retrieved it from her coat pocket and went up to her room to read it.

My dear Eliza,

You were careful to release me from any sense of obligation, but of course I wish I could be with you all at this difficult time, and I have naturally discussed the possibility with Daniel. For his part, he's unwilling to leave Bristol at present. He has been ill of late – a persistent cough, nothing more, but he feels that undertaking the long journey to Edge Hall, particularly in this bitter weather, might worsen his condition, and he will not hear of me travelling alone. He is, as you know, temperamentally disposed to worry about his own health, but he also has it in his head that my constitution is delicate – a view he has held unshakably since he first met me, and which I long ago stopped trying to contradict.

I share his reluctance to make the journey, though for different reasons. If it were clear that Father's absence was the result of illness or accident, then, believe me, I should pack my valise this instant, Daniel or no Daniel, and be with you by nightfall. But so much of Father's behaviour over the years has been odd and unpredictable, and I don't think anyone should be surprised or unduly troubled by the development you describe.

Please write as soon as there is any resolution of the present uncertainty. You perhaps overestimate the extent to which faith informs my thinking, but hope seems entirely reasonable, and I would urge you not to lose heart.

Your loving sister,
Charlotte

An unexpectedly measured response, Eliza thought, and an appropriate one. She penned a quick reply and set off for town. She wasn't twenty yards down the drive before her mother threw up the sash of her bedroom window and called out to her.

'Where are you off to now?'

Eliza held up the letter by way of explanation.

'I want you to come straight home as soon as you've posted it.'

'I've nothing else to do.'

The window banged shut.

The change was unmistakable now – the chill gone from the air, a stiff wind driving from the west, smelling of rain. She breathed deeply as she walked down the lane, imagining the flush of new growth greening the meadows, birdsong spilling from the hedgerows. It will come, she thought, and at that moment she saw Morgan walking up the hill towards her, moving slowly, his head and neck bent forward as if he were bearing his troubles on his shoulders. He seemed unaware of her approach until she hailed him.

'Eliza,' he said. 'I've been thinking about you. About your family. This business with your father. Is there any news?'

'None to speak of. They're questioning Isaac Fletcher.'

'Seems they're questioning everybody. That new constable was up at the farm a couple of days ago, asking me if I knew anything. He said the police are leaving no stone unturned – that was his phrase – and I suppose that must be a kind of comfort to you. I wish I could have been more of a help to him.'

'The constable told me you'd seen nothing unusual, but even that may be helpful – a clue of sorts. I wondered, though, whether you might have seen any sign of Fletcher. He claims to know nothing about my father's whereabouts, but says he found his horse on our land on the evening of his disappearance.'

'Everyone knows Fletcher's a thief and a liar – anything he says would need to be taken with a sizeable pinch of salt.'

'True enough – the story about finding the horse on the estate wasn't the story he told at first. I don't imagine Constable Pritchard places much faith in his evidence.'

'No, but as I explained to the constable the other day, I don't consider myself an ideal witness either.'

'Really? I'd have thought—'

'My eyesight, Eliza. You remember how it was when you used to visit? – how you'd ask me to read you stories out of my newspaper, and how I'd be forever stumbling over the words. Not because I was a poor scholar, though you might have been excused for thinking so, but because even then something was wrong – a greyness or cloudiness, so that I saw the words a little unclear. In those days it never hindered me in my daily work, and these' – he tapped the glass of his spectacles with a dirty fingernail – 'helped with the reading; but then the greyness started to thicken, like a mist coming down. Nowadays the spectacles make hardly any difference. The doctor says I shall go blind sooner or later, and the only thing I can do is to hope it's not sooner.'

'So even if something had been going on when you came to collect the cart, you might not have seen it?'

'That was the point I made when the young policeman pressed me on the matter. Think of it, I said – me half blind, darkness coming on and anyone up to no good doubtless doing his best to avoid me. What would be the chances of me spotting anything?'

Eliza looked into his eyes. 'They don't know everything,' she said. 'The doctors. Maybe you won't lose your sight.'

He gave her a sorrowful smile. 'You're a good girl, Eliza, and a kindly one. Those days you used to visit, I grew to care for you like one of my own.'

'You know it wasn't by my wish that the visits stopped.'

'I knew well enough whose wish it was.' Morgan was moving away now, visibly distressed.

The rain had begun, great cold drops of it stinging her face and hands. Eliza hurried downhill but by the time she reached the post office she was soaked to the skin.

Sixteen

Three days of driving rain, thawing the frozen ground and turning the stream into a foaming torrent. The sky seemed to bear down on the earth: a grey veil dimmed the woods and parkland and blotted out the world beyond the gates. Eliza moved from room to room, driven by an intolerable restlessness. She would take down a book, riffle through its pages and replace it on the shelf, or go to the window and stare out into the rain for a few minutes before resuming her aimless wandering. She conversed civilly enough with her mother at mealtimes, but avoided her company when she decently could. There was no word from Dafydd.

And Brand was missing. She'd first noticed his absence the day the rains began but had thought nothing of it at the time – his forays into the woods and fields often kept him away for hours on end. Three days on, however, she was fretting about him.

'He's never been away this long before,' she said. She was down in the kitchen, watching Mrs Pugh flatten out a thick slab of pastry. 'And in this kind of weather he'd normally keep to the barn.'

Mrs Pugh dipped her hand into the flour sack and dusted her rolling pin. 'Maybe he's in someone else's barn, waiting for the rain to stop,' she said. 'In any case, you've more important things to worry about than a lost cat.'

Eliza took her words as a reproach. 'Worrying about Brand doesn't mean I'm not thinking about Father,' she said. 'I think about him all the time.'

Not absolutely true, she reflected later that afternoon, sitting in her room with her pen poised over her notebook, but close enough to the truth.

I miss Father, she wrote. *Nothing stops the missing, and I'm more certain than ever that he's gone for good. How can I be so sure? How can I know it when there's nothing to know it by? It's a feeling, a sense that he's not in touch any more, as if the thread that tied me to him had snapped clean off; as if he'd fallen out of the world.*

It frightened her, setting it down like that, but she felt compelled to continue.

Does Mother have the same feeling, I wonder – the certainty of him being gone? I think not. She frets, she cries, but she still thinks, or half-thinks, she'll see him again – hopes for it, maybe, but without completely wanting it. My own situation is simpler, but bleaker. I really do want him back, and I know that what I want is impossible.

She raised her head and looked out of the window. The light was fading from the sky but the rain had stopped. She ran downstairs, snatched her coat from the hallstand and went out to the stable. No sign of Brand; the milk she'd put out for him was still in its bowl, lightly filmed with dust. She called his name twice, softly and without hope.

She waited, listening. Only the horses shifting in their stalls, the squeak and skitter of rats in the loft. She imagined him there at her feet, butting at the skirts of her coat, rising on his hind legs to rub his head against her outstretched palm, and knew suddenly that she wasn't going back to her room. She unhooked the lantern, pocketed the matchbox and set off across the parkland, stumbling over the sodden ground, careless of her trailing skirts. At the wood's edge she stopped and peered into the gloom.

'Brand! Brand!'

Her ears were still ringing with the sound of her own voice when she heard something else – a quick flurry of movement somewhere among the trees, something brushing the undergrowth. She called again and leaned over the fence, willing him to come.

Nothing now but the patter of raindrops falling from the canopy above. It had been a badger she had heard, maybe, or a gust of wind; perhaps nothing more substantial than her own longing, but she needed to know. She ducked between the rails and plunged into the wood.

Immediately the darkness thickened around her. She moved forward uncertainly, picking her way between the trees, at each step feeling for the flat ground between their gnarled roots. After a moment she set down the lantern, took the matchbox from her pocket and lit the candle.

She moved in deeper, holding the lantern out at arm's length, still calling, but with less and less conviction. He'd have come running by now, she thought, if he'd been anywhere nearby. But suppose he'd been hurt, suppose he was lying somewhere in the dark, hearing her voice but unable to get to her. Pure invention, she knew, but the notion, once formed, was impossible to dislodge. She pressed on, sweeping the lantern from side to side, searching for a sign among the wavering shadows.

When she reached the fallen ash trunk she stopped. Illogical, she knew, to think he'd still be there, but she stood a long time, watching and listening, until the faint hope flickered and died.

The wind was rising, tugging at her hair and clothes. She turned to go and as she swung round she glimpsed through the undergrowth, at the outermost edge of the lantern's range, a subdued glimmer like the pallor of fungi. She made her way towards it, keeping her gaze fixed on the spot. Something out of place, she thought as she drew closer, something... She raised the lantern and craned forward.

A breathless instant of incomprehension, and then she let out a stifled cry. The lantern dropped from her hand and smashed, plunging her into darkness, but what she had seen in its gleam was so indelibly imprinted that it seemed she was still looking at it. Her father lay huddled against the knobbed bole of an oak, his face twisted towards her so that she saw the distortion of his features – his nose and left cheek flattened, his right eye closed and swollen, his lips drawn back from his teeth in a stiff grin. His hair was clumped and matted, raked forward across his brow. He seemed to be bound in some way: a stout rope circled his body, passing beneath his left arm and trailing away into the undergrowth.

Eliza turned and stumbled away, moving blindly, anywhere, whipped and snagged by twigs and briars. A voice was crying out in the darkness, the same words over and over – *no, it wasn't, it wasn't, no, no no* – and even when she recognised it as her own she was unable to silence it. Numb with horror, hopelessly disorientated, she blundered on through the drenching undergrowth and at last found her way back to the wood's edge.

She ran up the slope to the house, sobbing, labouring for breath, and tried to open the front door. Locked. She hammered on the panels with her fists, and after a moment heard her mother's voice, high and tremulous with anxiety.

'Who is it?'

'Eliza. Let me in.'

The key turned in the lock, the door swung back. 'For heaven's sake, girl,' her mother began, and stopped. She stared into Eliza's face, and then her own face seemed to crumple, as though she already knew what she was about to be told. Eliza stepped forward and took her in her arms. 'It's Father,' she said. 'He's dead.'

Her mother's howl brought Mrs Pugh and Carys running from the kitchen. 'What is it?' asked Mrs Pugh, hurrying across the hall, and at that moment Hannah slumped forward over Eliza's shoulder. 'Help me,' shouted Eliza, struggling to keep her from falling. Mrs Pugh darted forward, thrust her hands under Hannah's armpits and lowered her to the floor. She turned to Carys. 'Fetch the smelling salts,' she said. 'Quick as you can.'

By the time Carys returned Hannah was sitting up, looking dazedly around her. 'Help me to the sitting room,' she said. She waved away the bottle of salts. 'I just need to be quiet for a while.'

They raised her to her feet and walked her slowly through. 'The sofa,' she said. 'I'll sit there.' She let them ease her onto it and lay back against the cushions, staring at the ceiling. The quick rasp of her breath seemed to fill the room.

Mrs Pugh turned to Eliza. 'What's happened?'

'I've found him. Father. In the woods. He's dead. I wanted it not to be him, I wanted him not to be dead, but I know what I saw.'

Mrs Pugh sat down abruptly at the foot of the sofa. Carys hid her face in her hands and began to cry, moaning and snuffling. Eliza stood watching, deathly calm now, feeling as though she were seeing it all from some vast distance.

Hannah reached out and caught her by the hand. 'We need Owen here,' she said. 'Go up to the cottage and fetch him.'

'No, Mother, we need a constable.'

'Carys can run down to the police station. You fetch Owen.'

But Carys was backing away, shaking her head. 'Please, ma'am, don't make me go. He'll be walking out there, I know it.'

'He won't,' said Eliza coldly. 'I told you, he's dead.'

'His spirit, Miss. You know what I'm saying.'

'I know you're talking nonsense.' She didn't want to think of him wandering feelingly through the world, knowing himself unbodied and homeless in it.

Hannah closed her eyes and turned away, burying her face among the cushions. Mrs Pugh seemed to gather herself together. She rose from the sofa.

'I'll go for the police,' she said. 'Eliza will fetch Owen. Carys, you're to stay here with Mrs Mace and tend to her.' She marched out of the room with Eliza following close behind.

'Wait,' said Eliza. She pulled the door shut behind her. 'Let me go to the police station. I'll be quicker than you.'

Mrs Pugh shook her head. 'It's too far for you in the state you're in.' She took Eliza gently by the shoulders and steered her to the mirror. 'Look at you.'

Like my own ghost, thought Eliza. Her face was as white as chalk, her eyes dark and staring; her hair hung in damp tangles about her shoulders. She felt a rush of gratitude for Mrs Pugh's solid presence.

'Ask for Constable Pritchard,' she said.

'I'll bring whoever's on duty. Go on now, Eliza. The sooner Owen's here, the better.'

* * *

As she climbed the path to Owen's cottage the rain started up again, and by the time she knocked on the door she could feel the chill of it seeping into her neck and shoulders through the cloth of her coat.

'Eliza! What are you doing here?' Owen's concern was obvious, but when she made to step inside he stood firm, blocking the doorway.

'I've found Father,' she said. 'Dead, in the lower wood. Mother wants you to come over.'

'Of course, of course. Wait there while I fetch my coat.' He swung the door to, leaving her on the step.

She stayed outside for a minute or so and then pushed her way in and stood dripping on the doormat, glad of the warmth from the hearth and the steady light of the oil lamp. She stared around her at the clutter of Owen's life – the framed engravings of farm animals on the walls, the shelf loaded with tarnished brassware, the books jumbled on the table among dirty crockery and spoons, the newspaper lying on the arm of the settle. A London newspaper, she noticed, and she was about to move in to look more closely when Owen came clumping down the stairs and bundled her out with him into the rain.

'What a terrible business,' he said, setting off at a pace so brisk that she had to scurry to keep up. 'And how horrible for you to have been the one to find him.'

'At the time I was frightened, but now I'm glad. I can't quite explain, but I feel he'd have wanted it to be me.'

'He was fonder of you than of anyone.'

Was – the word hung in the air like the boom of a tolling bell. From now on, she realised, her father would be spoken of in the past tense only. 'I loved him,' she said. 'With all his faults.'

They arrived back to find Hannah wandering around the hallway as though she were looking for something. 'Oh, Owen,' she cried, holding out her hands. He took them in his own and held them, gently, decorously. 'What should we do, Owen? Should we bring him in?'

'No,' said Eliza. 'We must wait for the police. They'll want to see him the way I found him. Where's Carys?'

'I sent her down to make tea. Such a display of weeping and wailing – I wanted her out of my sight.' Hannah gave a little sideways stagger; Owen drew her towards him and gripped her by the elbow.

'Maybe you should sit down,' he said. She let him lead her back to the sitting room and help her to the sofa.

The tea, when it eventually arrived, was lukewarm and overbrewed, but Eliza drank it gladly. She had barely set her cup back on the tray when she heard a knock at the side door. She ran into the hallway to find Dafydd coming towards her down the passageway with a lighted bull's-eye in his hand.

'I took the liberty of letting myself in,' he said. 'I left Mrs Pugh to follow at her own speed.' He stood awkwardly in front of her, fiddling with the catch of the lantern. 'Eliza, I'm very sorry to hear about your father. You must feel—'

'I don't want to think about my feelings now. I have to show you where he is.'

'There's no need for you to come out again. Just give me directions. I'll find him.'

'No,' she said, 'I want to come.' She stood stubbornly in front of him, watching the rainwater drip from his cape and puddle on the floor.

'You must be exhausted, Eliza. Mrs Pugh said that Owen—'

'Owen can come too. But I have to see Father again. Do you understand?'

Owen must have been listening. He stepped out into the hall, buttoning the collar of his greatcoat. 'I'm ready,' he said.

Dafydd led the way down the slope, but when they reached the fence he held out his lantern to Eliza. 'I'm glad you insisted,' he said, peering into the denser darkness among the trees. 'I might have stumbled around in there for hours without finding him. Would you guide us?'

Graciously done, she thought with a sudden flush of warmth, knowing the gesture was for her sake. She slipped between the bars and took the lantern from him. 'This way,' she said, striking off at an angle through the woodland.

She pressed forward quickly at first, propelled by a grim and brittle energy, but as she approached the place her legs began to tremble and she slowed almost to a standstill.

'Here?' asked Dafydd, drawing up alongside her.

'A little further.' She took a deep breath. 'I have to prepare myself.'

'There's no need for you to see him.'

'There is, Dafydd. Truly, there is.'

She gave herself a little shake and walked on until the beam of the lantern picked out the trunk of the fallen ash. 'Just there,' she said. 'Beyond that clump of brambles, against the oak tree.' She lifted the lantern high and stepped forward with her heart hammering in her chest.

Whatever she had been preparing herself for, it wasn't this. 'He's gone,' she said. She moved the lantern wildly to and fro, scanning the shadows, angry and perplexed. 'He was here and now he's gone.'

'Could you have mistaken the place?' asked Owen.

'I'm telling you, he was here.' She scuffed at the swollen roots of the oak with her boot. 'Just here. And look' – she swept the beam outward – 'that's the lantern I had with me. I dropped it when I saw him.'

'We'll make a thorough search of the area,' said Dafydd. 'First thing tomorrow.'

'No, I want to find him tonight.' She grabbed at his sleeve. 'Please, Dafydd.'

'If we charge about in the dark we risk destroying important evidence. I'll be over at first light.'

Whatever had held her together over the past hours snapped suddenly like a strained fiddle-string. She stood there in the pelting rain with her face in her hands and let the tears come. Dafydd took her gently by the shoulders and turned her around so that she faced back towards the edge of the wood. 'Come on,' he said. 'We'll take you home.'

Seventeen

She lay sleepless, rigid among the tangled bedclothes, knowing it over and over again – her father's face rising towards her from the shadows, the fall of the lantern from her numbed fingers, the splintering glass, the engulfing darkness. After a while she rose, lit the lamp and went over to the desk. She took her notebook from the drawer and began to write in a frenzy, desperate to get the words down, to give shape and order to her whirling thoughts.

Useless. After a while she set down her pen and returned to her bed where she lay with her jaw clenched and her eyes wide open until the sky began to lighten; then she dressed and went downstairs.

She sat at the dining room window, waiting for Dafydd to appear. A flock of redwings huddled on the ground in the lee of the shrubbery, almost motionless under the steady rain. Watching, she imagined them more stoical than herself, their small lives less troubled than her own.

When Dafydd eventually arrived, it was with company – Sergeant Williams at his side and, a few paces behind, two men in shabby working clothes, each bearing a spade over his shoulder. The group left the drive almost immediately and cut across the parkland. She watched until they were lost to view behind the curve of the wood; then she put on her coat and went out.

They were in the far corner of the parkland, where the laneside hedge met the wood. Dafydd and Sergeant Williams stood against the fence, apparently deep in conversation; the other two were digging, slowly and carefully, piling the upcast against the hedge. Dafydd looked up as she approached, then hurried towards her.

'Better you don't come any closer,' he said.

'Why not? Dafydd, what's happening?'

'I think we've found your father. We'll know very shortly.'

'Is he buried here?'

'Almost certainly. After I left you last night I came back and walked the length of the fence down to the lane – just looking, not for anything in particular, but with the idea that some clue to the night's doings might show up somewhere along the boundary – a footprint perhaps, or a snagged thread. In the event, I found a good deal more than that – found myself up to my ankles in a patch of freshly turned soil. If I've guessed rightly – I'm sorry, Eliza, I'm not insensitive to your feelings, but you'll understand that recovering your father's body would be a significant step forward for us.'

'Of course I understand. You've a job to do.' She glanced again towards the corner of the field and saw one of the men down on his knees, scrabbling in the dirt like a dog. As she watched, he rose to his feet and took a step back. 'Here,' he called and she knew at once, from the tone of his voice, that the search for her father was over.

Dafydd turned. 'You stay put,' he said, breaking into a run, but she was already at his heels, slipping and stumbling on the wet grass. Sergeant Williams was stooping over the diggings but he straightened up and looked round as she drew near. She saw him raise his hand as if to warn her off but she ignored the gesture.

'You shouldn't be here,' said the sergeant, catching her by the arm as she came level with him. She shook herself free.

'I want to see my father.' She pushed forward and saw what the men had uncovered – a coat cuff, a wrist, a hand with the fingers splayed and bent as though clutching at the wet earth.

'I wonder,' said Dafydd gently, 'if you'd mind fetching Owen.'

'I want to see Father properly. I want to see his face.'

'Leave us to our work now. We'll let you see him before we take him away. Tell Owen that we'll need transport.'

'There's only the gig. I'm not sure—'

'No, probably not appropriate. I suggest borrowing Morgan's cart again. Ask Owen to arrange it. And then you ought to let your mother know what's happening.'

She hesitated.

'Please, Eliza.'

She turned and walked back up the slope. Through the window of the dining room she could see her mother standing at the sideboard, her shoulders hunched and her head bowed. She hasn't seen me, thought Eliza, and she quickened her step, hurrying through the yard and up the track towards Owen's cottage.

As she unfastened the gate Owen appeared at the cottage door, settling his hat on his head. 'I was about to come down,' he said. 'I thought you'd need help with the search.'

'They've already found him. Buried in the bottom corner, down by the lane. They're digging there now. Dafydd wondered whether we might borrow Gwilym Morgan's cart again – wondered whether you might ask him.'

'Of course. How has your mother taken the news?'

'She hasn't heard yet. I'm going to tell her now.'

Owen was dithering on the doorstep, vague and distracted. 'You run on down,' he said. 'I've just remembered something I need to do here. I'll go and see Morgan as soon as I've attended to it.' He banged the door shut, leaving Eliza standing bewildered in the darkness.

'Owen,' she called, but there was no answer, and after a moment she turned and made her way back down the track.

* * *

She arrived at the Hall to find her mother at the table, staring out of the window with her breakfast almost untouched in front of her.

'Where have you been, Elizabeth?'

'With the police. Father's been found.'

'Where? Not where you first saw him?'

'No, but not far away. He's been buried down by the lane. They're working there now.'

Hannah rose and went over to the window. 'I've seen nothing,' she said.

'They're in the far corner. You can't see from here. I don't think it will take them long – the body's very close to the surface.'

Hannah's face seemed to crumple suddenly; she pressed her hands to her eyes. 'What's going on?' she said. 'I feel I'm in some frightful dream and can't wake myself up. Your father found and lost and found again, all in the space of a few hours, the police coming and going, you running off first thing without a word to anyone and then arriving back with your face set hard and your talk of burial and the body – your father, Elizabeth, your own father – as if all this were a newspaper story and not our lives, as if it had nothing to do with you.' She turned away from the window, bent in on herself with her shoulders heaving.

Eliza stepped forward and took her mother in her arms, feeling her stiffen in resistance. 'I'm just doing what I have to do,' she said. 'You ask what's going on – well, I'm asking the same question. I know there are answers – Uncle James says everything in life has an explanation – but I also know I won't find them if I turn my face from the facts or lose myself in my own misery.'

'It's not your job to look for the answers, Elizabeth. That's what the police are here for.' Hannah drew away and seated herself again at the table. 'Sit down and eat something. You'll make yourself ill, running around on an empty stomach.'

'Later.' Eliza was already making for the door.

'Where are you going now?'

'I might be needed out there.'

'Needed by whom? Leave the police to do their work – they won't want you getting in their way.'

'But surely it's right for his family to be there. You must feel that too.'

'No, Elizabeth, I don't. It's a question of propriety. Of course there must be a time for the family to gather round and bid him farewell, but that time isn't now. Surely you can see that?'

Eliza made a show of considering the matter before moving off. 'I have to go,' she said. 'I'll be back as soon as I can.'

* * *

Her father's body had been lifted and laid on its side on the trampled grass, facing towards the hedge. The skirts of his coat were rucked up almost to his waist – his good coat, she realised, soaked through now and caked with loam – and she had to repress the urge to step forward and straighten them. Absurd, she knew, but she would have liked to look after him in some small way, to let him know he wasn't beyond her caring.

'A terrible business,' said the sergeant, moving in alongside her and placing his hand on her shoulder. 'Our hearts go out to you and your family.'

'Amen to that,' said the younger of the two labourers, pausing in the act of cleaning his spade. 'No-one could say Mace was a good man, but who'd wish this on anyone?'

His companion shot him a warning glance. 'It's not for us to judge him,' he said.

'That rope around his chest,' said Dafydd, cutting in quickly, 'is something of a mystery. You don't recognise it, do you, Eliza?'

A filthy length of hemp, perhaps ten feet in all, knotted to form a noose that circled her father's chest just beneath his armpits.

'Only from seeing it last night. It was there when I found him.' She stooped to look more closely. 'I can't see anything special about it — it might come from anywhere. Could it have been used to kill him?'

'We think not,' said Dafydd, 'though it seems likely that strangulation was the cause of death. There are two distinct bruises on his throat, one on either side of his windpipe. Thumbmarks at a guess. We'll know more after the autopsy.'

Eliza walked round to look at her father's face. Nobody tried to stop her but a tense silence fell on the little knot of men around her.

This time there was no sense of shock, but an immense sadness swept over her as she stared at the bruised and muddied features, the outstretched arm, the palm upturned to the teeming rain as if her father were begging for something that could never now be given to him. She stood there with her head bowed, lost in her own private grief, until Dafydd stepped up beside her, took her by the arm and gently drew her away.

'Go back inside,' he said. 'You've done all you can out here. If the dead know anything about the world they've left, your father will understand that you've done your duty by him, and more. Get warm and dry, have something to eat. Tell your mother I'll call in this afternoon.'

Eliza nodded. She felt exhausted now, but with a sense that something important had been accomplished. She turned away and, carefully, a little unsteadily, began to climb the slope towards the house.

She had hoped to slip up to her room unnoticed but as she crossed the hall her mother called out to her from the dining room. Eliza opened the door and peered in.

Hannah was at the window again. 'Tell me what's happening,' she said. 'I don't really want to hear, but I can't bear not knowing.'

'They're going to take Father into town. There's to be an autopsy.'

'Are they certain it's murder?'

'No-one has used the word, but I don't think anyone believes otherwise.'

Hannah shook her head. 'That man,' she said. 'The shame he's brought on our family.'

Eliza's anger flared, guttered and died. 'I'm so tired,' she said. 'I need to sleep. Wake me when Constable Pritchard comes. He says he'll be here this afternoon.'

Over her mother's shoulder she could see Owen, down at the far edge of the parkland, leading Morgan's horse towards the corner of the field with the cart bumping and rocking behind. Father will be heaved in, she thought, and laid on the bare boards like a slaughtered animal. For a moment she imagined herself running back down to supervise the men, to see that they observed such decorum as the miserable circumstances allowed, but she knew that the effort was beyond her. She closed the door and made her way slowly up the stairs to her room.

Eighteen

She woke in a state of bewilderment, uncertain whether the footsteps that echoed through her head belonged to the waking world or to the confused dream she was emerging from. The steps came closer, ringing out clearly now on the cobbles below; the side door was opened and quietly closed again.

Late afternoon, she thought, judging by the light. She dressed in a daze and went downstairs. From the sitting room she heard the sound of her mother's voice, earnest and insistent. She pushed open the door.

She was so certain of seeing Dafydd there that when her uncle turned to greet her she simply stopped dead in the doorway and stood gawping at him. James stepped forward and folded her in his arms.

'My poor girl,' he said. 'Your mother has been telling me what happened last night.'

Eliza broke away and crossed to the fireplace. She held her hands out to the blaze. 'I wasn't expecting you,' she said. 'I didn't hear Owen take the gig out.'

'I walked from the station.'

'In this weather?'

'Why not? I've been out in worse. And rain or shine, there's no better remedy for a chestful of filthy London air than a few miles' brisk walk through country lanes. I'm sorry I wasn't here last night, Eliza – sorry it was you who found him. The whole business must have been a nightmare for you. I hope you'll be able to put it from your mind.'

'Not for a while, I imagine. Certainly not until we know what happened. And of course there's the funeral to plan for.'

'You can leave the funeral arrangements to me, Eliza. And let's leave it to the police to find out what happened to your father.'

'I've said as much,' snapped Hannah, 'but she won't be told. She was out there with them this morning in the pouring rain, quite unnecessarily and completely contrary to my advice. You should sit down, I told her, sit down and eat your breakfast, but she wouldn't listen. And then she comes back limp as a dishcloth with her clothes wringing wet, too exhausted to walk straight, and—'

'Yes,' said James, 'she's had a terrible time of it.' He turned to Eliza. 'Have you eaten anything at all today?'

'Not yet. I'll have something at dinnertime.'

'You'll have something now. Come with me.' He took her by the arm and led her through to the dining room. 'Your mother's grief,' he said, closing the door firmly behind them, 'is venting itself as anger, directed largely against your father but also against you.' He went over to the chimney breast and tugged on the bell pull. 'I suggest you leave us to talk together for a while. In any case, you must eat something – you look half-starved.'

'I'm not hungry.'

'That's hardly surprising, but it's essential that you keep your strength up. When the mind is disturbed the body resists nourishment, but that doesn't mean it has no need of it.'

A light tap on the door and Carys entered. 'You rang for me?'

'A bowl of broth, please, for Miss Elizabeth.'

Carys gave a little bob of her head and retreated. James made as if to follow her out, but stopped at the door and turned back to Eliza. 'One other matter,' he said. 'Your mother expressed the view that your behaviour towards her – your disobedience as she calls it – is attributable to your infatuation with Constable Pritchard. I assured her that no such infatuation exists. I'm sure you'll give her no grounds for imagining otherwise.'

'I'm not responsible for Mother's imaginings.'

A momentary pause before James replied. 'Quite so,' he said. 'We'll speak again later, when you've eaten. *Bon appétit.*'

* * *

Eliza was finishing her broth when she saw Dafydd striding up the drive towards the house. She put down her spoon and ran to let him in.

'I've been longer than I intended,' he said. He stepped inside, loosening the chinstrap of his helmet. 'It's been an eventful day.'

'Do you have news?'

'Patience, Eliza. Where's your mother?'

'In the sitting room. With my uncle.'

'Your uncle's back?'

'Since this afternoon.' She led him across the hall. 'Constable Pritchard is here,' she said, ushering him in. 'He has news about Father.'

'Indirectly, yes,' said Dafydd, 'though today's developments mainly concern others.'

James motioned him to sit down. 'Thank you, Mr Mace,' said Dafydd, 'but it's better I stand. This endless rain – I haven't dried out all day.'

'Others?' prompted Hannah.

'To begin with, Isaac Fletcher. I was already doubtful that he was our man – he'd lied in the first instance about the horse, obviously with the intention of playing down the theft, but his second story had the ring of truth. The horse, he said, had been tied to a tree in the wood – an odd and unexpected detail, and his account seemed the more credible for that reason. I'd begun to think of it as offering a clue to the circumstances of Mr Mace's death.'

James leaned forward in his chair. 'I don't see what's so odd about tethering a horse in woodland.'

'Think about it in specific terms. Your brother rides up the lane towards the Hall. He's drunk – perhaps a little less so than when he was helped into his saddle outside the Bull, but drunk or sober he'd have no chance of getting the horse into the wood from the lane, even supposing he wanted to. You know the lie of the land there – a high bank either side of the lane, more or less vertical and topped by briar and hawthorn. So we have to imagine him taking the obvious route home: up the lane to the gate, in at the gate and then – what? We don't know exactly but if we accept Fletcher's story someone, at some point, takes the horse down to the fence – to the throughway you showed me, Eliza – leads it into the wood and tethers it there. And that does seem odd to me, Mr Mace – odd enough to set me wondering.'

'A known malefactor gives the police unsubstantiated information about his own actions, information which, even if true, doesn't rule out other, darker deeds – forgive me, Pritchard, but if you're arguing on that basis that Fletcher couldn't have killed my brother—'

'I haven't said anything as definite as that. I'm simply building up a picture from the limited evidence at our disposal. And that picture must now include one telling and incontrovertible detail: although it's not entirely clear what was going on last night, we know that Fletcher couldn't have been involved. He's been under lock and key since his arrest.'

'But he wasn't in gaol at the time my brother disappeared. It's surely possible that Fletcher killed Robert and an accomplice buried the body?'

'It's my job to examine every possibility, and I've naturally examined that one. I'd be examining it more closely if I thought the effort worthwhile. The fact is that when we brought Fletcher in I considered it likely that he was directly responsible for Mr Mace's disappearance, but the more we've questioned him the further I've retreated from that view. Our latest discoveries put it beyond doubt that we're dealing with murder and they fall short of proving Fletcher innocent of the crime, but they confirm me in the direction in which I was already moving. So much so that when Mrs Fletcher visited the station this morning to tell me, at considerable length, that her husband wasn't a murderer – she'd just heard about the discovery of the body – I went so far as to say that I believed she might be right. I know I'm right, she said. When will you let him out?'

Hannah had been slumped in her chair, gazing into the fire, but now she jerked upright and swung round to face Dafydd. 'Let him out? Surely—'

'Mere wishfulness on Mrs Fletcher's part. Even if Jacob Todd were to confess to the murder tomorrow, Fletcher would still be facing a spell in prison for the theft of the horse. I had to set the poor woman right on that score.'

'You mentioned Todd,' said Eliza. 'There's no trace of him, I suppose?'

'I mentioned Todd with good reason, though I was getting a little ahead of myself. I'm pleased to say we have rather more than a trace – we found him this afternoon.'

Eliza started. 'Found him? Where?'

'Under our noses. In Clem Weston's cottage. You'll remember that Todd stayed with Weston on the night of your father's disappearance and left, according to Weston's testimony at the time, before first light the next morning. In fact, he didn't leave at all – he's been holed up there since he arrived, with Weston's connivance.'

'I know Weston a little,' said James, 'and always thought him a decent enough fellow. Why would he risk his reputation on Todd's account?'

'Friendship, he says. By the time he came to see us this afternoon it was clear to him that he'd made a serious error of judgement, but I could see how the situation had arisen. When Todd first approached him, Weston was simply agreeing to give temporary shelter to a friend who'd lost his job. The next morning he was early in town buying provisions when he heard of the previous evening's events in the Bull. It seems that when he told Todd that Mr Mace hadn't returned home after leaving the inn, Todd became agitated and asked to be allowed to lie low in the cottage for a further day or two. He claimed he was in danger of being arrested – wrongfully arrested, he insisted – on account of having had dealings with Mr Mace the evening before. When pressed by Weston as to what those dealings were, he told him he'd made Mr Mace pay what he owed him.'

'It strikes me,' said James, 'that that comes very close indeed to an admission of guilt.'

'Apparently that's not the way it struck Weston. Within a few hours of hearing Todd's story he was lying to protect him – that nonsense about his departure has wasted a good deal of our time – and in grave danger of being arrested himself. As he tells it, Todd persuaded him that he'd had a right to what he'd taken, and that the taking of it had caused Mr Mace no serious harm.'

'No serious harm? What does that mean? One thing's for certain – Robert wouldn't willingly have handed over that money. There must have been a struggle.'

'Todd admitted to Weston that he'd pulled him off his horse and shaken him up a little but says there was no more to it than that. I'd imagine your brother wasn't in a fit state to resist. Todd told Weston that he'd taken exactly what he was owed, no more, no less, and then helped him back into the saddle and sent him on his way.'

'And Weston believed him?'

'The story's not entirely implausible, but if Todd's innocent of your brother's murder he's going to have the devil of a job to prove it.'

'An innocent man would have come forward at once, not hidden himself away.'

'People don't always trust the law to get things right, Mr Mace, and that applies particularly to the poor when they find themselves suspected of crimes against gentlefolk. Besides, even if he's innocent of murder, he's certainly guilty of something close to highway robbery. There's a right way and a wrong way to go about retrieving a debt, and the fact that Todd can't afford to go about it the right way doesn't justify his actions in the sight of the law. He must have known that, and so, no doubt, did Weston. If I say that I can see why Weston was unwilling to betray his friend, it's because I know from experience that a man's moral sense is coloured by his place in society, and by allegiances that he himself may not fully understand.'

'Even so, Weston eventually chose to come to you. Something must have brought him to his senses.'

'True. Todd had initially held out the prospect of your brother's likely return and then, after Fletcher's arrest, an alternative possibility – that responsibility for Mr Mace's disappearance would soon be proved against a man known to the whole neighbourhood as a rogue. But today the town was buzzing with news of our discovery of the body, and once Mrs Fletcher had spread the word – perhaps with embellishments – that I believed the case against her husband wasn't entirely secure, Weston began to wonder whether he was harbouring a murderer. I think it was a sense of being out of his depth, and an understandable fear for his own safety, that brought him to our door this afternoon.'

'So Todd's now in custody?'

'Sergeant Williams is questioning him as we speak. I hope to have further news for you by tomorrow morning.'

'Until tomorrow,' said James, rising from his chair. 'Thank you for your time, Constable Pritchard.'

Eliza darted to the door. 'I'll see the constable out,' she said.

'Do you really think Todd killed my father?' she asked as she followed him down the passageway. 'It's hard to imagine. Mother used to say the pair of them were thick as thieves.'

'Maybe, but the whole town knows of their recent quarrel. It's a fact of life, Eliza, that even close friendships between equals can turn sour, and this certainly wasn't a friendship of equals. As I understand it, the quarrel arose directly from Todd's dismissal.'

'So you think he's guilty?'

'I said just now that he'd have a job to prove his innocence, and I stand by that. What's clear is that he's the last person known with certainty to have seen your father alive. Also that when he caught up with him after following him from the inn – caught up with him in fading light, on a deserted stretch of lane on the outskirts of town – he hauled him from his horse and lightened his purse for him. You can feel the noose tightening around Todd's neck already. But that's not all. Unlike Fletcher, he has no alibi for yesterday evening. Weston was out repairing the roof of his sister's cottage in the afternoon and stayed on for supper with her. He's vague about the time of his return, but believes it to have been no earlier than eight. So there's nothing to say that Todd wasn't up here at the time of yesterday evening's events. I can't tell you whether or not he's guilty, but I can tell you that men have been hanged on far flimsier evidence.'

A faint click; she could hear the sitting room door being eased open. Dafydd glanced up, over her shoulder. 'I must be going,' he said. He turned quickly and stepped out into the dark.

As Eliza crossed the hallway, making for the stairs, her uncle emerged from the sitting room. 'Won't you rejoin us?' he asked.

'For dinner, yes, but I must write to Charlotte first. I must tell her about Father.'

'Of course. I just wanted to remind you of our earlier conversation. About Constable Pritchard.'

'I don't need reminding.'

'Your mother thinks otherwise.'

Fatigue enveloped her like a smothering mist. She moved on without replying.

Nineteen

Eliza was walking up the high street towards the post office when she became aware of someone at her back, moving with a brisk step and closing on her. She stopped and turned.

'Good morning, Eliza.' Dafydd seemed awkward out there in the street, a little uncertain of himself. 'I was wondering whether you might have a moment to spare when you've done your errands.'

She held up her letter. 'I must send this to my sister, urgently. That's my only errand.'

'I'll wait for you here. Perhaps we might walk up to the Hall together.'

'Do you have news?'

'I have questions. I want to wander over the grounds again, to get a clearer sense of what might have happened there. Your company – your knowledge – would be particularly helpful to me.'

More than a hint of flattery, she thought, but she blushed all the same. 'I shall be back in a moment,' she said.

By the time she returned from the post office she had steadied herself. They walked along discussing the improved weather and the signs of approaching spring until, as they began to climb away from the town, Dafydd swung the conversation abruptly back to the subject they had been skirting.

'There's been no progress with Todd,' he said. 'No change to his story. He was asking to speak with you – says you'll back him up.'

'Back him up? How?'

'A good question. He says you know about the money owed him by your father.'

'I know what Todd told me and I've no particular reason to doubt his word. But my knowledge of the debt can't help him. It doesn't prove he didn't commit the murder.'

'That's exactly the point I put to him, but they say a drowning man will clutch at a straw, and in my experience a man facing the gallows may clutch at even less.'

'There's no reason for me to see him, is there?'

'I think any visit would be a distraction from more important matters, and the truth is that we've no time to waste. Now that we know we're dealing with murder, Sergeant Williams is talking of bringing in a detective. I'd like to forestall that if I can.'

'I don't see what's wrong with having a detective on the case.'

'I wouldn't expect you to, Eliza, but you can take it from me that detectives are less perceptive, less intelligent and a good deal less scrupulous than popular fiction would have us believe. A nasty, interfering breed, cutting in at the last minute to snatch the credit for work painstakingly carried out by others. I regard this as my case, and I don't want it taken out of my hands.'

'Your case? Your hands?' Eliza came to a halt in the middle of the lane. 'It's my father you're talking about. I want to know who killed him, and you can think of nothing but your job, your reputation. I don't care who discovers the truth. I don't care who gets the credit. I don't care who gets a shiny feather to stick in his cap.' She smudged away a tear with the cuff of her coat.

For a moment Dafydd stood staring at her, visibly taken aback. When he spoke again his voice had softened.

'I'm sorry, Eliza – I can see how thoughtless my words must have seemed. But the plain fact is that we both want the same thing. I shall do everything I can to ensure that your father's murderer is brought to justice. I hope you'll be willing to help me.'

It was clear that he took her silence as assent. 'What troubles me,' he said, 'is that we have no evidence for the timing of the murder.' He set off again and she fell into step beside him.

'Can't we assume that he was killed on the evening of his disappearance, on his way home from the Bull?'

'We've worked on that assumption so far and we may well be right to do so, but the evidence is missing. The cold weather around that time complicates the matter. The autopsy suggests that the body had been partially frozen, and that allows us to say with certainty that your father was killed during the hard frost – before the thaw set in. But the process of decomposition would have been arrested, or at least dramatically slowed, during the period following his death, which makes it unusually diffi-cult to establish exactly when the death took place. And there are oddities – the rope around his chest, for instance, or your discovery of the body in the lower woodland when, according to your uncle, he and Owen Meredith had searched both upper and lower woods from end to end in the immediate aftermath of your father's disappearance. Tell me, Eliza, do you think it's remotely possible that your father's body could have been there all along – where you discovered it the other evening?'

'It's out of the question. I was in exactly the same place a few days earlier – the day you came to tell my mother about Fletcher. While you were in the house I walked down to the wood and sat awhile on the fallen tree. I'm certain I'd have seen the body if it had been there at that time.'

Dafydd took his notebook and pencil from his pocket and jotted something down. 'That's useful information,' he said. 'Very useful indeed.'

'You mentioned the rope. Is that important?'

'The fact that we can't explain it makes it important. For a while I wondered whether your father might have been held captive before his death, but that seems unlikely. There are no rope marks on his wrists or ankles, and if his hands were free the slipknot that was used wouldn't have detained him for more than a couple of seconds. I'm hoping' – they had passed through the gate and he was steering her across the parkland towards the wood – 'that careful examination of the area will give us a clearer understanding of what happened to your father, both before and after his death. I realise this will be difficult for you, but would you mind if we revisited the spot where you found the body?'

'I'll do whatever's needed.' She entered the wood and picked her way between the trees with Dafydd following at her heels.

'I've been considering,' he said, 'what might have been done with the body immediately after the murder. The ground was frozen rock-hard. Ditch-digging and tillage had come to a standstill, and what was difficult for honest labourers would have been all but impossible for a murderer intent on concealing his activities. Even if digging had been practicable, the sound of a pickaxe on frozen earth would have travelled hundreds of yards in the stillness. So he had to wait for the ground to thaw, and during that time the body had to be kept from view. Somewhere in these woods, I imagine. Not, as we've established, in the place that you found it, but surely not far away.'

'We know where Father was buried, but he could have been killed and hidden anywhere between here and the Bull.'

'If a murderer has to move his victim he's unlikely to take him further than is necessary. The fact that your father was buried close to home – not by any means the safest choice – suggests that he was killed close to home, and that the body lay hidden hard by in the days between the killing and the burial.'

'But if my uncle and Owen searched the woods and found nothing—'

'Then we might conclude either that the body was remarkably well hidden or that their search was less thorough than it should have been.'

As she drew nearer to the place, Eliza's heart quickened and her pace slowed. Dafydd must have sensed her unease. He came alongside her and placed his hand lightly on her arm.

'Are you all right, Eliza?'

She kept on walking. 'Just there,' she said. 'You remember? Against the oak.'

Dafydd broke away and squatted down at the base of the tree, peering closely at the ground. 'Nothing very obvious,' he said. 'If you hadn't seen the body, we'd have no idea it had ever been here.'

She crouched beside him. 'That's true,' she said. 'And look around – there's so little evidence of disturbance anywhere. But that tells us something. Uncle James says a trail is like a poem – we have to learn to read between the lines. And what I read here tells me that my father was carried. If he'd been hauled along the ground we'd see clear signs of it – drag marks in the leafmould, a swathe of damaged vegetation leading to and from the spot.

The few signs I can see – this scuff here, this snapped twig – may be the tracks of the murderer, but they're not the marks of my father's body.'

Dafydd took out his notebook and pencil again. 'Of course,' he said. He wrote quickly, resting the book on his knee. 'I was coming to the same conclusion myself.' He rose and began to move away, scanning the ground.

'It might be better,' said Eliza, 'to try to follow the trail back in the other direction. We already know where Father was taken after I found him here. What we need to find now is the trail that shows where he was brought from. Look at the way this ash seedling has been bent over – that may be a start.' She stepped carefully forward. 'Yes, look here – you see how these aconite shoots have been crushed?'

'That's aconite? How do you know? It's barely showing above ground.'

'Even so, I recognise it. We learn naturally about things that interest us. Curiosity and observation – Uncle James says they're the foundation of all knowledge, and I realised very early that knowledge was what I was after.'

'You're close to your uncle, aren't you?'

'I owe him a great deal. See here – another scuff mark, quite unmistakable. We're definitely on the right track.'

She hadn't gone another twenty paces before she realised where the trail was leading. 'The ice house,' she said. 'Can you see? Up ahead – that long mound.'

Dafydd squinted into the shadows. 'Is that where you're taking us?'

'It's where the trail seems to be taking us.' She felt something coming clear in her mind, as though light were breaking through a pall of mist. 'It makes sense.'

Even during her childhood the ice house had shown signs of neglect and it had deteriorated further over the intervening years. The keystone of the arched entrance had slipped and the stucco had peeled away in patches from the jambs, leaving ugly scars; the trees had encroached and the mound covering the structure, which she had once been able to climb, was now overgrown with a tangled mass of briars.

'I love this place,' she said. 'As a child I was frightened of it, but I couldn't keep away.'

She placed her hand on the jamb and peered into the darkness. 'Do you have your lamp?' she asked.

'I had no idea I'd need it. I have matches.'

'Matches will do.' She ducked under the arch and began to move down the passage, feeling her way along the damp walls.

'I can't see a thing.' He was close behind her, blocking the light from the entrance. She heard the rattle of the matchbox.

'Not yet, Dafydd. Wait till we're there.'

'There?'

'You'll see.' She was moving carefully now, testing the ground with her foot, feeling for the stone lip of the shaft. 'Here we are.'

She pressed back against the passage wall, allowing him to stand alongside her. 'Now,' she said. 'Strike it now.'

A quick rasp and the match flared. Above, the building's domed vault; at their feet the shaft, packed with broken ice to within a few feet of its rim. Dafydd stared wide-eyed. 'I can see why you're drawn to the place, Eliza, but it gives me the shivers. Maybe because my father – damn it.' The match dropped from his fingers and went out.

She heard him fumbling with the box, felt his elbow brush her side. 'Your father,' she prompted.

'Just that his stories about what went on in the mines used to frighten me. Stories of broken props and firedamp, men buried underground.'

Rasp and flare. The hand that held the match was shaking. Eliza bent over the rim of the shaft. 'Here,' she said, dropping to her knees. 'Bring the match closer. I need more light.'

He squatted beside her, holding the match low. 'What is it?'

The flame touched his fingers and they were in darkness again. 'I don't know,' she said. 'Strike another.'

In the light of the third match she saw it plainly – a line a couple of inches wide and perhaps six in length, paler than the stone on either side, running inward from the edge of the lip. She stretched out her hand and touched it.

Yes,' she said. 'Feel it. The stone's naturally slimy down here, but at that point the coating has been rubbed away. Recently, by the look of it.'

'Something to do with getting the ice into the shaft?'

'No. Todd unloads the cart at the entrance and shovels the ice down the passage. This is something much more precise.'

Dafydd blew out the match. 'I want to get out of here,' he said. He turned and made his way towards the light.

She was stepping through the archway when it struck her. 'The rope,' she said. 'It's the mark made by the rope. Father must have been thrown into the shaft – hidden there after the murder, while the murderer waited for the ground to thaw. The rope would have been brought in on the night he was moved, to make it easier to drag him out.'

'Possibly. Well, probably.'

Eliza looked hard at him. 'You don't like it when I do that, do you?'

'When you do what?'

'When I see something you've missed.'

His face clouded, just for an instant, and then he threw back his head and laughed. 'You're sharp as a tin-tack, Eliza. No, I suppose I don't like it. But that's absurd, of course. I ask for your help, you give it – and then I lack the grace to admit that you're a step ahead of me.'

'It doesn't matter who picks up the clues. What's important is that we arrive at a clearer understanding of what happened to Father.'

'I think we're doing that. Let's suppose you're right. The body's hidden here and, once the ground is soft enough to dig, the murderer returns for it under cover of darkness. The tree roots make it more or less impossible to dig in the woodland, so the grave has been dug in the open – probably in advance. The murderer has gone to some trouble to find the one piece of parkland tucked away out of sight of the Hall, and he doesn't want to break cover when he brings the body down. So he carries it through the woods—'

'—which is when I hear him.'

'You heard the murderer?'

'I'm almost sure of it. A rustling in the undergrowth.'

'And he would have heard you.'

'Certainly. I was calling my cat.'

'Which is why he set down the body in the place you found it. He must have hidden himself close by, so you'd have been in some danger. If the murderer had—'

'You're very scrupulous, Dafydd.'

'Scrupulous?'

'The murderer this, the murderer that – you never name him. I understand your reasons but – between ourselves – we know it's Todd, don't we? You said as much yesterday.'

'What I said was that the evidence was against him. I stopped short of saying he was the culprit.'

'But you believe it, don't you?'

In the hush before he spoke she heard the front door of the Hall bang shut. 'I don't know,' he said at last. 'If you were to ask me who is more likely to have killed your father, Fletcher or Todd, I'd say Todd. But when you ask me, straight out, whether I believe that Todd is the murderer, I find myself hesitating. There's an odd circumstance – a detail that keeps nagging at me, though I know it may turn out to be unimportant. Todd has insisted throughout that he took no more nor less than his due from your father, and the detail seems to bear him out. The fact is that your father's purse was still in his jacket pocket when we took him from the ground – and not just the purse. Inside it we found a shilling and three sixpenny pieces.'

'Well, Mother had given him fifteen shillings. He'd then given three to Todd in part payment and we know he must have spent a fair sum on drink before Todd relieved him of the four still owing. The figure seems about right, doesn't it?'

'The amount isn't the point, Eliza. What I keep asking myself is why any money at all should have been left in the purse. Let me put it to you as a question: what kind of man throttles his debtor, seizes his purse and then, having effectively put himself in the hangman's hands for the sake of a few shillings, carefully counts out the money he's owed and returns the remainder to his victim's pocket?'

'Of course – I wasn't thinking clearly. I see what you mean. But that doesn't tell us that Todd's innocent of the murder, does it?'

'You're right. The detail may complicate our thinking but it certainly doesn't prove that Todd's telling the truth. And since he had both motive and opportunity, he's still very much – is that somebody calling?'

She held her breath, listening.

'Eli-za!' – the voice urgent but softened by distance.

'It's my uncle. I expect Mother has sent him to look for me. I've been out longer than I'd planned and she'll be anxious.'

'Of course. Tell me, Eliza, what time did your uncle arrive back at the Hall yesterday?'

'I couldn't say exactly. Sometime in the late afternoon. Why do you ask?'

'Curiosity. I'm as curious as you are, and as eager for knowledge.'

'Eli-za!' Her uncle's voice was closer now.

'I must go.'

'I'll come with you.'

'It's better you don't.' She broke away, leaving him standing.

As she emerged from the wood her uncle came hurrying towards her. 'Eliza! Your mother's been worried about you. To be honest, so have I. Where have you been?'

She glanced back towards the woodland. 'Walking,' she said. 'I needed time to think.' Not exactly untrue, she told herself as she climbed the slope to the house at her uncle's side, but lying awake in bed that night she saw with unsettling clarity that the evasion had been a form of betrayal.

Twenty

As Eliza came downstairs the next morning, Carys bustled into the hallway.

'Please, Miss Eliza,' she said, 'Mrs Pugh sent me to tell you the cat's come back.'

'Brand? Are you sure it's him?'

'You can see for yourself, Miss. He's out in the stable. Thin as a rake he is, but I've given him a dish of scraps and he's tucking in.'

Eliza pushed past her and hurried out.

It was Brand all right, but he barely looked up from his food as she squatted down beside him. She reached out and stroked him, feeling the knobbed arch of his spine, the angular hip bones. She waited until he had licked the dish clean and then lifted him into her lap.

'You're as light as a bird,' she whispered, dipping her head to brush her cheek against his fur. He was wary, resisting her touch. She wanted to hold on to him but he twisted free and slipped away into the shadows at the back of the stable.

Down in the kitchen Mrs Pugh was frying a panful of eggs. She looked up as Eliza entered.

'It's a small consolation,' she said, 'but in dark times we must take what we can get. I know what the animal means to you, Eliza, and I'm glad of his return for your sake.'

Eliza placed the empty dish on the table. 'Thank you, Mrs Pugh. Could you see that he's fed regularly until he's well again?' Her eye was caught by a small paper package, tied neatly with string. 'What's this?'

'A pie from last night's baking. It's for Todd.'

'Does Mother know you're sending food down for him?'

Mrs Pugh seemed preoccupied with the eggs. 'Because,' continued Eliza, 'I'm not sure she'd approve.'

'It's to keep his health and spirits up. I don't know what kind of food they serve him down there, but I can't imagine it's anything any of us would willingly eat.'

'Yes, but we're not—' She checked herself, but it seemed Mrs Pugh had already caught her drift.

'Maybe he's guilty, maybe he isn't, but one thing's for certain: he suffered at your father's hands. I remember when he first came here – a nice lad in those days, not at all clever but hard-working, trying to make something of himself. From the start it was obvious how your father played him – promising him the world, giving him nothing. One day Todd would be telling me how he'd be made footman when your father's business deals came good, the next he'd be sitting in that chair there, crying like a child because your father had threatened to sack him. As time went by something seemed to go bad in him – there'd be a nastiness in his talk, a simmering kind of bitterness that annoyed us all. In the end I had to tell him he wasn't welcome in my kitchen any more and we never really got on after that, but I still think back sometimes to the lad he was when he arrived. I'm not saying Todd shouldn't be where he is, Eliza; just that there's reasons for him being there, not all of his own making.' Mrs Pugh slid the eggs deftly onto a plate. 'And whatever he might have done, it's simple kindness to ease his burden as best we can.'

'Go back far enough and you'd find the boy my father was, with his own hopes and dreams. Maybe there are reasons there too, reasons we'll never know.'

'Maybe.' Mrs Pugh held out the plate of eggs. 'Would you mind taking this to the dining room?'

'Where's Carys?'

'Lighting the fires. She's already behind on account of the cat and at this rate I can't see her getting away before lunch.'

'Getting away?'

'She'll take Todd's food down when her duties allow.'

Eliza spoke almost without thinking. 'There's no need,' she said. 'I'll take it to him.'

* * *

Just a flicker of surprise in Dafydd's eyes as she entered the police station, and then he was on his feet and advancing to greet her.

'I thought I should spend the day here,' he said quickly and with a hint of apology, as though her visit were some kind of reproach. 'All this' – he indicated the scatter of papers on his desk – 'is an attempt to build a clearer picture from my notes. There are a few indisputable facts here, but so much still seems to be guesswork. You've not brought news, have you?'

She pulled the package from her pocket. 'No news,' she said. 'Just a pie. Mrs Pugh baked it for Todd and I offered to bring it down.'

Dafydd smiled and stretched out his hand. 'I'll make sure he gets it,' he said.

'I'd prefer to take it to him myself. I thought I might have a word with him.'

'I wouldn't advise it, Eliza. The lock-up's no place for a lady, and Todd's in no mood for civilised conversation.'

'You said yesterday that he'd asked if I could visit him. Talking to Mrs Pugh this morning, I realised I owed him that small kindness, at least.'

'You owe Todd nothing, Eliza. And you can do nothing for him.'

'I can listen to him. Please, Dafydd.'

Dafydd grabbed a bunch of keys from a hook on the wall. 'You understand,' he said, 'that this won't be a private conversation I'll be close at hand.'

'Is that necessary?'

'I can't leave you in there unsupervised. Besides, we occasionally pick up useful information in a situation of this kind. A prisoner who has kept up his guard under questioning may let something slip in the course of an informal conversation.'

This wasn't, she thought, quite the way she'd imagined her visit, but she followed Dafydd out into the yard. 'And of course,' he said, slotting a large key into the door of the lock-up, 'there's Fletcher. He'll be listening too.'

The smell hit her immediately. She wrinkled her nose: kerosene, urine, the mouldiness of unaired cellarage. Dafydd led the way down a short flight of stairs and stood aside to let her pass. 'That corridor on the left,' he said. 'First cell you come to. Don't get too close to the bars. Call if you need me.'

Todd was huddled in the corner of his cell with his head sunk on his chest. 'Todd,' she whispered.

'Miss Eliza!' He hauled himself to his feet and limped towards her. 'They said you wouldn't come but I knew you would. I have to talk to you.'

A hoarse voice from further down the passage. 'Is that Eliza Mace?'

'Fletcher?'

'Come here, girl.'

'I'm here to visit Todd, not you. What do you want?'

'Only to tell you I'm sorry for your loss.'

'Thank you, Fletcher.'

'You know, don't you, that I had no hand in your father's death?'

There seemed to be no appropriate response. Eliza turned back to Todd. 'I've brought you a pie,' she said. 'From Mrs Pugh.'

'She's been kind to me. Will you give her my thanks?'

'Of course.' She pushed the package between the bars, remembering how the children would cluster around the chimpanzees' cage when the circus came, holding out tidbits filched from their parents' pantries.

He tucked the pie inside his shirt. 'Safest place,' he said. 'Put food down and the rats will be on it before you can say knife.'

'If there's anything else you need—'

'That's what I want to talk to you about. Listen, Eliza, you have to help me get out of here.'

'Even if I wanted to, Todd, I can't do that.'

'You could put in a word for me. You know I was good to you. Will you tell them that?'

'What I know, Todd' – she lowered her voice – 'is that you laid hands on me.'

'And I'm truly sorry for it, believe me. But when you were small, didn't I look after you then? Remember? – riding up alongside me on the haycart or helping me look for plovers' eggs in the meadows. I was good to you then, wasn't I? – took you along with me when no-one else had time for you. Surely that counts for something?'

'Not in the way you want it to. Not in these circumstances. I'm sorry, Todd, but you must see that I can do nothing for you.'

'Please, Miss Eliza.' He thrust his arms between the bars, reaching towards her. His face, pressed hard against the rusted iron, was horribly distorted. 'If they hang me, they'll be hanging an innocent man. Do you want that on your conscience? Can you live with that?'

She heard Fletcher stumbling across his cell, calling out. 'Let the girl alone, Todd. She's told you how it is. Even if you're innocent – which I take leave to doubt – she can't help you. There's no sense in railing at her. Let her be.'

Todd took a pace backward, raised his arms high and struck at the bars. Eliza flinched, feeling his rage and pain as though they were her own. 'You shut your bloody mouth, Fletcher,' Todd shouted. 'Nobody asked you for your opinion.'

A clatter of footsteps echoing off the walls; she looked up to see Dafydd hurrying along the passageway towards her. 'Come on, Eliza,' he said. 'It's best you leave now.' He took her by the elbow and guided her back up the stairs.

She heard Todd strike the bars again. 'Like father, like daughter,' he yelled. 'Cutting a man loose as if he'd nothing to do with you, not caring what happens to him.' He was still shouting as Dafydd ushered her out into the yard.

'Wild words, Eliza.' He locked the door and stuffed the keys into his pocket. 'It's fear makes him speak like that. You mustn't take any of it to heart.'

'You warned me and I didn't listen. I've only myself to blame.'

'You did as you thought best, but the man's wound tight as a watchspring and not fully in control of himself. There's violence there, no doubt of it; the question is whether it was turned against your father.'

'And, if it was, whether the blame lay only with Todd. There was violence in my father too – his attacks on Fletcher and my uncle weren't entirely out of character, and there were times when—'

'What's that, Eliza? Your father attacked your uncle?'

'A couple of weeks ago. Didn't Uncle James tell you?'

'I've heard nothing of it. A physical attack?'

'A few punches. Owen stepped in and there was no great damage done, but it shook us all.'

'Understandably. What was the argument about?'

'Money was at the root of it. Money and property. It was my parents' quarrel – nothing directly to do with my uncle, but his intervention angered my father.'

'You're certain that your uncle has no stake in the property?'

'None that I'm aware of.'

Dafydd fumbled in the pocket of his tunic. 'Your notebook's on your desk,' said Eliza. 'Propped against the lamp.'

'Of course. You've a sharp eye, Eliza, and a quick mind. I've no doubt I shall have further occasion to make use of both.'

'I have to go now. Please make sure that Todd's as comfortable as his circumstances allow. Whatever he thinks, I do care what happens to him. I don't like seeing him in that filthy place. And even if he's guilty, I don't want him hanged.'

'If he's proved guilty,' said Dafydd, 'he'll hang. Neither you nor I will have any say in the matter.' It seemed to Eliza that his bluntness bordered on brutality, but if he regretted his words he gave no sign of it.

Twenty One

She was roused next morning by a hollow knocking, wood on wood. A broom head, she realised as she surfaced unwillingly from sleep, a broom head striking the skirting board in a nearby room. She threw her dressing gown over her shoulders and went out onto the landing.

'Carys?' Eliza pushed open the door of Charlotte's old room and peered in. Carys had pulled the bed away from the wall and was sweeping the accumulated dust into a small heap at her feet. She looked up as Eliza entered.

'You wouldn't believe how it gathers,' she said. 'In an empty room. Where does it all come from?'

'Does this mean we've heard from Charlotte?'

'By telegram, first thing. I looked in to tell you but you were sound asleep and I thought it best not to wake you. She'll be here this afternoon. Such a to-do in the kitchen – so little warning and not a spare scrap in the larder – Mrs Pugh said as much to your mother's face – and now I've to clean two rooms – your brother-in-law's coming too – and get the fires burning in them, and that's before I even start on the regular jobs. They'll have to take us as they find us, Mrs Pugh says, but your mother—'

'Get on with your work, Carys. I'm sure Charlotte and Daniel will be willing to make allowances.'

'Your sister, yes, but I'm not so sure about Mr Logan. Nothing's ever right for him, is it? You remember his last visit here – how he was almost thrown out for ordering us around? I saw it all. Your father had him pinned against the wall, down in the hallway. My wife and I can run this house without your assistance, he said. Nasty it was, but your father was right, Mrs Pugh said when I told her about it – right to stick up for the household. We can't be at Mr Logan's beck and call, she said, with him wanting everything done just so, and done yesterday. She thought your father—'

'That's enough, Carys. Whatever Mrs Pugh said at the time would have been intended to protect you and Alice, not to suggest that my brother-in-law shouldn't be treated with civility. I hope we can rely on you to give him the respect due to any guest.' Eliza turned and hurried away before Carys could answer her.

* * *

It came to her as she sat staring out of the dining room window after a hurried luncheon that the household was too busy with its preparations to acknowledge the absence at its heart, too busy to allow her to mourn her father's passing. She could hear her mother in the corridor issuing orders, Carys's quick footsteps as she scurried to and fro, a clatter and rattle of pans and cutlery from the kitchen, and she was suddenly filled with an immense longing to be clear of it all. She ran out into the hallway, snatched up her coat and was down the front steps before her mother could stop her.

She hurried down the slope and blundered through the wood, half blind with grief and rage; but once at the far side, looking out to where the flooded water meadows gleamed like polished silver, she felt her breathing slow and deepen. She stood there for a long time, drinking it all in, letting it work on her until her mind grew still.

When she felt ready to face the jangling life of the Hall again she turned and retraced her steps, taking her time now, moving more lightly. She stopped at the door of the ice house, sniffing as though some clue might be borne up to her on the dank air rising from the shaft; then, on an impulse, she changed tack and walked towards the lane, scanning the woodland floor and undergrowth for signs, picturing her father's body slung across his murderer's shoulder like a sack of meal and jolted unceremoniously downhill. When she reached the corner she ducked back through the fence and stood at the edge of the empty grave, her head bowed as if in prayer.

She barely noticed it at first, a glint of light at the margin of her vision; then she shifted her gaze and the thing came into focus – a sliver of glass on the surface of the spoil heap, sparkling like a diamond in the pale sunlight. She stooped and picked it up.

A tiny fragment, not a quarter of an inch in length, tapering to a sharp point. She took out her handkerchief and wiped it clean. It could have come from anywhere, she told herself, but she wrapped it carefully in the handkerchief and was tucking it into her pocket when she heard the rattle of the gig's wheels on the rough surface of the lane. She ran along the hedgerow, reaching the gate just as the gig swung into the drive.

'Charlotte!'

Owen brought Tinder to a standstill. Charlotte got down and hurled herself into her sister's arms. She was shivering, Eliza noticed, her whole body vibrating like a plucked string.

'Such a journey, Eliza – a missed connection, the hotel last night so cold we might as well have slept in the fields, and

Daniel' – she lowered her voice – 'Daniel in the foulest mood, haranguing porters, cursing the hotel staff for a bunch of incompetents, twisting Father's murder into a weapon to beat me with, as if the whole miserable business were my fault. He even suggested—'

Eliza squeezed her arm. Daniel had climbed down from the gig and was walking stiffly towards them.

'Good afternoon, Eliza.' He took her by the hand but there was no warmth in his touch. 'Such a tragedy. I can't begin to tell you how—'

'Thank you, Daniel, but there's really nothing to be said.' Eliza broke away and went over to the gig. 'Would you take Mr Logan up to the house, Owen, and help him with the luggage? I need to talk with Charlotte. Tell Mother we'll be with her in a few minutes.' They watched as the gig drew away.

'Oh, Eliza,' said Charlotte, 'do you think that Father's murder was a punishment for his misdeeds? That his behaviour brought about the violence that destroyed him? That's what Daniel says, and although I resist the idea I can't help wondering if he's right.'

'When we know exactly what happened we may have some kind of answer. It seems quite possible that someone wronged by Father took a terrible revenge. But if Daniel's implying that Father's death was in some sense appropriate – well, I don't subscribe to that, and neither should you.'

Charlotte nodded. 'You can't imagine,' she said, 'what a relief it is to see you. To talk with you. Sometimes it seems to me that Daniel's is the only voice in the world – that I can't even hear myself think for the noise of it, let alone speak out against it. But what about you? You don't look well, Eliza, and I'm not surprised – what a frightful time you must have had of it.'

'I'm well enough. Tired, it goes without saying. I'd love to put the whole thing behind me, to step away from it all, but of course that's out of the question at the moment.'

'Come and stay with us for a few weeks. Once the funeral's over—'

'It's not just the funeral. I need to find out what happened. I can't rest until we've tracked down Father's murderer.'

'But that's not your job, Eliza. It's the responsibility of the police – it's what they're paid to do.'

'There are things the police don't see, things they don't understand. And in any case, I want to be involved, to feel I'm doing something to help. I owe it to Father.'

'Daniel won't have it that we owe Father anything. For myself, I shall mourn him dutifully, as a daughter should, but that's all. I didn't love him, Eliza, and though I know you did, I'd be sorry to see you wear yourself to a shadow on his account. As soon as the ceremony is over we shall return to Bristol, and I hope you'll come with us.'

Eliza took her by the arm. 'Mother will be so pleased to see you,' she said. 'Let's not keep her waiting.'

* * *

'I hadn't realised,' said Charlotte, 'that the police have already made an arrest.'

They had slipped away from the others and were sitting beside the fire in the dining room, drinking tea. From across the hall Eliza could hear Daniel's voice, loud and monotonous, explaining some point of law. *The relict*, he kept saying, *the deceased* – as though Hannah and James weren't in the room with him, as though the world existed only as an abstraction.

'Two arrests if you count Fletcher.'

'Fletcher? The gamekeeper?'

'Former gamekeeper. He was dismissed some time ago. He's been charged with theft – he made off with Tinder on the night Father disappeared.'

'But he wasn't involved in the murder?'

'It seems unlikely. I suppose the reason Mother spoke only of Todd is that he's now the focus of enquiries.'

'It's hard to believe. Todd was closer to Father than anyone. And he was always fond of us – of you especially.'

It crossed Eliza's mind that she might tell Charlotte about the assault, about Todd's dismissal, but she dropped the idea at once. The episode seemed part of another world now, an irrelevance. 'It's always possible,' she said, 'that he'll be found innocent.'

'Mother seems to have no doubt of his guilt. Do you doubt it?'

'Not really. But when I visited him in the lock-up—'

'You went to the lock-up? Do you think that was wise?'

'I didn't consider the wisdom of it. I took some food down to him, that's all.'

'Weren't you afraid?'

'Not afraid, no. Disturbed, perhaps.' She saw it again – the shadowy cell, Todd's distorted features, his arms raised to strike the bars. 'I felt sorry for him. Sorry that anyone should be shut up in a cage hardly fit for an animal.'

'If he killed Father he deserves no better.'

'And if he didn't?'

'You must stop fretting about it, Eliza. Let it all go – Todd, Father, the whole miserable mess. Others can deal with it. A few weeks away will do you the world of good.'

The logs settled in the grate, sending up a fountain of sparks. Eliza fixed her sister with a hard stare. 'I shall go nowhere,' she said, 'until we know the truth.'

Twenty Two

A sorry affair, thought Eliza, counting the mourners straggling up through the graveyard from the church. Not that she had expected a better showing, but it saddened her to see evidence of her father's unpopularity so clearly displayed.

The mourners were regrouping at the graveside when Eliza heard the click of the gate latch and looked up to see a figure striding towards them. Dafydd, she realised after a moment's uncertainty, handsomely dressed in a long black overcoat, a bowler hat in his gloved hand. He glanced across at her as he joined the group, then bowed his head in an attitude of prayer.

It struck Eliza as the coffin was lowered into the grave that she should be crying, but her eyes were dry. Charlotte's too, she noticed: her sister was staring stonily out across the graveyard as though none of this – the gash in the trodden turf, the sombre knot of mourners around it, Mr Benson's thin monotone as he committed her father's body to the earth – had anything to do with her. Eliza wondered whether her mother had given way to tears, but the face behind the dark veil was inscrutable.

As the ceremony drew to a close it began to rain, a soft, insidious drizzle drifting in from the west. Mr Benson shepherded the family down to the shelter of the church porch where they stood as the other mourners filed past, each offering a word or two of condolence. Dafydd was the last in line. He approached Hannah with an odd hesitancy, clutching his hat to his chest with both hands.

'I must apologise,' he said, 'for my late arrival. It was unavoidable. Pressing matters concerning—'

'It was good of you to come at all, Mr Pritchard. Beyond the call of duty. And now, if you'll excuse us' – Hannah was pulling on her gloves – 'we need to leave. We can't keep our guests waiting.'

'Of course not. Good day, Mrs Mace.' Dafydd bowed stiffly, then turned and walked away down the path.

'You might have been more gracious,' said Eliza. 'He came to pay his respects and you treated him with contempt.'

'Hardly contempt. I don't want to encourage Mr Pritchard to consider himself a friend of the family – that's all. He didn't know your father, so to whom is he paying his respects? It's a reasonable question, Eliza, and I think you know the answer to it.'

'I wonder,' began James, laying a hand gently on Hannah's arm, but Eliza was already out of the porch and making for the gate. She ran down the lane as fast as the heavy skirts of her mourning dress allowed and caught up with Dafydd at the corner of the high street.

'I'm sorry,' she said. 'I'm afraid Mother's grief makes her careless of the usual courtesies – she meant no offence.'

'No offence taken, but I'm glad you came after me.'

'Do you have news?'

Dafydd shook his head. 'Todd continues to protest his innocence, but if he can't prove it, his only chance of escaping the rope, short of a miracle, is the discovery and arrest of a more likely culprit.'

'So you're still searching?'

'Sergeant Williams believes we already have our man, but I'm not entirely persuaded. So yes, I'm still searching, though I know I may be wasting my time.'

'Searching for something that incriminates him, or for proof of his innocence?'

'Searching for the truth.' He glanced back towards the church. 'Listen Eliza, this isn't the moment for what I have to say, but I do need to talk to you. I wonder whether we might meet again soon. Tomorrow morning perhaps?'

'We have an appointment with Mr Wells – my parents' solicitor – at ten o'clock. We could call in at the police station when the meeting finishes.'

'If you don't mind, I should like to speak to you alone.'

'That might be more difficult. Mother has taken to watching me like a hawk. She's concerned about my welfare – endlessly fretting over imagined dangers.'

'Dangers? You'll be in the company of a police officer, in the safety of a police station. Surely—'

'Look, I'll meet you in the wood – at the ice house – after lunch tomorrow. Cut through from the lane – don't come up the drive. Shall we say two o'clock?'

'Very well. I'll be there.' He tipped his hat, turned and walked briskly away.

* * *

Nothing would be wasted, of course, but the sight of so much uneaten food was dispiriting. 'It's like that at funerals,' said Mrs Pugh as she gathered up the plates. 'Nobody's really hungry. They come to talk, not to eat.'

In fact, Eliza reflected, watching the last of the guests disappear down the drive, there had been precious little conversation.

197

Scarcely a dozen of the local worthies attending, and most of those showing an understandable reluctance to speak in any detail about her father's life, let alone his death; yet it had seemed difficult to talk about anything else. 'I wonder,' she said, opening the door to let Mrs Pugh through, 'whether we might retire to the sitting room.'

They had barely seated themselves around the fire when Hannah turned on Eliza.

'How dare you, Elizabeth? Running after the man – what were you thinking of? And at your father's funeral too, with everyone watching. What kind of behaviour is that?'

'No-one was watching, Mother. And if your own behaviour had been better, there'd have been no need for me to run after him at all. I went to apologise on your behalf.'

'On my behalf? I had nothing to apologise for. Your intervention was not only unnecessary, it was presumptuous and disloyal. What did Pritchard say?'

'He said he hadn't been offended.'

'Exactly. The matter couldn't be clearer. There was no offence taken because none had been given. I'm tired of it, the way you're forever trying to turn the tables, blaming others as a means of avoiding censure yourself. It's the way of a child, Elizabeth, not a grown woman. I've asked Charlotte to take you in hand while you're in Bristol – to give you the guidance you so obviously need.'

Eliza glanced across at Charlotte, who was looking steadily at the floor. 'I've already told Charlotte,' she said. 'I'm not going anywhere until we've found out what happened to Father.'

'Charlotte has conveyed your wishes to me, but it's obvious that you're not the best judge of the matter. She and Daniel share my concern for you and have kindly offered their hospitality for as long as it takes you to recover.'

'I'm not ill, Mother.'

'You're in an unhealthy state of mind, and when the mind sickens it's only a matter of time before the body follows suit.'

Daniel leaned forward in his chair. 'Your mother's right,' he said. 'My own body suffers abominably after any blow to the spirits – isn't that so, Charlotte? – and in your case, Eliza, given the circumstances...'

He sank back, apparently satisfied with his contribution. James leaned over to Eliza and placed his hand on hers. 'Listen to those who love you,' he said. 'We all have your best interests at heart.'

'If you loved me you wouldn't be trying to send me away. And anyone who loved Father as I do would understand why I can't go.'

Hannah jerked her head back as if she had been slapped. She started to speak but Eliza was already on her feet and making for the door.

Up in her room she took her notebook from the desk, opened it up and laid it flat. As she pulled out her chair she heard a faint tap at the door.

'I'm busy. What do you want?'

'I want to talk to you. May I come in?'

Charlotte gave her no time to reply. She stepped inside and perched on the edge of the bed. 'Come and sit down,' she said. 'Here, with me.' She patted the coverlet. 'Please, Eliza.'

'Did Mother send you? Are you here to talk me round?'

'You mustn't blame me. I told her I'd invited you to Bristol and that you'd declined the invitation – nothing more than that. I had no idea I'd be stirring up trouble for you. Even so...' She cleared her throat, shifted uneasily on the bed. 'The fact is, Eliza, everyone's worried about you. If you're not taking good care of yourself – and we can all see that you're not – then please let others take care of you for a while. I don't hold with everything Mother says, but it's obvious that you need rest. There's no shame in it. The human spirit can take only so much, and a woman being the weaker vessel—'

'Let me be the judge of what my spirit can take, Charlotte. If I leave now I shall feel I've left something undone, something there might be no chance to do later. Dafydd is trying to get at the truth of Father's death, and he needs me to help him.'

'Dafydd? The constable?' Charlotte was silent for a moment, plucking at a loose thread in the coverlet. 'Eliza, you'd tell me, wouldn't you, if there was any justification for Mother's anxieties on that score?'

'Mother will hang her anxiety on any peg she can find. There's no need for you to follow her example.'

Charlotte eyed her narrowly. 'Come away with us,' she said. 'Please.'

'I've heard you out, Charlotte. Now you can go down and tell Mother you've done your duty.'

Charlotte's eyes brimmed with tears. 'You've grown hard,' she said. 'Hard and hurtful. Could I at least tell her that you're considering the matter?'

'You can say whatever you like.'

Charlotte rose to her feet. 'We're leaving in two days' time,' she said. 'I'd be sorry to leave without you.'

Eliza listened as her footsteps receded down the corridor; then she took up her pen and began to write.

I'm setting it down here so no-one can take it away from me. The facts matter. That's what Uncle James taught me, and I've never been more certain that he was right. Dafydd believes it, I know.

Searching for the truth, what could be more important? To serve the truth — to discover it, to bear witness to it: if we have a purpose in life, it's surely that. Whatever they say, I must stay.

She was cold, but she wouldn't go down. She drew her shawl around her and sat staring out of the window at the darkening sky.

Twenty Three

The solicitor's office was small and crammed with furniture – dusty cabinets lining the walls, a table piled high with books and papers, six chairs arranged in an untidy arc in front of a heavy oak desk. Mr Wells sat at the desk with the light from the window behind him making a halo of his white hair. 'Please,' he said, beckoning them in. 'Take a seat.'

Hannah entered, with James at her shoulder. Daniel held the door for Charlotte and Eliza, then squeezed in after them and pushed it shut. Hannah put back her veil and sat down. Her face was pale and when she spoke her voice was tired and flat.

'You know my brother-in-law and daughters, Mr Wells. And this is Mr Logan, Charlotte's husband. I've asked him to accompany us. I hope you have no objection.'

Mr Wells leaned back in his chair, put his hands together and rested his chin on the tips of his fingers. 'Entirely as you wish, Mrs Mace. We're just waiting for Mr Morgan to arrive and then we'll begin.'

'Mr Morgan?' asked James. 'Gwilym Morgan from Dene Farm?'

'Your neighbour, yes.'

'What interest can Morgan possibly have in our affairs?'

'He's named in your brother's will, Mr Mace. It seems right that he should be present. However—'

The door opened again and Morgan entered, awkward and hesitant. He had trimmed his side-whiskers and slicked down his hair. His broad chest strained against the buttons of a worsted jacket that had clearly been made for a smaller man. He peered uncertainly around the room.

'Please take a seat,' said Mr Wells, indicating the vacant chair. He opened a drawer and pulled out a thick file of papers. 'First, my heartfelt condolences to the family. A terrible affair, with unfortunate effects, some of which I'm in the unhappy position of having to address today. You probably know, Mrs Mace, that over a number of years your husband entered into a variety of business partnerships, financing each new enterprise with loans from external sources. I oversaw a number of contracts on his behalf, invariably giving him the benefit of my advice. Latterly that advice was simple – namely that the ventures he was so eager to embark on would result in his ruin. He gave short shrift to my warnings, arguing that he had nothing to lose – I understood him to mean this in the most literal sense – and that his salvation lay, despite all evidence to the contrary, in persistence. It's possible, of course, that one or more of these ventures bore fruit, though from what I know I believe that to be unlikely. Mrs Mace, do you know of any money earned and put by, either at Edge Hall or in some bank account unknown to me?'

'My husband had no money of his own.'

'We can be certain of that,' said James. 'He was dependent entirely on my sister-in-law.'

'As I thought. In one sense the will is straightforward. Originally drafted in favour of three members of the family – that is, his wife, his elder daughter and his brother – it was amended to include Elizabeth at the time of her birth. A later codicil adds Mr Morgan to the list of beneficiaries.'

'How much?' asked Morgan, drawing himself up in his chair. 'How much has he left me?'

'The amount is irrelevant, as are the proportions allocated to the four family members. You'll understand from what I've been saying that, unless funds or assets currently unknown to us are brought to light by chance or further research, Mr Mace's will has no practical effect. To put it bluntly, there's nothing to distribute.'

Morgan leaned forward. 'He said I'd get the money I was owed. I don't know why I believed him – the man broke promises as easy as the rest of us break bread.'

James cleared his throat. 'I appreciate your disappointment,' he said. 'I apologise on my brother's behalf.'

'Apologies cost nothing and they solve nothing. Apologies won't put food on the table. Apologies won't keep Jevan at school as the lad wants.' The blood was rising to his face and his voice was edged with anger. 'I hope the family will see fit to accept the terms of the will as far as my share's concerned.'

'You mean you want us to settle my brother's debt?' James turned to Mr Wells. 'I don't see why we shouldn't—'

'It's not a small sum, Mr Mace.' The solicitor glanced down at the file. 'Two hundred pounds to be precise.'

A moment's silence before James spoke again. 'In that case,' he said, 'we'd have to examine the claim carefully. At the very least we'd need to see proof of the loans.'

'There's no loans,' said Morgan. 'And the proof you want is on your doorstep, Mr Mace, if you'd only the eyes to see it and the wit to make sense of it.'

'I don't understand you, Mr Morgan.'

'Maybe not, but she does.' He twisted to face Hannah, his big hands gripping the arms of his chair. 'You know, don't you, Mrs Mace? You know what's been hidden from the world all these years. I kept his secret, and it was partly on your account – yours and your children's. I raised the boy with as much love and care as if he'd been my own, and when your husband stopped paying his due and started to come to me with excuses and empty promises – always to do with this or that business deal, never anything an honest farmer could be expected to understand – still I kept quiet. I could have gone through the courts and made him pay for Jevan's upkeep that way, but I held back, not wanting to bring the whole thing crashing down about our ears, hoping all would come good in the end. Well, I see now what a fool I've been. The money is rightfully mine, payment for what I've already done for the boy and for what's still to do, and if you won't give it willingly I'll go to law to get it from you.'

Hannah had been gazing fixedly at the far wall, her face impassive, but now she turned to Morgan. 'No doubt Mr Wells can shed light on the matter,' she said, 'but I'm not aware of any law that compels a widow to provide for her husband's bastard.'

It seemed to Eliza that what followed was taking place at a distance, as though she were watching a play from the gallery – Morgan rising abruptly, oversetting his chair as he stumbled towards the door, James reaching out a restraining hand as he brushed past, the door banging back against the wall with such force that the panelling shook. She heard the outer door open and slam shut, heard Morgan's footsteps fade away down the street. She tried to catch her sister's eye but Charlotte was hunched in her chair with her head down, clutching the fabric of her dress in her fists.

James rose to his feet. 'The best thing now,' he said, 'would be for the family to retire to consider these matters. I need hardly say how important it is that none of what we've just heard should be communicated to anyone else, at any time. Am I right in thinking, Mr Wells, that the immediate business is now concluded?'

The solicitor nodded. His face was grey; his hands trembled as he slipped the will back into the file. 'I had no idea,' he said. 'None at all.'

'Of course not.' James reached across the desk and shook him by the hand. 'Thank you for your assistance. We shall notify you if we need further advice.' He took Hannah by the elbow and steered her briskly out, leaving the others to follow at their own speed.

* * *

Luncheon was eaten in a silence so palpably tense that Mrs Pugh, entering the room with the coffee pot as Carys cleared the plates, stopped in her tracks and shot a questioning glance at Eliza. Eliza lowered her gaze and fiddled with her napkin, but when the servants were gone she sat back in her chair and looked round the table.

'Are we not to talk about it?' she asked. 'Uncle James said that we shouldn't discuss the matter with anyone outside the family, not that we shouldn't discuss it at all.'

Hannah set down her cup. 'There's nothing to discuss, Eliza. Your father's dead and buried, and as far as I'm concerned that brings the whole sorry business to an end.'

'How does that end it? His child – my half-brother – lives a hundred yards beyond our gates, in a household afflicted by sickness and poverty. Aren't you going to do anything about it?'

'I have neither the means nor the inclination to support a child fathered by my husband on another man's wife. Is that my responsibility? No, what took place between your father and Rebecca Morgan was their responsibility, and theirs alone.'

'But Morgan suffers. Jevan suffers.'

'They must bear their suffering, as I bear mine. You can't imagine the pain it gives me, even now, to think of it – the betrayal, the humiliation. I did nothing to deserve it but I suffer all the same.'

'Your suffering isn't an argument against helping others. You say you don't have the means but that's not true. Sell a little land—'

'If I sell anything, Eliza, it won't be for the Morgans' benefit. My responsibility is to you and Charlotte, and in time to come you'll thank me for that.'

'If I might intervene,' said Daniel, 'I'd like to offer a little practical advice. I think Hannah is absolutely right to want to put the whole thing behind her. You can't touch pitch without being defiled by it, and any involvement with your dubious neighbours, however well-intentioned, risks bringing this family – our family, if I may – into disrepute. Eliza's fine feelings do her credit, but she doesn't understand how the world works, or how it judges. The sooner we dissolve our unfortunate connection with the Morgans – a connection that nobody around this table had any hand in creating – the smaller our chance of being sucked into their lives.'

Eliza glared at him. 'That's cold counsel,' she said.

'It's good counsel. It's worth remembering that you're the most vulnerable member of the family – I mean that you still have to find a husband. You could marry well, Eliza – you're an intelligent girl, with the kind of looks some men find attractive; but if you really want to profit from your natural advantages you need to keep yourself free of the taint of this unpleasant business. You must get on with your life and leave the Morgans to resolve their own problems.'

'If you think—' began Eliza, but James cut across her.

'I wonder,' he said, 'whether Daniel and Charlotte might like to retire to the sitting room. Thank you for your advice, Daniel. We'll bear it in mind as we continue our discussions.'

Daniel reddened but said nothing. He rose and escorted Charlotte from the room. James waited, listening, until the sitting room door clicked shut. 'Now,' he said, 'we can discuss the matter more sensibly.'

'I have to say,' said Hannah, 'that Daniel's advice made perfect sense to me.'

James shook his head. 'Practical advice, he says, but surely you can see that even from a narrowly pragmatic point of view he's wrong. Morgan kept the secret for as long as he could hope for payment; take away his hope and he may well decide to talk. I don't imagine for one moment that he has the funds to initiate legal proceedings but he's certainly capable of dragging the family name through the dirt.'

'If I understand you, James, you're suggesting that we buy the man's silence.'

'I'm suggesting that we give him what Robert should have paid him. It's a considerable sum but it seems reasonable in the circumstances. Robert had no realistic prospect of discharging the debt, but the codicil to the will makes clear his intentions. I appreciate that fulfilling my brother's wishes may be the last thing on your mind but there's no better way of freeing ourselves from the burden he has laid on our shoulders.'

'Forgive me, James, but the money you're so eager to dispose of is mine.'

'If I had any of my own...' James spread his hands wide in a gesture expressive simultaneously of the desire to give and the impossibility of doing so.

'Listen,' said Eliza, placing her fingertips lightly on her mother's wrist. 'Now that Father's gone you've no reason to hold back. Land must be sold so that we can discharge our debts. And when you have the money in hand, you'll go to the tradesmen in town and pay up – you wouldn't consider withholding what's due to them. Why shouldn't Mr Morgan be treated the same as the butcher or the grocer? We owe him money and must pay it – it's as simple as that.'

'I'm glad you think it's a simple matter. If I see it differently, that may be because I've been more deeply wounded by your father's actions than you ever were.' Hannah rose from the table, pressing her hand to her forehead. 'I don't want to continue this discussion, Eliza – I'm tired and headachy and I can't think clearly. I'll give the matter my attention as soon as I can but for the moment I just want to rest.'

Once she had left the room James turned to Eliza. 'Heaven alone knows how she has suffered – knowing the truth, unable to speak of it.'

'Not even to you?'

'She never breathed a word. I don't believe she'd ever have spoken of it at all if Morgan's disclosure hadn't made silence impossible.'

'You'd think her suffering would make her more sensitive to the suffering of others but it doesn't seem that way. It's obvious that the Morgans need our help – Jevan especially. To think how I used to hold the little mite on my lap and never guessed, though I see it clearly enough now. To know that he's kin to me—'

'I hope there'll be no more talk of kinship in your mother's hearing, Eliza. She may come round to the idea of giving Morgan the money, but I doubt whether it would be on those grounds.'

Out in the hallway the clock struck two.

Eliza leapt up. 'I'm sorry,' she said, 'but there's something I have to do.'

'Can't it wait?'

'I shall be back in ten minutes.' She rushed from the room and was out of the house in seconds, struggling into her coat as she ran.

Dafydd was waiting by the entrance to the ice house. 'I thought you might have forgotten,' he said. 'Not that I'd have blamed you – I can imagine how difficult all this has been for you.'

'You can't, Dafydd. You can't possibly imagine it.' She was flustered, breathless. 'Listen, I don't have much time – my uncle expects me back in a few minutes. What was it you wanted to say?'

'It's a delicate matter. I should have liked to discuss it at greater leisure but we must make do with the time we have. In brief, I'd like to enlist your help again.'

'You know I'll do anything I can.'

'Something particular. If I'm in the office when Carys brings Todd's food to the station I make a point of engaging her in conversation. Twice now she has hinted at a suspicion concerning your mother and your uncle. I think there's something there that she feels she should tell me, but if I press her on the matter she retreats, saying there's probably nothing in it, she's not one to spread rumours, it's hard to imagine it of them, and so on. I'm sorry to have to raise this with you, Eliza, but do you know of anything untoward in your uncle's dealings with your mother?'

'Of course not. It's servants' gossip, that's all.'

'Even so... you once told me that your mother was more at ease with your uncle than with your father.'

'My father was a very difficult man. Nobody was at ease with him.'

'I understand that, but your mother and uncle are obviously close. In the churchyard yesterday, watching them walk down to the porch with their arms linked, I thought how anyone might mistake them for husband and wife.'

'My mother's health isn't good at the best of times, and recent events have made it worse. If she needed to take my uncle's arm, that's hardly surprising in the circumstances. Nothing you saw yesterday should raise questions of the kind you're asking.'

'You would tell me, wouldn't you, if you knew anything – anything that might have a bearing on the subject?'

'Don't you understand? There's nothing to tell.'

'And if you were to see or hear anything in the future – you'd tell me about that, wouldn't you?'

'I don't like this conversation, Dafydd, and in any case I have to get back. My uncle will be waiting for me.' She turned quickly and hurried away.

As she approached the house the front door opened. Her uncle came running down the steps and strode out to meet her.

'What was it, Eliza? Where have you been? What was so important that you had to break off our discussion to attend to it? If this has anything to do with Constable Pritchard—'

'He asked to see me. He had a couple of questions he thought I might be able to answer.'

'If he has questions, let him come up to the house and ask them. I don't want you chasing off for private meetings with the fellow. Don't you see the impropriety of it, Eliza? Can you imagine what people might think?'

'There was no impropriety.' And I defended you, she wanted to say, against the same charge; but she held her tongue.

When he spoke again his tone had softened. 'I believe you, Eliza. But please try to see how your actions might be misinterpreted. I speak as one who loves you, one who knows from experience how hard it can be to square our own human needs with our duty to the wider world.'

Her throat was tight; she was holding back tears. He reached out and took her gently by the arm. 'Let's go in,' he said.

Twenty Four

They were finishing breakfast the next morning when Hannah, who had sat in silence until then, turned to Eliza.

'Have you packed?' she asked.

'I've told you, Mother, I'm not going anywhere.'

'I know what you've told me. Now I'm telling you: you're going to Bristol with Charlotte and Daniel. Their invitation stands despite your ingratitude. They'll be leaving in half an hour.'

Charlotte reached over and touched Eliza's hand. 'Please,' she said. 'There's nothing more for you to do here.'

Eliza glanced across the table in dumb appeal to her uncle. 'I think you should go,' he said. 'It's for the best.'

Daniel was staring at the tablecloth, studiously avoiding her eye. She set down her knife and fork, rose to her feet and swept out of the room.

Up in her bedroom she grabbed pen and paper and scribbled a note.

Charlotte – just go. Don't miss your train. Don't look for me. Don't worry about me. Thank you, E.

She ran to her sister's room and placed the note on her valise. As she stepped back into the corridor she heard the door of the dining room open, and then her mother's voice rang out, sharp and impatient. 'Well, we must make sure that she does. Please see to it, Charlotte.'

Eliza hoisted her skirts and hurried up the stairs to the attic. She unbuttoned her dress, stepped clear of it and stuffed it into the gap between two crates. She opened the window and squeezed out onto the roof of the bay; then she pulled the sash down to within a couple of inches of the sill.

The sun was well up but the air was chilly. She felt it again, fleetingly – the familiar exhilaration, the giddying sense of space and light – and stepped to the parapet to look over. Then the fear of discovery moved in like a raincloud; she drew back and huddled down against the wall.

Footsteps echoing up through the house, doors opening and closing, a general sense of bustling movement. After a few minutes she heard her mother's voice rising from the landing below.

'And definitely not in the kitchen?'

'Daniel has been down to ask. Mrs Pugh and Carys both say they haven't seen her.'

'She must be somewhere, Charlotte. What about the attic?'

Eliza stiffened. Charlotte murmured something she couldn't quite catch, and then Eliza heard her light footfall on the staircase. The attic door creaked open.

For a long moment there was no sound from inside. Eliza held her breath. And then the footsteps again – Charlotte moving towards the window. Eliza pressed her shoulders hard against the wall and hugged her knees tightly to her chest, but she knew she'd been found.

Charlotte lifted the sash and leaned out. As their eyes met, Eliza opened her mouth to speak but Charlotte ducked quickly back inside. The door opened again, and Eliza heard her descend to the landing. 'She's not there,' Charlotte said. 'Why would she be? Perhaps she went out.'

'We'd have heard the door.'

'Not if she hadn't wanted us to.'

'That would only bear out my view, Charlotte – that she's behaving like a child, treating life as some kind of game. She needs to understand...'

As her mother's voice died away Eliza stretched out her legs and eased the stiffness in her shoulders. She was shivering with cold. She scrambled to her feet and was making for the window when she heard the gig come rattling across the cobbles of the yard and out onto the drive. She dropped down again and hunched tight, keeping her head below the level of the parapet. The gig came to a stop outside the front door.

'Unfortunately not,' Charlotte was saying as the door opened. 'Daniel has a number of important appointments at the office tomorrow.'

'Then just wait a little. You've a good ten minutes in hand.'

'I don't see the point, Mother. She won't return until she knows we're on our way.'

'Supposing she has come to some harm?'

'I don't believe that and neither, I'm sure, do you. I imagine she saw the futility of arguing with you and has chosen to retreat until the matter has resolved itself.'

'There's no resolution, Charlotte. There never is, and there never will be until she learns to respect other people's advice. But the girl's unteachable – I might as well try to reason with a block of wood.'

The thud of heavy luggage being loaded. A flurry of farewells and then Owen clicked his tongue and the gig began to move. Eliza waited until the front door had banged shut before raising her head. She peered over the parapet and saw the gig swing out of the drive and disappear down the lane. Once she was satisfied that it was safely beyond calling distance she clambered back through the window, put on her dress and went downstairs to face her mother.

* * *

Early afternoon, and Eliza was at her desk. *My dear Charlotte,* she wrote,

I got off more lightly than I'd expected – Mother's anger is obvious but she has said very little about this morning's doings, while Uncle James has merely urged me to take more thought for others, and more care of myself. I think I mollified him a little by admitting that, on the former point, I was certainly at fault; but I felt obliged to add that my strategic withdrawal had been intended to avoid an ugly scene that could have had only one result – for I was determined not to leave – and would have blighted your departure.

Which brings me to my chief reason for writing. My dear sister, I owe you thanks and an apology. The thanks are, of course, for not having given me away this morning, when you might so easily (and perhaps with a clearer conscience) have spoken out. The apology is for my harsh words the other day, when you came to my room. I think you were right – I have indeed grown hard. You of all people will surely understand that a degree of obduracy has been necessary for me to weather the storms of our unhappy household, but I say this simply by way of explanation – I don't pretend that it's an excuse for the way I treated you. I spoke without thought and without sympathy,

hearing in your words only your opposition to my wishes and not your
care for my well-being. I'm very sorry for that, and hope you will find
it in your heart to forgive me.

   As for my decision to remain here, it isn't easy to explain – I'm
not sure I can entirely explain it to myself – but I want you to know
that it wasn't lightly taken. Believe me,

                              Your loving sister,
                                      Eliza

She had hoped to leave unnoticed but as she was fastening her coat the sitting room door flew open and her mother stepped out into the hall.

'Where do you think you're going now, Eliza?'

'I have a letter to post.'

'A letter to whom?'

'To Charlotte.'

'Let me see it.'

Eliza hesitated for a moment before handing over the letter. Her mother scanned the address on the envelope and handed it back. 'You behaved badly towards her,' she said.

'I know. The letter's an apology.'

'I'm glad to hear it. I hope the day will come when you'll see fit to apologise to me.'

A few seconds of tense silence, before Eliza turned away. 'I shan't be long,' she said.

                        *   *   *

It was drizzling again and the high street was almost deserted. She was barely a minute in the post office and might have got home without delay, but as she emerged she heard someone call her name and looked up to see Dafydd hurrying down the street towards her.

'Do you have a moment?' he asked.

'Not really. Not today. And if it's about my uncle and my mother—'

'I'm afraid I expressed myself clumsily yesterday. If I can't detain you, at least let me accompany you. Are you on your way home?'

Eliza nodded. She moved on and he fell into step beside her.

'You must understand,' he said, 'that police work sometimes requires us to break the rules that govern polite society. We can't always afford the luxury of tact. We push our snouts into all kinds of stuff, trying to rootle out the truth. We upset people, inevitably, but I hope we don't upset them any more than is necessary. If I ask questions about your family, it's not because I know there's something amiss there, but because I need to be sure that there isn't.'

'But the way you spoke of my uncle and mother made me think you suspected them of some form of wrongdoing. And surely – since it's my father's murder that you're investigating – that must mean complicity in the crime.'

'You put it more strongly than I would. I see questions that need answering; I don't yet have the answers.'

'Even so, the questions you ask tell me something about the kind of answer you're looking for.'

'What I'm looking for is the truth – no more, no less.'

'Yet when it comes to your dealings with me, I don't feel you're being entirely honest.' She stopped dead and turned to face him, blocking his way. 'Tell me straight, Dafydd – do you have evidence of any wrongdoing on my uncle's part? Or my mother's?'

'Not so loud, Eliza.' Dafydd glanced over to the other side of the street where a little knot of grimy children stood watching them. 'Let's walk on.'

'So you won't answer me? What am I to deduce from that?'

'I will answer you, all in good time. Wait until we're clear of the town. You know what they say: walls have ears.'

They were a good hundred yards up the lane before he spoke again. 'The straight answer,' he said, 'is that I've nothing you could call evidence, but I've often felt that something's not quite right there. I can't put my finger on it, but the feeling has been strong enough to set me thinking about possible motives.'

'Motives? So you really do think Uncle James may have killed my father. Let me tell you, Dafydd, that no-one who knows him could possibly imagine him killing anyone. And his own brother...'

'If you're familiar with your bible, Eliza, you'll remember that the first murder was a fratricide. You can't rule out your uncle on those grounds. And yes, I do think he may have killed your father – just as I thought Fletcher might have done, just as I think Todd might have done. Both of those men considered themselves ill-used by your father; both were in need of the money he had about him on the night he died. Each might be said to have a motive, but that's not the same as saying that either is guilty. So when I speak of your uncle's motives you must understand that I'm exploring, probing, testing possibilities – nothing more than that. And if I ask for your help, it's because you're in a position to see what I can't.'

'What I can see, Dafydd, is that you're barking up the wrong tree. What reason could my uncle possibly have had for killing my father?'

'If you're willing to open your mind to the possibilities, I'd be happy to list them. Let's start with the brothers' well-attested dislike of one another. They spend much of their time under the same roof, sharing your mother's company, with your uncle apparently having the lion's share. Think about the understand-able resentment on your father's part, a resentment culminating, as we know, in a physical attack on your uncle. Think about the possibility of retaliation. Then ask yourself this: what might your uncle have to gain materially from his brother's death? When I ask myself that question I move from what I know to what I can only imagine, but that's the way detection works. So I imagine this: a woman with a troublesome husband admires or falls in love with the husband's brother. Her feelings may or may not be reciprocat-ed, but suppose she's the owner of a substantial property: whatever her brother-in-law's feelings for her, he's likely to recognise the advantages of stepping into her husband's shoes. And whether or not she's complicit in the murder itself, she may be complicit in a deception that allows her to benefit from the crime. If her own life suddenly becomes easier as a result of her husband's death—'

'This is just a story, Dafydd, one of hundreds that might be invented to account for what happened to Father. Stories don't take us anywhere. We need facts. We need the truth.'

'We invent stories in order to arrive at the truth. I tell myself this particular story because it fits neatly with what I know at present. If I find that it no longer fits I shall have to look for a new story.'

Eliza found herself trembling with anger. 'I'll tell you what doesn't fit,' she said. 'You've made up a story about criminals – the kind of story you read in the penny dreadfuls. But my mother and uncle aren't criminals. They're good people, quite incapable of the kind of behaviour you're accusing them of.'

'I've made no accusations, Eliza. As you rightly say, I've told you a story and, as I've admitted, the story may eventually have to be changed. But when you say that your mother and uncle are incapable of acting in the way I've described I have to say bluntly that opinions of that kind are usually discounted in police investigations, and with good reason. We hear it again and again – a relative's incredulity that someone they think they know so well could possibly be an embezzler, an impostor, a murderer. A single fact can demolish a theory, but opinions have very little force.'

Eliza walked along in silence for a while, considering. 'Here's a fact,' she said at last, 'to explode your ridiculous theory. Even supposing Uncle James had a motive and an opportunity for the murder, you're forgetting that he was in London when I found Father's body. He couldn't have had anything to do with what went on that night.'

'I'm forgetting nothing. Your uncle's claim to have been in London isn't corroborated by anything I know of. And I'd go further: don't you think it a little odd that he should have turned up so soon after we'd found the body? Pure chance, perhaps, but that's not an explanation that satisfies me. I've been wondering whether the visit to London ever took place at all – whether your uncle might have been found far closer to home had anyone thought to look.'

'You could answer the question easily enough if you wanted to. Why not ask him for proof? He's bound to have something – his train ticket, a ticket for a London omnibus, evidence of that sort.' Something was stirring at the back of her mind. 'In fact,' she continued, 'I've just realised that the proof we need may be within easy reach. When I went up to Owen's cottage on the night I found Father's body…' She tailed off in a kind of panic, confusedly aware of the implications of what she had been about to say.

'What is it, Eliza?'

She hung her head, unable to bear the intensity of his gaze.

'Tell me,' he said. 'What were you going to say?'

'Nothing. I wasn't thinking clearly.'

'Nothing? Really?'

Her mind was whirling. 'Nothing of any importance,' she said.

'Whatever information you have, or think you have, I need to know what it is. Let me be the judge of its importance.'

It was clear that he wasn't going to let the matter rest. She took a deep breath. 'What I remembered,' she said, 'was that when I went up to the cottage to fetch Owen...'

'Go on.'

'There was a newspaper lying on the arm of the settle – a London newspaper. Why would Owen have a copy of the *Standard*? As far as I know, the only newspaper he reads is *Seren Cymru*. It strikes me now that the paper on the settle may have been brought back by my uncle.'

'Did you notice the date on it?'

'No. Everything was happening so quickly. And you have to remember that I'd just found Father, and I must have been—'

'Of course, of course. But surely you can see the significance of what you're saying? Depending on the date of the newspaper, it may well be possible to link its presence in the cottage to your uncle's movements. In which case I might have to concede that he went to London, but I might also be able to show that he misled us about the duration of his visit. Do you understand what I'm saying?'

Eliza nodded miserably; she felt sick with understanding. 'Perhaps,' she said, 'the newspaper had nothing to do with my uncle's journey.'

'It's possible,' said Dafydd, gently but without conviction.

They were approaching the Hall gates. Eliza dawdled, came to a stop. 'I'll go on alone,' she said, 'if you don't mind.'

'Perhaps we might talk again tomorrow? In the meantime I'd like you to think back over the events of that night – the night you found your father. Did you notice anything strange or unusual in anyone's behaviour during the time leading up to my arrival at the Hall?'

She shifted uncomfortably, remembering how Owen had left her standing on the step, closing the door on her while he'd gone upstairs for his coat; how she'd had to push her way in, uninvited, to get out of the driving rain; how brusquely he'd bustled her out again.

'I'll let you know if anything comes to me.' She made to go, but Dafydd reached out and caught her by the sleeve. 'Take your time,' he said. 'Don't dismiss anything as irrelevant. And don't mention this conversation. Not to anyone.'

She broke his hold and hurried away, but as she entered the drive she looked back to see him standing stock-still in the middle of the lane, staring after her.

Twenty Five

Eliza slept badly and was awake before dawn. Lying in bed, obsessively visiting and revisiting the previous day's conversation, she was able to tell herself that Dafydd's suspicions were absurd but couldn't quite dismiss them from her mind; and later, sitting across the table from her uncle as he ate his breakfast, she found herself watching him closely, searching his face for anything that might give a clue to his thoughts or feelings.

'I wonder,' said James when Hannah had left the room, 'whether the time might be right for us to resume our walks together. It would do us both good to turn our minds outward again.'

She hesitated for only the barest instant. 'I'd like that,' she said, and as she spoke she felt she wanted it more than anything – the refocusing of vision, the restoration of some kind of order in a household shadowed for too long by sorrow and uncertainty. 'I'll be ready in twenty minutes.'

But as she opened the door to her bedroom Carys came scuttling along the landing towards her.

'I've something for you,' she whispered. 'When I took Todd's bread and bacon down this morning the constable gave me this.' She thrust her hand into the pocket of her pinafore and pulled out a folded scrap of paper. 'He said I was to put it into your hands and no-one else's.'

'Thank you, Carys.'

'I can take a reply if you want me to.'

'It won't be necessary. Go back to your work.'

Eliza closed the door firmly behind her and unfolded the paper. A scribbled note: *I have news. Come to the station as soon as you can. D.*

James was still sitting at the table when she went down. 'You were quick,' he said. 'Let me fetch my coat.'

'Do you mind if we postpone our walk for an hour or two? There's something I have to attend to.'

'Something to do with Constable Pritchard?'

'Something to do with his enquiries, yes. He wants to see me at the police station.'

'You seem determined to ignore your mother's concerns, Eliza. Can't you see what troubles her? Can't you simply accept our advice? Ask Pritchard to come up to the house if he has questions for you. You shouldn't be running around like this, at his beck and call.'

'He's expecting me. I have to go.'

Her uncle opened his mouth to speak but she was already making for the door. 'I'll be back as soon as I can,' she said.

* * *

Dafydd was at his desk, writing busily, but he set down his pen and rose to his feet as she entered. 'Thank you for coming,' he said.

'It wasn't easy. My uncle doesn't like me being – as he puts it – at your beck and call. He thinks anything you have to say to me should be said at the Hall.'

'And in his presence, no doubt. There may be reasons for that, Eliza. I think you should know that I have further evidence concerning your uncle's movements. The newspaper you mentioned has come to light.'

'When you say it has come to light—'

'I brought it to light. Retrieved it from Owen's cottage.'

'Retrieved?'

'I searched the premises yesterday afternoon, while Owen was out.' He opened the desk drawer and brought out a copy of the *Standard*. 'As you noticed, a London paper. And look at the date.'

He flattened the newspaper on the surface of the desk and jabbed at it with his forefinger. 'You see this? The date here is the day you found your father's body – the day before your uncle's supposed return. I'm certain that he brought the paper with him from London, and that we can regard it as evidence that he was back here by the time you went up to the cottage to fetch Owen.'

'I understand your reasoning but I can't see why Uncle James would have wanted to mislead us.'

'Can't see or prefer not to see? Forgive me, Eliza, but you must realise where this is leading. If your uncle is lying about his whereabouts on the night you discovered the body, the chances are that his reasons have to do with your father's murder.'

'The newspaper doesn't prove that.'

'At the very least it suggests that something untoward was happening on the night in question, and that both Owen and your uncle were involved. Here's a theory – another story, if you want to think of it that way. Both men play a part in the murder – we know, after all, that they were out together on the night of your father's disappearance, supposedly searching for him – and are complicit in all subsequent attempts to conceal both the murder itself and their own involvement in it. When your uncle—'

'I've told you – my uncle isn't a murderer. And neither is Owen.'

'Let me finish. When your uncle goes to London it's not, as he claims, to find your father – he knows perfectly well where he is – but to keep himself out of the picture for a while. When the ground has thawed sufficiently to allow the body to be buried, he returns to help Owen with the job. He steers clear of the Hall for obvious reasons, lying low in Owen's cottage until dusk, when the pair of them go up to the ice house. Your father was a big man, but with two people sharing the weight—'

'You've missed something. Owen was at home when I walked up to the cottage after finding Father's body.'

'I've looked into the matter with great care. Carys can't remember exactly how much time passed between your return to the Hall and your departure for the cottage, but she reckons not less than twenty minutes. If we allow the possibility – the probability, I'd say – that Owen had already dug the grave, there was time enough for the two men to carry the body down and bury it before cutting up through the woodland to the cottage. And of course it may be that Owen returned alone at that point, leaving your uncle to backfill the grave. Owen would certainly have understood the urgency, the importance of being back at the cottage before anyone came banging at his door with news of your discovery.'

'Even supposing my uncle to be capable of such things – and I have to say again, Dafydd, that I don't suppose it – why on earth would Owen allow himself to be caught up in a web of murder and deceit? It makes no sense.'

'I've thought about that too. I saw from the outset that there was a deep split in the family – your father on one side and your mother and uncle on the other – but more recently I've come to understand that Todd and Owen were an important part of it all. Todd's allegiance to your father was perhaps a matter of practical necessity – of self-preservation, if you like – but I gather that Owen's loyalty to your mother runs deep.'

'That's true enough. The connection between his family and ours goes back a long way – his father was steward here before him.'

'Carys tells me that Owen's refusal to take orders from your father led to arguments with him. Would it be fair to say that he sees himself not simply as steward of your mother's estate but as guardian of her title to it?'

'I don't know how he sees himself. I know that he's a good man, and that your suspicion of him does you no credit.'

'I understand your resistance, Eliza, but let's suppose—'

'Suppose, suppose – I've had enough of supposing.' Eliza felt her face grow hot. 'What are you going to do – throw the pair of them into the lock-up along with Todd and Fletcher? On the strength of – what? – a newspaper? A theory?'

'Calm down, Eliza. You're right, of course – I need more evidence. I have to go back to Owen's cottage this afternoon. I don't suppose you know where he keeps the key to the bureau that stands to the left of the chimney breast?'

'How should I know that? Why don't you ask Owen to unlock the bureau for you?'

'You know perfectly well why I can't do that.'

'I know why you think you can't. But when you find you've been following a false trail you'll wonder why you didn't approach Owen and my uncle openly, why you didn't simply ask them to explain anything that seemed odd or unclear. Shall I tell you why you're clinging so tightly to your ridiculous theory? – it's because you're drawn to what's clever and complicated. Down below in the cells you have a man with a grievance and a pressing need for money, a man who followed my father from the Bull immediately before the murder and went into hiding immediately afterwards. Is that too obvious for you? I don't say it's certain that Todd's the murderer, but the evidence against him is a good deal more solid than the tale you're spinning about Owen and my uncle.'

For a while there was no sound in the room but her own quick breathing. Dafydd seemed to be considering her words.

'Please understand,' he said at last, 'that I haven't lost sight of Todd. But there's something else here, something that needs to be followed up.'

'Then you must follow it up alone. I don't want to help you any more, Dafydd. I don't want to spy on my own family. I don't want to say or do anything that might harm people I love. I'm going home.'

'I'm asking too much of you, I can see that. You may think me thoughtless, but that's not it. I've made use of your knowledge and insight, certainly, but I've always had an eye to your well-being. I knew there might come a time when you'd find it impossible to continue, but I also knew that you'd tell me when that time came.' He reseated himself at his desk and took up his pen. 'I'm grateful to you, truly grateful for all the help you've given me.'

She was halfway out of the door when he called her back.

'What is it?'

'Please be careful, Eliza.'

'Careful of what?'

'Of yourself. Your welfare means a lot to me.'

She hesitated for a moment on the threshold; then she closed the door firmly behind her and set out for home.

* * *

Her uncle was in the yard when she returned, squatting on the cobbles with his hand outstretched, trying to entice Brand towards him.

'He won't come,' said Eliza. 'Since his time away he won't let anyone touch him but me.'

James straightened up and the cat shot away into the stable. 'Maybe,' he said, 'but I'm making progress with him. Are you ready for our walk?'

'More than ready.' She turned and stepped back out onto the drive, and at that moment the sun struck through the clouds, gilding the parkland and the tops of the budding trees in the wood below. She breathed deeply and something in her breast seemed to lighten, dissolving like morning mist.

James fell into step beside her and they walked down together, squelching over the sodden turf, saying nothing. For as long as it took them to cross the parkland Eliza was able to persuade herself that this was the old, amicable silence, but as she was about to enter the wood he caught her by the arm.

'I want you to understand,' he said, 'that these private discussions with Constable Pritchard must stop.' His face was stern, unsmiling. 'When I told your mother where you were this morning – no, listen to me, Eliza – when I told her where you were, she was distraught. Don't you think she has enough to cope with at the moment, without you adding to her troubles? Don't you care about her?'

'Of course I care. But I can't be expected to live my whole life according to her rules.'

'Everyone needs rules, Eliza.'

'Do you imagine I don't have rules of my own?' She leaned against the fence, suddenly overtaken by fatigue. 'I don't want any more of this,' she said. 'If we're to walk together, we'd better drop the subject.'

Her uncle nodded. 'Agreed,' he said gruffly, and he ducked into the wood, leaving her to follow.

The trees and undergrowth were busy with birdlife; the air was vibrant with song. This was the time of year she loved more than any, when the earth's balance shifted and its delicate intimations of rebirth were transformed, almost overnight, into undeniable fact. With the quickening of small lives, the greening of woods and fields, some answering shift would take place in her mind or spirit, bringing her own life back into focus, sharpening her sense of who she was and what she might become.

But today, trailing after her uncle as he left the path and threaded his way deeper into the wood, she found herself dull and unresponsive. Nothing, she thought miserably, would restore the old ways. Something was gone – snuffed out, perhaps, with her father's life – and she was adrift in a world that held no meaning for her.

At the wood's far edge they stopped, as they always did, to look out across the meadows. Over towards the river a skylark hung high in the air, a tiny, trilling speck against a backdrop of ragged cloud.

'Something has changed,' she said.

'There's always change, Eliza. We change. The world changes. Nothing stands still, however much we want it to.'

'I never expected things to stand still. But I thought…'

'What?'

'I just thought the changes would be for the better, that's all. I don't know why.'

The lark was silent now, dropping back towards the earth. Her uncle turned to her.

'Where now?'

'Home,' she said, and the word rang hollow in her ears, as though no such place existed.

Twenty Six

Eliza spent the following morning moping around the house, unable to settle. 'You're sickening for something,' said her mother, entering the dining room to find her staring moodily out of the window. 'Either that or you've something on your conscience.' Eliza shook her head impatiently and left the room without answering.

But her mother hadn't been so far from the mark, she thought as she climbed the stairs to her bedroom. If she had hoped to clear her mind by distancing herself from Dafydd's investigations, the strategy had been singularly unsuccessful. She was still plagued by anxiety, troubled now by the thought that she might, by averting her gaze, miss some clue, some insight – might ultimately miss the truth she so desperately needed. Yes, and suppose Todd were innocent but went to the gallows for want of that truth – how would she live with her conscience then?

And there was something more. She saw now that by leaving Dafydd to continue the quest without her she had deprived herself of the sense of purpose that had kept her afloat in the tumultuous aftermath of her father's death. In its absence, she realised, she was depleted, a poor lost creature without focus or direction.

She sat on her bed for a long time, not so much deliberating as feeling her way forward. When she eventually rose to her feet she knew clearly what she had to do. She let herself quietly out at the side door and set off for the town.

* * *

She arrived at the police station to find Sergeant Williams standing on the steps, buttoning his tunic. 'I have a few urgent matters to attend to,' he said, pushing back the door for her, 'but Constable Pritchard will be able to give you news of the case. Better able than I am if truth be told. Speaking for myself, I think we already have our man, but the constable's nothing if not thorough, and I respect him for that.' He touched the brim of his helmet and strode away.

Dafydd looked up as she entered, but said nothing. The ticking of the mantel clock seemed to fill the room.

'I made a mistake,' she began. 'I mean, I spoke in haste when I should have taken time to consider. I've considered now. I want to go on helping you, the way I was doing before.'

Dafydd leaned back in his chair. 'Are you sure?' he asked.

'Absolutely. I want to find out the truth, whatever it is. I don't believe that my uncle had anything to do with my father's murder, but I have to be ready to believe it if you find proof. And if by any chance I should find proof...'

'If you find proof?'

'I should have to share it with you, regardless of the consequences. It was Uncle James who told me that truth must be honoured above all else. Without the highest regard for truth, he said, there can be no valid scientific endeavour or worthwhile social interaction. I set that down in a notebook at the time, and I turn to it often, the way a believer might turn to a holy text.

And if you ask me now why I'm so certain of my uncle's innocence, you'll find the answer there. A man who can't stomach a lie is hardly likely to plot a murder.'

Dafydd was staring at her, earnestly and with a kind of perplexity. 'I'm wondering,' he said, 'whether your first impulse might have been the right one – whether it might be better for you to keep your distance from the enquiry.'

'Is that what you want?'

'I'm thinking of you, Eliza.'

'Then listen to me. I've made my decision. That's why I'm here.'

Dafydd sighed. 'There are matters,' he said carefully, 'that may prove disturbing.'

'What – more disturbing than losing my father? More disturbing than stumbling on his body in a dark wood? More disturbing than seeing him grubbed out of the ground like a turnip or thinking of him bumping down the lane in a farm cart?'

'Calm down, Eliza. You've no cause for anger.'

'I'm angry because you're not listening. I tell you, Dafydd, I've made up my mind. Don't you want my help?'

'I want it very much indeed. But what I have to say about your uncle—'

'What you have to say must be said. I'll hear you out.'

'Very well.' He bent forward, pulled open a drawer and brought out a small green wash-leather bag, tied with a draw-string. 'When I went back to Owen's cottage yesterday afternoon, I found this.' He loosened the string and slid a silver pocket-watch into his palm.

'You found it in the bureau?'

'Yes. With the help of this' – he indicated a small brass imple-ment on his desk – 'I had the drawer open in half a minute.'

'You forced the lock?'

'I picked the lock. There's a difference. But the important thing is this.' He pressed with his thumb and the back of the watch sprang open. 'Look here.'

On the inside of the case an inscription in neat copperplate:

O.M. from J.M.

Love conquers all

'Owen Meredith,' said Dafydd, snapping the case shut again. 'And James Mace. Rather closer to one another than I'd realised. Did you ever have any inkling of this?'

She was silent, staring at the watch.

'You understand, don't you, Eliza?'

'I'm not a child. I understand what you imagine you've discovered about my uncle. Maybe he does admire Owen. I can't see what—'

'The word is love, not admiration. *Love conquers all*. It's the sort of motto a man might have inscribed in his sweetheart's locket.'

'And if he loves Owen in that way, what of it? Does that have anything to do with your enquiries into Father's death?'

'I think it does. Knowledge of their intimacy reinforces my belief that the two may have worked together, firstly in carrying out the murder and later in attempting to dispose of the body.'

'But their intimacy, as you call it, weakens another part of your theory: that my uncle had designs on my mother – that he killed my father in order to marry her.'

'There's nothing in what we've learned that contradicts that supposition. As I suggested, the marriage would have been advantageous to your uncle whether or not he had strong feelings for your mother. And think of the convenience of an arrangement that would keep him close to Owen while allowing him to present a façade of marital respectability to the world. No, Eliza, my theory isn't undermined by any of this.'

He set the watch down on the desk, face upward. 'It's broken,' said Eliza. 'The glass is gone.'

'Not only that. The hands are bent – see? It has obviously taken quite a knock at some time – which is presumably why it was in the bureau. A stroke of luck for us: if it had been working – if it had been tucked safely away in Owen's waistcoat pocket – we might never have known about the inscription.'

'Lucky, yes,' said Eliza absently. Her mind was working furiously, but on a different tack. She slipped her hand into her coat pocket and felt it through the fabric of her handkerchief – the tiny sliver of glass she had discovered on the day of her sister's arrival. She pressed the tip of her finger against the sharp point until it hurt.

'What is it, Eliza? What's the matter?' Dafydd was leaning forward in his seat, scanning her face.

'Nothing.' She gave herself a little shake. 'Truly, Dafydd. Nothing at all.'

* * *

The phrase was, as she had half-known, from Virgil. *Omnia vincit amor; et nos cedamus amori.* Love conquers all; let us, too, surrender to love. She had the Eclogues open on her lap when the sitting room door swung wide and her uncle entered.

She started guiltily and banged the book shut. 'You frightened me,' she said.

'I'm sorry.' He seated himself in the chair opposite. 'What are you reading?'

She held out the book with the spine towards him.

'Your hand's shaking,' he said. He took the book from her, flipped it open and scanned the title page. 'We need to talk,' he said. 'In private. Would you come to my room?'

'Why not talk here?'

'The servants. Your mother. The matter is one of considerable delicacy.'

'Better to stay where we are.' She was struggling to quell her unease, to keep her voice steady.

'As you like. Listen, I've been speaking with Owen. He tells me his pocket-watch has gone missing – taken from his home while he was out yesterday afternoon. A burglary, he thought at first, but there was something odd about it. The intruder ignored other valuables in the same drawer as the watch – a silver tie-pin, a couple of half-sovereigns. Strange, certainly, but not inexplicable.' He leaned towards her. 'Do you know what I think, Eliza?'

She stared into the grate, unable to meet his gaze. 'How should I know what you think?'

'Then let me tell you. I think this is the work of your friend Constable Pritchard. I also think – and believe me, Eliza, I'm sorry to think it – that you're involved in some way. Were you with him when he went to the cottage?'

'Of course not.'

'There's no of course about it. How can I tell what you're capable of? It seems to me I hardly know you these days. And even if you weren't at the cottage, I can be fairly certain that you know something of what's been going on. It's obvious that you've seen the watch. You have, haven't you? You've read the inscription. This' – he held up the book – 'can hardly be a coincidence.'

For a moment she said nothing, and then the hurt she had been nursing all afternoon swelled into rage. 'Yes,' she said, 'I've seen the inscription. I know about you and Owen. You tell me you feel you hardly know me – has it occurred to you that I must feel the same about you? All that time – all our walks together, all our talking – and you weren't here on my account at all, were you? It was Owen you wanted to be with, not me. I was your excuse, a convenient cover for something else – something you couldn't admit to. And all that lofty stuff you fed me, encouraging me to live my life under the banner of truth – yes, those were your words – while all the time you were hiding the truth about your own life. You made me believe I was following you into a new and better world, and now I look round and see you limping along behind me – not the noble leader you pretended to be but a feeble hypocrite. You made a fool of me – betrayed the trust I placed in you – and I won't forgive you for that, not now, not ever.'

In the hush that followed there was a light tap at the door and Carys peered in. 'The tea's made,' she said. 'Shall I serve it now?'

James turned to her. 'Thank you,' he said. 'You can leave it on the table.'

Carys set down the tray and left. Eliza listened as her footsteps died away along the corridor. Her uncle sat motionless with his face averted and downcast, so much like a scolded child that her anger began to drain away.

'You judge me very harshly,' he said. 'Not entirely without reason, perhaps, but I want you to know that our excursions together have meant as much to me as anything I've found in Owen's company. And since you chide me for my lack of openness, let me ask you this: how should I have told you about the way things stood with me and Owen? And when should I have told you? Even at sixteen, you're barely old enough to understand. In what terms could I have framed the truth for the child you were?'

She could see no way of answering his questions. 'I'll pour the tea,' she said.

They drank in awkward silence. It seemed to Eliza that the conversation was at an end, but as he set his cup and saucer back on the tray her uncle took up the thread again.

'You speak of hypocrisy,' he said, 'but that's too simple. If you're telling me that I've urged you to live your life in ways I've been unable to live my own, I accept that, but the path I set you on was the path I should have liked to follow if the world had allowed it. I'm forced to skulk in the shadows, but does that mean it was wrong of me to want you to walk in the light?'

'Does Mother know?'

'About me and Owen? I suppose so. We've never spoken of it, but she's no fool. Tell me, Eliza, do you suppose Pritchard means to expose us?'

'I've no reason to think so.'

'Then what does he want with the watch? Why did he enter the cottage in the first place? Is it possible that he suspects Owen of having had something to do with the murder?'

Yes, she might have answered, and not Owen alone; but Dafydd's suspicions were, after all, absurd. 'I doubt it,' she said. 'Constable Pritchard has a reputation for thoroughness. I think he's the kind of man who can't rest easy while any stone remains unturned.'

'Maybe you're right. And maybe he has other reasons for not bringing matters to a quick conclusion.'

'What do you mean?'

'Simply that once the case is closed he has no excuse for seeking out your company. Think about it, Eliza – Todd has been held for days now but only, as I understand it, on a charge of robbery. Why has he not been charged with murder? Why the delay? Can there really be any doubt of his guilt?'

'I suppose there must be. It's the only plausible explanation.' She set down her cup and saucer and stood up. 'I'm sorry for what I said earlier. I spoke in anger and I wish I hadn't.' She made to leave, then turned back to face him. 'There's something I have to ask you,' she said. 'That night – the night I found Father's body...'

'Yes?'

He knows already, she thought, watching his eyes; he knows what I'm going to ask.

'Were you there when I called to fetch Owen?'

'Why do you need to know?'

She stared hard at him, stared until he looked away. 'Yes,' he said. 'Yes, I was there.'

Twenty Seven

Yes, he said, he'd misled her, and her mother too, and was sorry for that, deeply sorry. He'd been there when she called and had slipped upstairs while Owen spoke with her at the door. Pure coincidence, he said, that he'd returned on the evening she'd discovered the body – no luck with his enquiries in London, and the opportunity to spend time at leisure with Owen. If he'd known, he'd never have done such a thing, never have put himself in such a position. She could imagine, couldn't she, the anguish he'd felt, hearing her at the door, hearing the terrible news, the anguish of wanting to speak with her, console her – and as he climbed the stairs he'd twice stopped in his tracks, wondering whether to turn back and face her – whether to confront her with the truth of the matter – before continuing to the bedroom. And then having to wait next day, wait in hiding until such time as it might seem credible that, having taken an early train from London – and even if credible, the fear of discovery, and then knowing himself tangled in the web of his own falsehood, unable to break free without betraying himself, without betraying Owen…

She had felt sorry for him then, hearing him stumbling over his long-winded explanation, all his eloquence gone. But later, lying awake in bed, wondering whether she would ever again be able to take him at his word, her rage came flooding back. Wasn't his deceit the worst betrayal of all? Wasn't she doomed now to live her life in a state of perpetual uncertainty, unable to forget how ground she'd once trusted had crumbled and folded underfoot? She lay rigid, staring into the dark.

After a while she relit the lamp and went over to her desk. She had hidden the sliver of glass in the drawer, and now she took it out and turned it between finger and thumb, examining it closely. Something solid, she thought, something to hold on to; and, just possibly, the key to her father's death.

Such a tiny flake, though – too small for her to be able to interpret. Holding it close to the light she wondered whether she could make out the faintest suggestion of a curved surface, but even if so – and the closer she looked, the more uncertain she became – that wouldn't mean much. The fragment was far more likely to have been chipped from a discarded flask or bottle than from a watch-glass and, for all she could tell, might have lain in the ground for years.

She would go down in the morning, she decided, down to the police station. She would show Dafydd the fragment and suggest a closer examination of the spoil heap. If further fragments were found, they might or might not prove relevant to the investigation; if nothing turned up, she would at least have done her duty. The possibility that any discovery might incriminate Owen and her uncle couldn't be dismissed, but hadn't she told Dafydd that she would hide nothing from him? And wasn't she already in danger of breaking her word? Yes, she thought, she would leave at first light. She returned to her bed, extinguished the lamp and sank almost immediately into a deep and dreamless sleep.

* * *

Someone was knocking. Eliza surfaced slowly. Sunlight pale on the counterpane; a clatter of crockery from downstairs.

'What is it?'

'I'm sorry to disturb you, Miss Eliza, but your mother sent me to ask you to come down for breakfast. She says she'd like a word with you.'

'Thank you, Carys. Tell her I'll be there in five minutes.'

She went down braced for argument; but entering the dining room she saw at once that that her mother wasn't in argumentative mood. Her uncle pulled out a chair and hovered attentively at Eliza's shoulder as she seated herself.

'Tea?' Hannah nudged the pot towards her.

'Thank you. Carys told me you had something to say to me.'

'Indeed I have. Your uncle and I have been discussing the future.'

'My future?'

'The family's future. It was you who urged me to sell part of the estate, and of course you were right to do so, though your timing was unfortunate. It's not as if we have any alternative. I need to consult further with Owen and of course' – she glanced across at James – 'with your uncle, but we think the sale of twenty or thirty acres will clear our debts and go a long way towards setting the Hall and its remaining lands in order again. I want to restore our reputation, to win back the respect we've lost. I want to be able to hold my head up when I walk down the high street, and I want the same for you.'

'And Jevan?'

'I've come round to your uncle's view on that subject. The boy will be taken care of.'

'Father wanted to leave two hundred pounds for his upkeep. Is that what he'll get?'

'I shall pay Morgan two pounds a month until the boy's sixteenth birthday, on condition that the arrangement remains a private matter. I shall keep my hands on the purse-strings, but the total sum is not ungenerous. It goes without saying that the boy is to be told nothing about his unfortunate connection with our family. I hope you'll bear that in mind, Elizabeth.'

'May I tell Mr Morgan about the money?'

'You may tell him to come and see me this afternoon. Say simply that I have something I wish to discuss with him.'

Eliza gulped down her tea. 'I'll go over to the farm later,' she said. 'Would you excuse me?' She rose to her feet without waiting for an answer and left the room.

* * *

Dafydd examined the flake of glass with polite interest but showed no enthusiasm for Eliza's suggestion that the spoil heap should be sifted for further fragments. 'How likely is it,' he asked, setting the flake down carefully on the rim of his inkwell, 'that this has anything to do with the case? When I had a garden in Cardiff I'd turn up any amount of glass in a morning's digging.'

'We're not talking about debris from an urban garden. This comes from open countryside, from a site we know to be associated with my father's murder. And if there's a chance that it's a clue to the murder – any chance at all, no matter how slender – it would be wrong to ignore it.'

'Maybe you're right, but I really can't imagine what connection—'

'Owen's watch – the missing glass. Listen, Dafydd, I have to know – does the fragment come from that?'

'Do you think it might?'

'I need to know that it doesn't.'

248

Dafydd took up the flake again and turned it in his palm, examining it from every angle. Even before he spoke she sensed the shift in his thinking.

'Very well, Eliza. You go back – I'll be with you shortly.'

She dawdled up the lane, stopping at intervals, listening for the sound of his footsteps behind her. She was almost home when he caught up with her, panting slightly, a garden spade held at an angle over his shoulder.

'An hour or two should do it,' he said. They turned in at the gate and followed the line of the hedge to the corner of the parkland.

He set to immediately, shaving the wet spoil heap carefully with the edge of the spade, watching closely as the damp earth peeled away.

'Stand here,' he said. 'Where you can see. Keep an eye on the soil as it falls. We're looking for anything out of the ordinary – anything at all.'

A snail shell, a bird bone, a streak of red rust; and then, catching the sunlight as it fell, a small piece of glass. Eliza pounced on it.

'Let me see,' said Dafydd, throwing his spade aside. He took the fragment from her and wiped it clean with his thumb.

She craned over it, her heart beating fast. 'Is it?' she said. 'Is it from the watch?'

'I think not. This edge here is unbroken – you see the smoothness of the arc – and if we project it, the curve seems very tight. Too tight, I'd say, for a typical watch-glass, though admittedly there's not much to go on.'

Eliza felt her breathing ease. 'You can't imagine,' she said, 'how relieved I am. Not that I ever really believed that Owen or my uncle could be guilty, but I couldn't be quite certain that they weren't.'

'You do realise, don't you, that this piece of glass offers no certainty on that score? You thought you might have stumbled on evidence of their guilt, and now – well, now it turns out that you haven't, that's all. It's not the same thing as finding proof of their innocence.'

He slipped the fragment into the pocket of his tunic, and at that moment Eliza looked up and saw her uncle striding towards them. Dafydd followed her gaze. 'It would be best,' he said quietly, 'to say nothing about our find.'

'It's a pleasure to see you again,' said James with awkward formality, approaching Dafydd with his hand outstretched.

'Better not,' said Dafydd, displaying his muddied palms. 'This is dirty work.'

'What are you doing?'

'Looking for clues around the grave. Eliza's idea, and a good one in principle.'

'But you haven't found anything?'

'Nothing we can connect to the crime.'

James turned to Eliza. 'Have you been over to see Morgan?' he asked.

'Not yet.'

'Perhaps this would be a good moment to do so.'

'Not really. I'm helping Constable Pritchard.'

For a moment the matter seemed to hang in the balance; then James turned back to Dafydd.

'I'd like a word with you,' he said. 'About Owen Meredith's watch.'

'The watch you gave him, Mr Mace?'

It was as if the air around them had suddenly darkened. 'Yes,' said James, 'the watch I gave him. The watch you took from his bureau drawer. I don't presume to know why you took it, and

I don't propose to insist on its immediate return, though I believe I'd have a right to do so. I simply want your assurance that none of this will go any further – that the nature of my connection with Owen Meredith will remain confidential.'

'All I know of the connection is that you've given a friend a gift, lovingly inscribed. I'd rather not know any more, Mr Mace, and unless the friendship has a bearing on the enquiry into your brother's death I shan't be looking for more. Does that satisfy you?'

James nodded. 'I'm grateful to you, Constable Pritchard. Very grateful indeed.'

Dafydd bent to retrieve his spade. 'If you'll excuse me,' he said, 'there's work to be done.'

James glanced at Eliza, opened his mouth as if to speak and then appeared to think better of it. He turned on his heel and strode away.

* * *

By the time the work was finished they had unearthed seven small fragments, all suggestive of a reasonably delicate object. 'Too fine for a bottle or a jar,' said Dafydd, grouping them in the palm of his hand and examining them closely. 'Maybe a lens or a little roundel from a leaded window. If any of these edges can be fitted together we might get a clearer idea. I'll see what can be done when I get back to the station.'

'I could help you. I have to run an errand for Mother now, but I can come down this afternoon.'

'I've a feeling your uncle would have something to say about that. Better to leave it for a couple of days. I'll let you know if there's any news in the meantime.' He transferred the fragments carefully to his pocket, shouldered his spade and moved off.

She stared after him, hoping for some further acknowledgement, but he turned out of the gate without looking back.

What was she looking for, she wondered, listening to his heavy tread as he went down the lane – what did she want from him, from her family? Respect, perhaps – recognition of who she was and what she was capable of. Yes, and freedom too – the freedom to move as she pleased through a wide, beguiling world she had barely begun to understand. In the end, she thought, they were all in it together – Dafydd, her mother, her uncle – telling her what they wanted of her, trying to keep her in what they imagined to be her place. She wiped her hands in the wet grass and set off for the farm.

Rebecca had brought out one of the parlour chairs and was sitting with her back to the farmhouse wall, her hollow face tilted to the sun and her eyes closed. Her hands, resting on her knees, seemed almost translucent in the pale spring light. Her eyes fluttered open as Eliza drew near; she jerked forward in her chair and rose unsteadily to greet her.

'Please,' said Eliza, 'don't disturb yourself. I've come with a message for your husband, that's all.'

'Give me your arm, Eliza. I'd like to walk a little. I'd like to talk with you but not here, not so close to the house. Gwilym's asleep in the parlour and I don't want to wake him.'

She slipped her arm through Eliza's and drew her away, back down the track towards the lane. 'Such terrible nights he's been having lately – sweats and nightmares – and then it's often as much as he can do to keep his eyes open during the day. Jevan's a blessing though, doing what he can to help with the farm work. He's been out in the top pasture every day this week, cutting back brambles, keeping an eye on the lambs.'

'How is he?'

'Well enough, but sorry to be kept from his lessons.'

'He shouldn't be missing school.'

'It's not what I want for him, but he's needed here. And now that we're certain there's no money coming...' She sagged suddenly and clung to Eliza for support; her body seemed small and light as a child's. There was a long pause before she spoke again.

'I know you know about him,' she said at last. 'That he's your father's son. I know Gwilym let the secret out. He regrets that, but I don't. There's no reason for silence any more, and I want to speak before time runs out for me. I'm sorry, Eliza, sorry for the shame I brought on your family, sorry for the shame I brought on my own. I've no excuses, but I've suffered for my sins, and I go on suffering. Perhaps I've suffered enough. If you could find it in your heart to forgive me, I believe I'd face whatever future I have with a lighter heart.'

'I bear you no grudge,' said Eliza gently. 'And if there's blame, it should be fairly apportioned. Father led you astray and should have borne responsibility for that.'

'To tell the truth it's hard to know who led who astray, but it's fair to say that your father should have done more for Jevan. He didn't have to acknowledge him as his own – he and Gwilym were of one mind on that subject – but he broke a solemn promise when he stopped supporting him.'

'I imagine the promise was made in good faith and then broken without much thought. I don't believe that my father was entirely without scruples but he certainly wasn't trustworthy.'

'Yet we trusted him, even after the payments stopped coming. We're just waiting for his ship to come in, Gwilym would say, looking to make light of the situation, though in truth it could hardly have been more serious. I went along with him at first, but as time passed I came to see how things really stood. He'll look after his own, Gwilym said one day, trying to cheer me, but I knew different. I think the endless pretence – the pretence that Jevan wasn't really his own – must have made your father careless of his duty towards him.'

'Possibly, but there was a clause in his will that suggested otherwise. Did your husband mention that?'

'Of course he did. Maybe I should give your father more credit for wanting to set things right but it was just empty words, and he must have known it. If your mother had seen fit to step in where he had failed us – if she'd offered us even a scrap of what was owed – the words might have had some meaning.'

'Perhaps my mother is more sympathetic than you imagine.'

'Her husband's bastard – that's how she spoke of Jevan, and with Gwilym there to hear it. My heart froze when he told me that, and not just because I knew there'd be no money coming. Is that the way she speaks of him to you? Is the child to go through life with my sin hung around his neck as if it were his own?'

She had begun to cry. She rummaged in the pocket of her apron and drew out a frayed scrap of cloth. 'For myself,' she said, dabbing at her eyes, 'I accept whatever blame your mother chooses to heap on me. Heaven knows I wronged her, and no doubt I deserve her contempt. But Jevan – how does he deserve it? As sweet-natured a boy as you could hope to meet – not what you'd call forthcoming with others but loving towards me and Gwilym, and such a help and comfort to us in our trouble.'

She was sobbing unrestrainedly now, her face in her hands. Eliza put an arm around her heaving shoulders.

'My mother spoke without thinking,' she said, 'and perhaps not quite as your husband's report led you to imagine. She meant no harm – certainly not to Jevan. In fact, the reason I'm here...' She paused, considering. Rebecca lifted her head.

'What were you going to say?'

'My mother has decided to make a sum of money available to you. For Jevan. I'm not supposed to talk about it, but if your husband calls at the Hall this afternoon she'll discuss the details with him.'

Rebecca stared up at her. 'Are you sure?' she asked. 'Does she really want to help us?'

'She has come to feel,' said Eliza carefully, 'that all of my father's debts should be honoured, without exception.'

'Then my prayers have been answered.' Rebecca swung round and tugged at Eliza's arm. 'Come back to the house with me,' she said. 'You must tell him yourself.'

'My mother will discuss it with him later. Let him know he's welcome to call at any time this afternoon.'

'Please, Eliza, tell him now. Just what you've told me. I'm not asking you to say more.'

'I shouldn't like to wake him.'

'He'd be glad to be wakened for this.' She led Eliza to the door and ushered her into the parlour.

Morgan was slumped in his chair beside the hearth, his chin sunk on his chest. A dog-eared book lay open on his lap; his spectacles rested on the chair-arm under his hand. Rebecca touched him lightly on the shoulder. He jerked awake and looked up at her.

'Eliza's here, Gwilym. She has news for us.'

'Eliza?' His gaze seemed to focus suddenly. He put his book aside and leapt to his feet, thrusting his spectacles into his jacket pocket as he rose. If he had been less flustered, if the manoeuvre had been less clumsily executed, Eliza might not have noticed the twisted frame, or the empty space where the left-hand lens should have been.

Twenty Eight

No, she kept telling herself as she walked back down the track, no, there's no reason to think it. If you asked around the town you'd quickly find a dozen people who had broken their spectacles at one time or another. And maybe the glass they had found wasn't a lens at all. But her thoughts ran on what she'd seen, and by the time she reached the lane her mind was in turmoil. She hurried past the entrance to the drive and on into town.

Dafydd glanced up from his desk as she entered.

'Eliza!' He dropped his pen and leapt to his feet. 'Eliza, whatever's the matter? You look as if you've seen a ghost.'

'I don't know what I've seen. I mean, I know what it is, but I'm not sure what to make of it. It may be nothing. I hope it's nothing, but I have to tell you about it.'

Dafydd pulled up a chair and motioned her to sit, but she shook her head. 'This won't take long,' she said. 'It's about Morgan. I was up at the farm – I'd gone to see him about a business matter – and while I was there I noticed...'

She paused, suddenly overwhelmed by the implications of what she was about to say. But it was too late to retreat. Dafydd leaned towards her.

'Go on, Eliza.'

She took a deep breath. 'Morgan's spectacles,' she said. 'One of the lenses is missing. The frame is damaged. It's probably pure coincidence but it struck me that—'

'I can see the connection you've made, Eliza, and I think you may well be right. Look at this.' He opened the top drawer of his desk. 'Once I'd fitted the fragments together it was obvious. Certainly a lens, almost certainly from a pair of reading glasses. Not necessarily Morgan's, but as long as we can get hold of the frame it should be a simple matter to find out whether there's a match. Do you think Morgan will have any idea of your suspicions?'

'I don't know. It's possible.'

Dafydd reached for his coat. 'I'm going up to the farm now. You go home. I'll come to the Hall later if there's any news.'

'Come in any case. Either way, I need to know.' She was at his heels as he swept out of the door, but couldn't keep up. He strode away towards the high street.

'Dafydd!' she called. 'There's something else.'

He stopped in his tracks, turned to face her.

'What is it?'

'That business I mentioned. I went to Morgan's farm with good news – news of a sum of money due to him. Because I'd already mentioned the matter to his wife I felt I had to repeat it to him even though I'd seen the spectacles. Maybe the two of them will be sitting there now imagining a better future for themselves, and then you'll bang on the door and everything will fall apart. It seems so cruel.'

'If our suspicions are unfounded, the Morgans' plans won't be affected. If, on the other hand, Morgan has killed your father he must face the consequences of his actions. None of this is your fault, Eliza. Don't torment yourself with it.'

She nodded, dumb with misery. She would have liked to walk up the lane at his side but he was off again, urgent and purposeful, leaving her standing in the middle of the street, gazing after him.

* * *

She was sitting at the dining room window with her book lying unopened in her lap when she saw Dafydd coming up the drive in the failing afternoon light. She put the book aside and ran to let him in.

His face gave nothing away. 'Tell me,' she said. 'Tell me what's happened.'

'All in good time. Perhaps we should sit down.'

She led the way through to the dining room and drew up a chair for him.

'It's good news,' he said, 'though I'm afraid you may not think so. We have our man.'

'Morgan?'

Dafydd nodded. 'He has confessed to killing your father. There are complications, but those are matters for judge and jury. From my point of view the essential facts are that the crime has been solved and the criminal apprehended.'

'It's almost unthinkable, though I suppose I've known since this morning. I suggested to Mother that he mightn't be able to accept her invitation today – busy with lambing, I told her – but I thought it best to say nothing else until I heard from you.'

'Where is your mother?'

'Upstairs, in her room. Should I have her fetched in?'

'Yes, and your uncle too, but not for a moment. There's something else I have to say to you, something you might wish to consider without their intervention. The fact is that Morgan wants to speak with you. He says it's about his son – says you hold the key to the boy's future.'

'I'll come down to the station with you when you leave.'

'Only if you're sure you want to, Eliza. If you refused to see him I'd understand entirely. But it might be useful. His confession was hedged about with hints that it wasn't the way it seemed, that the blame lay with your father – he was insistent on that point, but wouldn't explain himself. And now he's gone quiet, refusing to answer our questions altogether. I've an idea that if you were to visit him he might open up.'

She went over to the chimney breast and tugged at the bell pull. 'I'll come,' she said.

'That's good of you, Eliza. I'm very grateful.'

'I have my own reasons.'

'May I know what they are?'

Footsteps in the passageway. Carys opened the door and peered in. 'Did you want the lamps lit?' she asked.

'Not now. I'd like you to fetch my mother and my uncle. Tell them Constable Pritchard is here and wants a word with them.' She waited until she heard Carys's footsteps on the landing above before turning back to Dafydd.

'You said Morgan thinks I hold the key to Jevan's future. I don't suppose he gave you any clue as to what he meant by that?'

'None at all.'

'I have to find out,' she said. 'If I can help Jevan, I will.' And then, softly but firmly: 'Jevan's my half-brother.'

Dafydd frowned. 'Morgan's son?'

'My father's son. Morgan brought him up as his own.'

There was a long pause before Dafydd spoke again. 'Why didn't you tell me earlier?' he asked. 'You must have realised that the information was important.'

Voices on the stairway, in the hall. 'I'll explain later,' said Eliza as the door swung open and Hannah entered, with James at her heels. She advanced towards Dafydd.

'You must forgive me, Constable Pritchard. I was resting. I wasn't aware that you were here.'

'I arrived only a few minutes ago. Eliza let me in.'

'I assume you have further news for us.'

'Important news. We know who killed your husband.'

Hannah lowered herself into an armchair. Her hands were trembling. 'Who is it?'

'Your neighbour, Gwilym Morgan.'

Hannah stared up at him. 'Morgan? I'd have sworn it was Todd.'

'Morgan has confessed. We don't have much by way of detail, but the confession's enough for our immediate purposes. We may know more when Eliza has spoken with him.'

Hannah jolted upright in her chair. 'Eliza? What in heaven's name does this have to do with Eliza? Surely you don't imagine it's her job to question her father's murderer? I'll thank you to do your own work, Mr Pritchard, and leave my daughter out of it.'

Eliza stepped forward. 'Gwilym has asked to speak with me, Mother, and I've agreed. I shall go down to the station now.'

'You'll do nothing of the sort. Morgan can't be allowed to impose on you like this. I'm surprised the constable thinks it appropriate to convey his message.'

Dafydd turned away from Hannah and, with a glance, addressed himself to James. Eliza saw and intuitively understood – man to man, yes, but something more: she recognised in Dafydd's look the power of a man who holds another's secret in his hand.

James cleared his throat. 'I suppose,' he said, 'that Morgan may have something of importance to say, and if he has decided that Eliza is the person to whom he wishes to say it, it might be best to let her go. If the constable can guarantee her safety—'

'Eliza will be in no danger, Mr Mace. And the meeting with Morgan won't last a moment longer than she wants it to.'

Hannah seemed to be about to speak, but James cut in. 'It will be dark in half an hour. You'll see Eliza safely home, won't you?'

'Of course.'

Hannah was staring into the fire, her fists clenched in her lap. Eliza judged it best to leave without further discussion.

* * *

They were halfway down the drive before Dafydd spoke again. 'How long have you known?' he asked. 'About Jevan.'

'That's what I wanted to explain. I've only known for a few days. Since the reading of Father's will.'

'You should have told me at once.'

'My uncle said we weren't to discuss the matter outside the family. He was very clear about that.'

'But in the circumstances—'

'Have you thought about my circumstances, Dafydd – my own particular circumstances? Did you ever consider what it might feel like to be caught between you and my uncle, torn by conflicting loyalties, always off balance?'

'Your loyalty shouldn't have been to either of us, but to the truth.'

'And what was the truth? Not what you saw when you looked at my uncle and decided, too early and on too little evidence, that he must be my father's murderer. You didn't know the truth then, and you wouldn't know it now if it hadn't been for me. I don't care that you give me no credit – who'd ever know from your account just now that I had anything to do with finding the real culprit? – but when you turn on me—'

'I'm not turning on you, Eliza. I've spoken thoughtlessly, that's all. And if I say nothing about the part you've played, there's a reason for that. I want to protect you, if possible, from any formal involvement in the trial – from being called as witness. But of course I'm grateful to you, and I'm sorry if I haven't made that clear.'

An uneasy silence fell between them, unbroken until they reached the police station.

'If you don't mind,' said Dafydd, unlocking the door and showing her in, 'I'll bring Morgan up. That way you'll be able to talk in peace, without risk of interruption from Todd or Fletcher.'

'Todd? Hasn't he been released?'

Dafydd shook his head. 'There's the matter of the money – the money taken from your father.'

'Money that was rightfully Todd's.'

'We've established that. But he took it by force. Hauled your father from the saddle and buffeted him about until he paid up. He doesn't deny it.'

'But if you know the circumstances, surely you can let the matter go.'

'I've no authority to make a decision of that kind. Todd assaulted your father and will have to plead his case in court. There may be grounds for leniency, but I don't imagine he'll escape a gaol sentence. The way things work, he's at a serious disadvantage. If the master manhandles his servant the law may well turn a blind eye, but let the servant lay hands on his master and he'll be made to pay for it.'

'But that's not justice, is it?'

'It's what passes for justice. Listen, Eliza, I wouldn't shed any tears for Todd. He may not be a murderer, but he's a scoundrel, no doubt of it. Morgan, on the other hand, will almost certainly hang for murder, yet it seems to me that he's a decent man at heart.'

He stepped over to his desk and pulled out the chair. 'Sit here,' he said. 'I'll go and fetch him. I think he'll talk more freely if I'm out of the room, but I shan't be more than a few paces away, and I'll be listening closely. The minute you want to bring the conversation to an end, call out and I'll be in to take him back down. He'll be handcuffed to this' – he reached out and placed his hand on a rusted ringbolt set in the wall opposite her – 'so there's absolutely no danger. Are you ready?'

'Yes,' she said. 'You can bring him in now.'

When he had gone she leaned back in the chair and spread her hands on the surface of the desk. What would it be like, she wondered, to occupy the seat by right, to have a place in the world of men? For a few moments she let herself imagine it – the sense of purpose, the power to get things done – and then the door opened again and the dream faded.

Morgan peered uncertainly around the room until his gaze fell on Eliza; she could see the shame in his eyes. Dafydd took him by the wrist and deftly handcuffed him to the ringbolt.

'This isn't necessary,' said Morgan.

'It's for Eliza's protection.'

'Eliza knows I'd never lay a finger on her. Let me sit down and talk with her, the way I'd talk with her when she was a child.'

'That was another place, another time. Before you killed her father.'

Morgan staggered as if he'd been struck. He leaned back against the wall. 'That's what I have to talk to her about,' he said. 'About the killing.'

'I've no wish to hear about that,' said Eliza. 'The constable told me you wanted to speak to me about Jevan.'

'It's all bound up together. Now it's known I'm your father's killer your mother will surely want to withdraw her offer of help – now, when Jevan needs it more than ever. I don't ask for her forgiveness – she'll never grant me that, and I don't see that I deserve it – but I want her to understand what happened, and why. I want you to explain to her how it was, and to speak up for me – for Jevan. If what I have to say distresses you, I'm sorry for that, as I'm sorry for the grief I've already brought you, but please listen to me. For Jevan's sake if not for mine.'

Dafydd was hovering in the doorway. 'It's all right,' she said. 'I'll hear what he has to say. You can go now.'

Dafydd retreated, leaving the door ajar. 'Tell me,' said Eliza, turning back to Morgan. 'Tell me what I need to know.'

'Thank you, Eliza. You're a good girl.' He groped in his breeches pocket with his free hand, pulled out a filthy handkerchief and dabbed at his eyes. She waited, listening to the dull tick of the clock, steeling herself for whatever might follow.

'I find it hard,' he said at last, 'to believe that I've done this thing. At first I wondered if it was a nightmare I'd wake from; now I know for certain it's the daylight truth, but it still seems strange to me, as though what was done was the work of another man. You spent time with us, Eliza, you know what kind of life we led, what kind of man I was – honest, dependable, gentle with the children, no less with Jevan than with my own. That's the man I want you to tell your mother about – the man, you might add, who welcomed you into his home without thought of the harm your father had done him.'

'You and your wife treated me with great kindness. I know that. And yet my father is dead before his time, and by your hand.'

'I didn't go out that evening with the intention of killing him. I didn't even expect to meet him. I was on my way to carry down Todd's last load of ice as I'd promised, and to fetch back the cart. But as I reached the drive I saw your father riding towards me up the lane. I say riding, but he was slumped forward in the saddle, with the reins hanging loose and the horse ambling along at its own speed. I thought he must be hurt, so I tied Bess to the gate and went down to see what help I could give. Just a simple neighbourly act, but it was the start of it all, the moment things began to go wrong.

'I took hold of the reins and asked him was he ill. Beaten, he said, beaten and robbed. He tipped forward in the saddle and I caught hold of him, meaning to help him dismount, but he kicked out at me, telling me to take my hands off him or he'd have the law on me. That was when I smelt the drink on his breath. You're a bunch of thieves, he said, thieves and liars – shouting it out, right there in the middle of the lane. Someone needs to teach you a lesson, he said, and he kicked out again.

'I stepped back, wanting to stand clear of his boot and whatever argument was going on in his head, but thinking I should make sure he reached the Hall – the light was going and the air was bitter cold. He began ranting then, nonsense mostly, about his creditors – bloodsuckers, he said, and you too, Morgan, as bad as the rest of them. And I confess I felt a kind of anger at that, but nothing I couldn't control. Let's get you home, I said, and at that moment he slid from the saddle and fell to the ground, one foot still in its stirrup. I came forward again and freed him, wondering what damage he'd done himself – none, it seemed, for he scrambled to his feet and shoved me away, still shouting. I've told you, he said, there's money in the will for the boy, but you can't wait, can you? You want everything now.

'Since you mention it, I said, I do want the money you owe me, and I want it soon, but this isn't the moment to discuss the matter. You're blind drunk. Go to bed and sleep it off. We can talk about the money tomorrow. Not if I can help it, he said, and swore at me – a something leech, he called me. Still I held back, keeping my anger close. And then he brought Rebecca into it.'

Morgan paused, breathing heavily. 'What was it?' asked Eliza. 'What did he say?'

'Don't ask, Eliza. You don't want to know.'

'I have to know. You have to tell me.'

'You won't thank me for the telling but, in short, he said he'd been made a fool of. He said – though these aren't the words he used – that what Rebecca had done with him she'd doubtless done with half the men of the town, and that likely as not he was being asked to support another man's child. If you'd heard him speak the words he really used, if you'd seen the malice in his eyes as he stood there spitting them at me, you'd know why I lost control then, why I lashed out at him. I fetched him a crack on the jaw and he fell back against the bank, not badly hurt, I think, but shocked. He stared at me for a moment, without getting up. I'll make you pay for this, he said. I'll see you in prison for assault.

'It was a desperate threat, and an empty one. I told him so. You go to law, I said, and the whole story will be out – how you bent my wife to your will and fathered a child on her, how you've neglected your responsibility to the lad, ducking and dodging at every turn to avoid paying his keep. Is that a story you'd want spread through the town? A story you'd want to tell the magistrate?

'He hauled himself to his feet and brought his face close to mine. Are you threatening me? he asked. No, I said, I'm telling you what's bound to happen if you report this – you won't be able to stop the truth coming out, and neither will I. I could see him considering that, and then without any warning he was on me, swinging with both fists, battering at my head and shoulders. If he'd been sober he might have had the advantage, but the blows were wild and I put him down with a low punch that knocked the breath out of him. And that's when I should have stepped away.'

'But you didn't.'

'No, my blood was up and I wanted to hurt him, to get back at him for the misery he'd brought upon my family. Even then, though, I had no plan to kill him. To be honest, I had no plan at all, just the rage of a man unfairly treated – insult added to the old, festering injury. I dropped to my knees beside him and caught him by the throat, holding him down. Listen to me, I said, I want to see an instalment of the money. Tomorrow – bring it up to the farm first thing. I could see the fury in his face as I said it, but my own anger had made me reckless. He was pushing at my arm, trying to free himself, but I had him fast. And that's when it came to me that I might kill him. Just keep bearing down, I thought – and I could see that he was already fighting for breath – and he'll be gone.

'Somewhere at the back of my mind was the will, the money promised for Jevan. I'd always supposed that the promise was a sop to keep me quiet, but if it was true that we'd be provided for on your father's death, that would be reason enough, I thought, to finish what I'd started. Forgive me, Eliza – that makes it sound as though I was thinking it through with a clear head, but it wasn't like that. No, I was lost in a cloud, with the thoughts tumbling through pell-mell. I was half horrified by what was in my mind, half excited by the notion of doing something – anything – that might let me get my hands on the money I was owed. And it seemed at the time – though of course I know better now – that there was a kind of justice in what I was doing, looking down on him as if from some high place, watching his struggles grow weaker until he lay still.'

Morgan sagged against the wall and put his hand across his eyes. 'I can still see it,' he said. 'Almost as sharp as if it was happening now. And then there's the dreams – many nights I'm afraid to sleep, knowing I'll see his face again, see him twisting and turning in the gloom, trying to fight me off. I can't say he didn't suffer, Eliza, but if it's any comfort to you, I don't think he suffered for long. As for me, I'll go on suffering as long as I live.'

Eliza shivered and drew her shawl close around her shoulders. 'And then,' she said, 'you hid his body in the ice house.'

'You know that?'

'I worked it out.'

'Yes, I carried him to the shaft and laid him out on the ice as decently as I could, though I was shaking with fear by that time – knowing what a terrible thing I'd done, understanding how easily I might be caught with the body. Then I brought up the cart and piled its load on top of him. And all the while I knew I'd have to come back, knew I'd have to move him as soon as the ground had thawed enough for me to bury him, and that weighed on me – thinking I'd have to see him again, touch him again; wondering whether I'd have the stomach for the job.'

'You might have left him where he was.'

'Might have done, but he'd have been discovered as soon as the ice was needed in the kitchen, if not before. I knew that for as long as he wasn't found there'd be confusion and uncertainty, and I saw how that would serve my turn. If you hadn't come over to the wood that night, when I was carrying him down—'

'I came out to look for the cat.'

'I heard you call and it struck me to the heart – your voice on the air like an angel's, and me stumbling through the undergrowth

269

in the gloom with your father slung over my shoulder as if he'd been a flitch of bacon. That you found him there seems to me a thing more terrible, more truly unforgiveable, than the murder itself. I watched from the bushes – saw you find him, saw you turn and run. What can I say, Eliza? How can I make amends to you?'

The questions hung in the air, unanswerable. 'The grave you dug,' said Eliza briskly. 'It wasn't deep enough. If we hadn't found it, the foxes would have done.'

'I was in a hurry. Afraid of being seen. And if I'd been less rushed, if I'd taken more care, I wouldn't have stepped on my spectacles. You knew about that, didn't you?'

'I knew you'd broken them.'

'You knew more than that. You're a clever girl, Eliza – I always said so. And it's right that you should have been the one to find me out.'

The door swung open and Dafydd looked in.

'I think it's time I took you home, Eliza.'

'Not yet. Would you give us five more minutes?'

Dafydd nodded, withdrew. Eliza turned back to Morgan. 'Your wife,' she said. 'Did she know?'

'I told Rebecca nothing and I don't imagine she guessed. I believe she thought she knew me through and through, and knew me for a good man. And the fact is that up to the moment of the murder I'd never done anything to betray her faith in me.'

'As a girl I always saw you as utterly reliable – so different from my father.'

'Yes, but what strikes me now is how quickly it all fell apart. You remember how, quite early on, they arrested Isaac Fletcher? I'd hidden your father's horse in the wood while I took the cart back to the farm, planning to pick him up later – I was going to ride him to the edge of town under cover of darkness and tether him there. But Fletcher found him while I was gone and took the matter out of my hands. Well, I started to think that fortune was smiling on me, and all the more so when I heard that Fletcher was suspected of the murder.'

'Didn't that trouble you – that Fletcher might be punished for your crime?'

'It should have done, but what I'm telling you is that a thread had been cut and now everything was unravelling. I don't say it didn't cross my mind that I should give myself up to save him, but that thought didn't last half a minute. Would you believe it of me? – I was ready to let the man hang to save my own skin. That's how low I sank; that's how fast it happened. I'll make my case in court and plead for mercy, but I tell you, Eliza, there's times I wonder whether I deserve to live.'

She could hear Dafydd pacing up and down outside. 'I ought to go,' she said.

'You'll speak to your mother?'

'For Jevan's sake, yes.'

'Thank you, Eliza.'

She got up and went to the door. 'I'm ready to go,' she said.

It came to her, as Dafydd was unlocking the handcuffs, that she might never speak to Morgan again. There was more to be said, she felt, but the opportunity to say it was perhaps already gone. She watched in silence as he was led away.

Twenty Nine

'**B**ut you must see,' said Eliza, 'that the money is even more necessary to them now. Dafydd says Morgan will plead provocation but doesn't think it likely he'll escape hanging. And if he hangs, what will Rebecca and Jevan do then?'

Hannah took a sip of coffee. 'They'll shift for themselves as best they can,' she said. 'It's not our affair. Eat your breakfast before it goes cold.'

'If it was our affair before we knew that Morgan was the murderer, it's our affair now.'

'That's not true. What we've learned changes everything. You're asking me to support the wife and child of the man I now know to have shattered the lives of my own family. Think about it, Elizabeth – why should I be expected to do that?'

'Because the fact of the matter is that Jevan is your husband's child. Because he'll go hungry if you won't support him. Because whatever else he has done, Morgan had the grace and compassion to take on the child in the first instance and to continue caring for him in spite of Father's negligence. Shall I go on?'

Hannah was silent, staring stonily over the rim of her cup, her eyes fixed on the far wall. Eliza turned to her uncle. 'Please,' she said. 'Make her understand.'

'It's not my place to make your mother do anything, Eliza, and even if I agree with what you say I can't approve of the way you say it. If she's willing I'll discuss the matter with her later.' He glanced across the table at Hannah but there was no response. Eliza folded her napkin and rose from the table.

'Aren't you going to finish your breakfast?' asked James.

'I shan't eat while my brother starves.'

She saw her mother draw back her arm and dodged sideways, so that the cup went wide and hit the floor just behind her; she heard the shards skittering across the boards. Hannah's face was twisted with rage.

'He's not your brother,' she said, 'and I won't have you call him so. Do you hear me? The boy's none of my family.'

Eliza stood for a moment in shocked silence, then gathered up her skirts and stormed out of the room.

* * *

Rebecca must come down to the Hall, she decided as she sat brooding in her bedroom – must come down and speak with Hannah, plead with her if necessary, mother to mother, wife to bereaved wife. She knew the risk – that her interference might succeed only in intensifying her mother's anger – but calculated that a direct appeal from Rebecca might well prove more persuasive than her own arguments. The idea had no sooner presented itself than she was on her feet and running down the stairs. She let herself out at the side door and hurried along the drive.

It was Jevan who answered her knock. He opened the door the width of his own skinny body and stared sullenly up at her, making no move to let her in.

'May I speak with your mother?'

He pulled a face. 'She won't want to see you. You're not welcome here.'

A hand caught him by the shoulder and drew him back. Rebecca threw the door wide. 'You mustn't pay him any mind,' she said. 'You're always welcome in this house.' She stood aside to let Eliza enter.

Jevan had retreated to the far corner of the room and stood glowering in the shadows. 'You told the police,' he said. 'They came for him because of you.'

'Hush, child,' said Rebecca. 'The fault wasn't hers.' And then, turning back to Eliza: 'This whole miserable business – you must understand how it is for us. He woke in the small hours this morning, crying his heart out, calling for his da the way he used to when he was a tiny scrap of a thing. I tried to quiet him, but my own heart's in pieces and I've no comfort to offer. I can only hope Rhiannon will be able to do something for him.'

'Rhiannon? Is she here?'

'Just arrived. She's down at the lock-up, visiting her father.' She turned to Jevan. 'Go on now,' she said. 'Go and see to the sheep.'

He left without a word, slamming the door behind him. Rebecca dropped wearily into one of the fireside chairs and motioned Eliza to sit in the other. 'I know,' she said. 'You're suffering too, but Jevan won't see that. His thoughts run on his own father, not on yours.'

'He's very young. He can't see the full picture.'

'Which of us can, Eliza? We dwell on our own problems. When I cry for Gwilym there seems little room in my mind for thoughts of your mother's loss.'

She was silent for a moment, staring into the fire. When she spoke again her voice had a harder edge. 'Her grief may be as great as mine,' she said, 'but the difference is...'

Eliza waited. From outside, Jevan's voice, still touched with anger, insistently calling the dog to heel. 'Tell me,' she said at last. 'Tell me what you were going to say.'

'Only that your mother can go on living where she is. There'll be a roof over her head, food on the table. But where will I go? What can I do? I can't run the farm, can't pay the rent. Money from the sale of stock might tide us over for six months once I've paid off the arrears; after that we'll have nothing left but these few sticks of furniture and a chest of threadbare clothes.'

'I'm trying to persuade Mother to keep her word – to help you as she'd intended.'

'Why would she help me now? Even if she did, how far would the money go? And how could it make me well again?' She drooped her head and covered her eyes with her hands. 'Forgive me, Eliza. I know you want to do well by us, but we're beyond helping.'

She had begun to cry. Eliza leaned over and gently touched her hand. 'Nobody's beyond helping,' she said. 'Come back with me. Come back now and speak with my mother. Tell her how things stand with you.'

Rebecca raised her head. 'I can't,' she said. 'Even if I had the strength, I wouldn't have the nerve.'

Looking into her eyes, Eliza saw that further argument would be futile. She rose from her chair and went to the door. 'If you change your mind,' she said, 'you'll let me know, won't you?'

Only a watery smile by way of response. Eliza lifted the latch and stepped out into the sunlight.

She was halfway down the track when Rhiannon turned in at the entrance and came slowly towards her. Pregnant, Eliza saw at once, and heavy on her feet, moving slowly on the steep incline. Her eyes were downcast and Eliza was almost upon her before she looked up and registered her presence.

Rhiannon greeted her coolly but seemed willing to stop and talk. The baby was due in May, she said, and yes, she was well enough in herself but everlastingly tired, and now this business with her father, as she delicately put it, had thrown her into a kind of confusion. 'Not that I blame you for any of it,' she added hastily, and Eliza, seeing the colour come up in her face, knew they were on dangerous ground.

'I'm glad you're here,' she said. 'Your mother's in very low spirits.'

'She's mortal sick, Eliza – my da believes she won't see the summer out. She's worn to a shadow already, and I think she'd go willingly now if it wasn't for what's happened. It's the thought of Jevan that troubles her most – the thought of him orphaned and with nowhere to turn.'

'Couldn't you take care of him? You or your sister?'

'Grace has cut herself off from us, more or less. I'd take him, no question, but Abel – my husband – says he can't see us getting by with two new mouths to feed.' She placed her hand on the mound of her belly. 'Sometimes I wonder if he really wants this one; I can't imagine him giving houseroom to Jevan. My da says Abel has a duty to care for the child, but I can imagine his answer to that.'

'I saw your father yesterday. Did he tell you?'

'Yes. He was grateful for your visit – very grateful. There's not many, he says, would have done what you've done – an angel, he called you. The money for Jevan—'

'I haven't been able to persuade my mother. Not yet. But that money belongs to your family by right. It's a debt left unpaid by my father – a debt we must discharge now that he's gone.

And there's something more. Whether my mother likes it or not, Jevan is a link between our two families, as much my brother as he is yours. There's nothing angelic about what I'm doing – any sister would do the same.'

Rhiannon smiled. 'There were times – those days you used to come over – when you seemed like one of our family. I loved that – the way you sat with us at table, the way you made my da laugh, the way you held Jevan. Tell me, Eliza, did you know?'

'About Jevan? I found out only a few days ago – though I wonder now whether I might have glimpsed the truth long before, but didn't dare think it. And you?'

'I thought it for years, but didn't dare say it. He's so like you, Eliza, and there was such a bond between you.'

'That way he had of looking at me – I used to imagine he was reading my thoughts.'

Rhiannon put her hands on her hips and arched her back. 'I need to go in,' she said. 'Take the weight off my feet. I leave tomorrow morning but I'll return for the trial.' She started off towards the farmhouse, then turned back to face Eliza. 'They'll hang him, won't they?'

Her face seemed to fold suddenly; her eyes filled with tears. Eliza, finding nothing remotely consoling to say, ran up and clasped her clumsily to her breast.

* * *

Her uncle was at the sitting room table with a scatter of books and journals spread out in front of him. He was reading, but he set his book aside as she entered.

'Your mother's furious,' he said. 'Where have you been?'

'At Morgan's farm. I went to see whether Rebecca Morgan might come down and have a word.'

'Have a word?'

'Argue her case. Explain to Mother how desperately she needs the money.'

'That's not a good idea. Certainly not at the moment.'

Eliza shrugged. 'Good or bad, it makes no difference. She won't come.'

'I've spoken with your mother on the subject. Briefly and tactfully. Note that, Eliza – tactfully. I think she'll return to a more enlightened understanding of the situation, but only if you don't antagonise her. I suggest you leave the matter in my hands. I'll try to resolve it before I leave.'

'Before you leave? Where are you going?'

'Your mother thinks it advisable that I go away for a while – until the trial is over, at least, though it's possible I shall be away for considerably longer. I've been thinking of a walking tour, perhaps in the Pyrenees. The spring flora—'

'But you can't. You can't be planning to miss the trial.'

'It's your mother's view that no member of the family should be present. I agree with her. None of us, it seems, will be called as witness. Justice will almost certainly be done. Why cause ourselves unnecessary distress by attending?'

'What if the distress isn't unnecessary? Maybe it's important to feel it. We can't simply detach ourselves – we need to understand what's happening around us.'

James sighed and leaned back in his chair, fixing her with a gaze suggestive simultaneously of impatience and concern. 'I wonder,' he said, 'whether you fully appreciate the situation. This will be no ordinary trial. Your father's unpopularity can hardly be overestimated and it's no exaggeration to say that, for many in the town, the villain of the piece isn't the murderer, but his victim. There will be a good deal of sympathy for Morgan in the public gallery and your mother is worried that our presence there might invite the anger of the crowd. It's not an unreasonable anxiety, Eliza, and I hope you'll fall in with her wishes as I, for my part, intend to do.'

He picked up his book, and Eliza, realising that he regarded the matter as closed, turned on her heel and left the room.

Thirty

In the days following her uncle's departure Eliza spent as much time as possible out of doors, wandering aimlessly through the woods and meadows, staying out of her mother's way. She moved in a fog of guilt and anxiety, troubled by thoughts of the Morgans' present sufferings and the suffering still to come, desperate to help yet apparently powerless to do so. But one thing was clear to her: whatever took place in the courthouse would be as much her business as anyone's. She would be there.

On the morning of the trial she was at her dressing table, pinning up her hair, when her mother entered and stood at her shoulder, stiff as a poker.

'Are you going out, Elizabeth?'

'Yes. To the courthouse.'

'I thought your uncle had discussed the matter with you.'

'We discussed it, yes. I gave no assurance that I'd stay away.'

In the mirror Eliza saw her mother's face harden. 'I forbid you to go,' Hannah said. 'I absolutely forbid it.'

'I need to be there. I have my reasons.'

'And I have my reasons for preventing you.' She gave Eliza's shoulder a vicious little squeeze, then stalked away. Eliza heard the door slam, heard the key turn in the lock.

She ran to the door and tried the handle; she beat on a panel with the flat of her hand. 'You've no right,' she shouted. 'Let me out.'

She waited, one ear to the panel, but there was no response. After a while she went to the window, raised the sash and looked out.

As a child she'd been a fearless climber of trees but there was nothing here between her and the wet cobbles below, and only a rusted downpipe to assist her descent. She eyed the pipe narrowly, judging its distance from the edge of the window, calculating the angle she'd have to lean at before her outstretched hand could make contact. Dangerous, she thought. Was it worth the risk?

She drew back. For long minutes she deliberated, pacing back and forth like a caged animal, whipping herself into a fury that seemed, in the end, to answer the question for her. She dragged a chair to the window, hitched up her skirts and positioned herself astride the sill, her left leg inside the room and her right dangling above the yard. Grasping the window frame with her left hand, she ducked under the sash and leaned out into the cool morning air.

She looked down. There was still time to reconsider. For a second or two she sat poised between possibilities; then she launched herself out and sideways, reaching for the pipe.

She had misjudged it. Her right hand struck the pipe but closed on air; her left, still clutching the frame, held her while she groped for purchase. For what seemed an age she hung there, fumbling at the pipe's cold surface, knowing she had come too far to haul herself back to safety but not far enough to be able to relinquish her hold on the window frame.

She had time to imagine the fall – her hands clawing at the wall or the streaming air, the sick jolt as her body hit the cobbles – and then her fingers, finding the far side of the pipe, hooked and held. She brought her left hand over, gripped the pipe and let her left leg slide from the sill.

She was ready this time for the shift in her body's centre of balance. She lurched sideways but steadied herself at once and then, leaning outward, stopping at intervals to kick free of the encumbering folds of her skirts, inched down the wall until she stood on firm ground.

* * *

She could hear it as she entered the town, a buzz of voices, faint at first but growing progressively louder as she advanced up the high street. Rounding the corner into Broad Street she slowed, disconcerted by the sight of the crowd milling about outside the courthouse; then, taking a deep breath and drawing back her shoulders, she marched on.

A few heads turned as she approached but it was only when she tried to force her way between the jostling bodies that she felt herself becoming the focus of the crowd's attention. An ill-dressed woman, clearly the worse for drink, positioned herself squarely in her way, deliberately blocking her progress. She brought her red face up close to Eliza's.

'What's so special about you, young Miss? – barging in and shoving people around as if you owned the place.'

'I have to get into the courthouse. Please let me pass.'

'They'll not let you in,' said another woman. 'The room's packed to the rafters.'

A man's voice from close behind her: 'It's Mace's girl. Let her through.' And then another, harsh and angry, cutting across the first from somewhere over to her left.

'That doesn't give her any rights in the matter. She can wait out here with the rest of us. And while she's among us, let her hear this: there's a man in there will hang for doing what half the town would have liked to do.'

'That's dangerous talk,' said the first, 'dangerous and cruel, and the girl shouldn't have to hear it. I said let her through.'

A moment of breathless tension and then the red-faced woman stepped back and the crowd parted, leaving a clear path to the door. Eliza walked up the steps, head bowed, careful to avoid meeting anyone's eye.

Sergeant Williams stood guard just inside the public gallery, his broad frame blocking the doorway, but he stepped aside to let her enter. 'The benches are crammed,' he whispered, closing the door quietly behind her. 'I'm sorry, Miss Eliza, but you'll have to stand. Not for long, I'd say – the judge is summing up.'

'Already?'

'Morgan might have spoken for longer, made more of a case for himself, but His Honour seemed in no frame of mind to listen. Said the jury would need facts, not excuses, and cut him short.'

'...needn't detain us,' the judge was saying. 'Gentlemen of the jury, we live in tumultuous times. Over the past few years we have seen what happens when, across the land, men – yes, and women too – band together and rise up against the established order. Threats against rural landowners, violence in our towns and villages.'

Morgan put his hands on the rail and leaned towards the judge. 'This has nothing to do with my case,' he said. 'Nothing at all.'

The judge fixed him with a ferocious stare. 'I'm addressing the jury,' he said, 'and I'll brook no interruption. You've had your chance to speak.'

Morgan opened his mouth as if to say more but the judge was pressing on.

'And if we don't uphold the rule of law, if we offer leniency where stringency is most needed, we imperil the whole fabric of society. The defendant would have us believe that Mr Mace was the primary aggressor, but where is the evidence? We have the defendant's say-so, nothing more. And against his confused plea for leniency on grounds of provocation we must set his actions after the event. As we have heard, he went to great lengths to conceal his crime, dragging his victim's body from one part of the estate to another, finally bundling it unceremoniously into a makeshift grave. Moreover, he permitted the police investigation to continue when he might have stepped forward at once. Do these sound like the actions of an honourable man?'

He paused and looked around the courtroom, as if assessing the effect of his words on his audience.

'And one further detail,' he continued, turning back to the jury. 'You should bear in mind that the defendant stood, in theory at least, to gain materially from Mr Mace's death. His claim that he did not know the contents of the will prior to the solicitor's reading of it is mere sophistry. As Constable Pritchard's testimony makes clear, the defendant knew enough to suppose that he might be a beneficiary of any will made by Mr Mace, and that should be a factor in your deliberations.'

There was a subdued stir – a shifting on the crowded benches, an audible release of breath. 'That's it,' murmured a young man to his neighbour. 'The poor devil's done for.'

Eliza looked across to where Morgan stood in the dock, impassive now, his head up and his eyes fixed on the high windows behind the judge's seat. The judge leaned towards the jury box.

'I see no reason to prolong this trial,' he said. 'I must now ask you to retire to consider your verdict.'

As the jury filed out a subdued whispering arose from somewhere over to Eliza's right. The judge glanced up. 'We shall wait in silence,' he said.

The wait was just long enough for Eliza to entertain the possibility that Morgan's plea for leniency had carried sufficient weight to tip the scales in his favour, but scanning the men's faces as they trooped back into the courtroom she saw a grim resolution that told her otherwise.

The judge turned to address the foreman. 'Have you considered your verdict?' he asked.

'We have.'

'And do you find the prisoner guilty or not guilty of the charge of murder?'

'Guilty, Your Honour.'

'Is that the verdict of you all?'

'It is.'

There was a stifled sob from the front row of the benches. Eliza craned forward and saw Rhiannon doubled up as if under a great weight, her face in her hands and her shoulders heaving. She wanted to go down and comfort her – for an instant she imagined herself raising the weeping girl and gathering her into her arms – but this, she knew, was neither the time nor the place.

'...and thence,' the judge was saying, 'to the place of execution, and that you be hanged by the neck until you are dead...'

By the neck: something in the phrase – so exact, so ordinary – struck her with the force of revelation. She felt the noose around her own neck, rough against the soft skin of her throat, knew the agony of the wait, the drop, the jolt as the rope jerked tight. The courtroom seemed to recede and for a moment she thought she might fall. She stepped back and leaned against the wall, waiting for the world to reconstitute itself around her.

'Take the prisoner down.'

How terrible a thing it must be, she thought, watching the judge rise from his seat, to hold a man's life in your hands; how much more terrible to cast the life away. She scanned his face for signs of emotion but there was nothing in his blank gaze to suggest that he had been touched in any way by the ritual over which he had just presided.

The benches were emptying; the spectators were making for the door. Eliza ducked out ahead of them, anxious to be off, but immediately found her way blocked by the noisy, jostling throng outside. An old woman grabbed her by the sleeve.

'Is he to hang?' she shouted above the clamour.

'It seems so. Please let me pass.'

The woman pushed her way to the balustrade, leaned over and conveyed the information in broad pantomime to the crowd below, one hand clenched beside her ear, her neck bent sideways and her tongue protruding. 'Shame,' someone yelled, and others took up the cry. Eliza plunged into the crowd, fighting her way down the steps and out onto the street, desperate to get free of the press of bodies and the battering din of voices.

She was almost clear when she tripped and stumbled. She would have been hard put to it to say, in all that confusion, whether the foot that tripped her had been extended deliberately, or whether there was malice in the blow that struck her glancingly across the shoulders as she fought for balance, but as she pitched forward among the trampling feet she knew she was in danger. She huddled on the cobbles, her arms shielding her head, unable to rise until – quite suddenly, it seemed – the hubbub quietened and a little space opened up around her. She struggled to her feet and saw Dafydd's head and helmet bobbing above the crowd as he carved a path towards her from the courthouse.

'Back,' he shouted as he broke through. 'Stand back, the lot of you.' He grabbed Eliza by the arm and dragged her after him until they were out of it all, with the open street ahead. She wanted to slow down, to gather herself, but he hustled her relentlessly on, not stopping until they reached the corner of the high street.

Eliza leaned against the wall of the corner shop, breathing heavily, trying to steady the wild pounding of her heart.

'Thank you,' she said at last. 'I don't know what might have happened if you hadn't turned up.'

'I saw you go down. I was standing on the courthouse steps. Were you attacked?'

'Maybe. I don't know.'

'I wouldn't be surprised. It's a rabble. These people have no idea what they want but they've no shortage of grievances. A landowner is killed and their muddled minds make a hero of the murderer. The law takes its course and they cry foul.'

'But surely you can see that Morgan doesn't deserve to die?'

'The law says he does.'

'And what do you say?'

'I serve the law. That's my job. What I feel in any given case is neither here nor there.'

'You think feelings are unimportant?'

'That's not quite what I said.'

He was distracted, she could see, his attention half on her and half on the crowd behind. 'Go back,' she said. 'You have your duties to attend to.'

'Let me see you to the lane. I need to know that you're safe.'

She shook her head. 'It's better I go alone.'

At the top of the high street she looked back and saw that he was still at the corner, gazing after her. She might have acknowledged his concern – a nod would have been enough – but she turned away in sudden, inexplicable confusion and the moment was gone.

Epilogue

An afternoon in late June, the sky a milky blue, the air shimmering with heat and humming with insect life. Eliza dawdled up the lane towards the Hall, stopping at intervals to wipe the sweat from her face with the sleeve of her blouse.

She heard them before she saw them. *There, see, running along that branch* – Jevan's voice, high and excitable, and then Rhiannon's soft burr: *Quietly now. We don't want to waken him.*

As they came into view round the bend in the lane Eliza saw them for an instant as if they were strangers, as if their lives and hers had not been inextricably linked. The little group might have figured in a sunny watercolour as an emblem of rural ease – the young mother walking sedately along with the sleeping baby in her arms, the boy at her side swinging lazily at the hedgerow nettles with a peeled stick. And then, as she drew close, Eliza saw the haunted look in Rhiannon's eyes, and the illusion faded.

No, said Rhiannon, there was no news, but her mother was growing a little weaker with every day that passed. She was silent for a moment, watching Jevan as he wandered on down the lane. 'We're getting to the end,' she said, 'no doubt of it. I'll stay now until she goes.'

'What will happen to Jevan?'

'It's decided he'll live with us after all. Abel came with me on my last visit and was won over within an hour. Jevan's an odd child, Eliza, but anyone can see how sharp he is. Practical too, as he's had to be, and that weighed with Abel. It's true there'll be another mouth to feed, he says, but there'll also be another pair of hands to help with the vegetable plot. My mam cried when I told her and I thought I'd somehow done wrong, but it was relief, she said, relief that he'd be properly housed and fed when she was gone.'

'I'm sorry I wasn't able to persuade my mother to pay anything towards his keep. Even my uncle couldn't shift her.'

'I know you've tried, Eliza, and I'm grateful for that. It will be a struggle but we'll manage without.'

The baby stirred, opened its eyes. Eliza leaned over. 'He's lovely,' she said. 'What's his name?'

'Aaron. I wanted Gwilym for my da's sake but Abel wouldn't have it. It will be a shadow, he said, a shadow cast on the child's life. We argued about it at the time but I've come to see that he was right. A new life, a fresh start.'

Eliza nodded. 'I've been thinking about your father a good deal lately. About my own father too. Although they'd never have wished it, they've both harmed us. We'll always live in the shadow, you and I, but we must hope that Aaron will grow up free of it all.'

The baby was twisting in Rhiannon's arms, its small mouth working. 'He'll want feeding,' said Rhiannon. 'I'd best get back to the house.'

Down the lane Jevan was beckoning, calling: *Come and look, come and look*. 'I'll go,' said Eliza. 'You take Aaron home.'

She walked back to where Jevan stood peering into the hedge. He looked up as she approached. 'It's Rhiannon I was calling,' he said. 'Not you. I want to show her something.'

'Rhiannon had to see to the baby. Will you show me?'

'Here,' he said sulkily. 'A nest.' He turned away but she caught him by the arm.

'Show me properly.'

He pointed. 'There. Where the twigs fork.'

'Yes, I see it now.' Four eggs, sky blue and flecked with black. 'Song thrush. I expect you knew that, didn't you?'

He nodded. 'We have to go now,' he said, 'or the mother bird mightn't come back.'

'Quite right. I'm going back to the Hall. Do you want to walk with me?'

She set off and after a moment's hesitation he fell in alongside her and began to talk, shyly at first but with increasing confidence, about the local wildlife. He spoke knowledgeably and with a quick turn of phrase, and it struck her as they walked how easily they might have got along as brother and sister, roaming the woods and meadows together, attuned to each other and to the small lives around them.

As they reached the Hall he turned his head to look up the drive. She caught the movement and spoke on impulse.

'Would you like to come in?'

He stood stock-still, staring. 'Am I allowed?' he asked.

'Of course you're allowed. You're with me.' She took him by the hand and led him through the gateway.

As they crossed the bridge she glanced up the slope and saw her mother sitting in the shade at the edge of the shrubbery. She was reading, bent over her book, but raised her head at their approach. Eliza saw her shoulders stiffen. She put the book aside and sat upright in her chair, waiting, still as a statue.

Eliza affected not to notice her obvious displeasure. 'I've brought Jevan,' she said.

'So I see. For any particular reason?'

'I want to show him the grounds. I want you to meet him.'

Jevan gave an awkward little bow and held out his hand. Hannah took it absently, her eyes fixed on Eliza's. 'I wonder,' she said, 'whether we might have a word in private.'

Eliza turned to Jevan. 'Why not go and explore the stream? I often see warblers there.'

'Will you come?'

'In a few minutes. When I've spoken with my mother.'

Hannah waited, watching as Jevan moved nimbly down the slope through the flowering grasses. 'Don't you see?' she said at last. 'Don't you see the distress you cause? The boy's the spit of your father – can you imagine how I feel, seeing him here? You never think, Elizabeth, you never think about the feelings of others.'

'I'll tell you what I'm thinking. I'm thinking about Jevan – where he'll go from here, what help he'll receive on his way. I find it strange that he's been brought up lovingly by a man my father wronged—'

'A murderer, remember that.'

'—by a man my father wronged, and that he'll be supported now by his sister's husband, a man who might reasonably say he owes the child nothing. Others step forward while we turn our faces away and pretend he has no connection with us.'

'What your father did—'

'Father's dead. The question is, how shall we make amends for what he did? An allowance would be a start. You've just sold thirty acres of land and we barely miss it. We can easily afford to keep Jevan clothed and fed.'

'The money's not the point – you know that perfectly well. You talk as though the manner of your father's death were an irrelevance.'

'What has the murder to do with Jevan? He's no more responsible for Morgan's actions than he is for his true father's. Look at him down there – how can you see him and not want to help?'

Jevan was standing at the edge of the stream, carefully parting the sedge stems. He seemed utterly absorbed but as they watched he turned, as though he had sensed their attention, and his gaze met theirs. He raised one hand in a small, hesitant gesture of acknowledgement.

'I can't bear it,' said Hannah. Her eyes had filled with tears. 'Send him away.'

'Let him stay a little longer.'

Hannah rounded on her with sudden fury. 'You heard what I said, Elizabeth. Get him out of my sight.'

'Hush, he'll hear you.' Eliza broke away and hurried down the slope to where Jevan stood waiting for her, his eyes bright and his cheeks faintly flushed.

'Reed warblers,' he said. 'I saw them up close.'

'They nest here every summer. I'm glad you've seen them, but I'm afraid you have to go now. I'll come to the lane with you.'

They walked in silence until they reached the gate. Jevan turned and looked back across the sunlit parkland.

'I shan't be allowed in again, shall I?'

'One day you will.'

'But your mam doesn't want me here. I heard what she said.'

'She's upset, that's all. And things change. If they don't change of their own accord we can make them change.'

'Rhiannon says I'm to live with her in future. What if I never see you again?'

'You'll see me, Jevan.' She wanted to say more but held her tongue.

He turned, thrust his hands deep into his breeches pockets and walked away. She watched him go, hoping he might look back, knowing he wouldn't.

* * *

By the time she returned her mother had regained her composure and had taken up her book again. Eliza flopped down in the shade and lay on her back with her hands pillowing her head. Hannah sighed.

'Shall we ever make a lady of you, Elizabeth?' The reproach was unmistakable but her tone was lighter now and this was familiar territory. Eliza breathed more easily.

'I've been thinking,' continued Hannah, 'about the boy. I spoke harshly just now, and shouldn't have done. But imagine it, Elizabeth – meeting my husband's child face to face, the shock of it, the distress.'

'I'm sorry. It was thoughtless of me.'

'Not entirely. You were right to think that I should meet him. Difficult as it was, I'm relieved now. Perhaps I should have met him earlier.'

'You'll help him, then?'

'I didn't say so but yes, I believe I shall. I want to begin again. I woke this morning with a feeling closer to happiness than anything I've known in years, grateful for the chance to refashion my life without your father endlessly sapping my spirits and hindering my plans. It's a terrible thing to admit, but I want to leave him behind. And the fact is, I'll do that more easily if I pay off his debt to the Morgans than if I carry it with me. I don't want to bear that burden, Elizabeth, and I don't want you to bear it either.'

'I had it in mind – it was a kind of dream – that I might one day be in a position to help Jevan myself.'

'That won't be necessary, but we do need to consider your future. Doubtless you'll marry in due course, but I'd like to suggest that while you're waiting for a husband to turn up you take full responsibility for the running of the Hall. That will leave me free to devote myself to the management of the estate, as I must if we're to rebuild the family's fortunes and restore its good name.'

Eliza looked out over the shimmering grasses, taking in the sweep of the woodland below and then, across the river, above the roofs of the town, the far hills glowing like molten gold. She let her eyes rest on the distant prospect for a moment before turning back to her mother.

'Thank you,' she said, 'but I have other plans.'